UNDYING DESTINY

THE ENCLAVE

Undying Destiny

The Enclave

Jessica Lee

Entangled Publishing, LLC
2614 South Timberline Road
Suite 109
Fort Collins, CO 80525
Visit our website at www.entangledpublishing.com.

Edited by Erin Molta
Cover design by Kim Killion

Manufactured in the United States of America

First Edition June 2013

To the Alpha Male who rocks my world at home, this is for you, sweetheart. Your love and support, no matter how crazy of an idea I have, mean everything to me. I love you — Always.

•

Chapter One

"Whoever you are, you'd best have a damn good reason to continue breathing," Kenric rumbled.

It took balls for someone to enter his secured, private quarters within the compound while he slept. A part of him respected the bravado, but he despised games.

The cold edge of serrated steel trailed down his midsection. "Now, Kenric St. James, is that any way to speak to your sire?" An unmistakable female voice whispered at his ear.

He lunged.

Kenric's momentum propelled them both across the shielded darkness of his bedroom. Her head smacked the wall with a satisfying crack *followed by the* thud *of the blade against the hardwood floor.*

With his hand constricting her throat, Kenric hissed through descended fangs, "Death is all that awaits you here, Marguerite." The thundering beat of his heart filled his ears. "I will *see you pay for murdering Annice. And I'll have revenge for every other life you've destroyed."*

A wicked smile curled her lips before she laughed. Ready to purge three centuries of vengeance from his gut, he tightened his grip.

His hand collapsed around dead air. "Son of a bitch!"

Seconds later, a force slammed into his chest, propelling him across the room. His back struck the mattress. A naked, grinning Marguerite appeared, straddling his hips. Her hand slid between their bare bodies.

Kenric snatched her wrist. "That will never happen again." Tossing her off him, he leaped to his feet.

"Maybe this would be more to your liking?" Marguerite's form shimmered. Her black-as-sin hair morphed into long blonde ringlets. Her body transformed. Layers of white satin and lace soon covered her nakedness.

His gaze followed the familiar white dress down to her small slippers, then up again, following her soft curves and slight bosom. A sorrow-filled lump, the size of his heart, formed in his throat. His breath hitched. The gown was exactly like the one Annice had been wearing the day he'd proposed—more than three hundred years ago.

Large blue eyes, almost too large for her face, met his gaze. He grabbed the nearest bedpost, steadying his legs. Kenric stepped forward before his mind even registered he'd moved. But reality slammed into his brain and he yanked on the brake.

How could Marguerite be this *evil? What the hell was he thinking? Marguerite Devonshire didn't give a shit. She didn't care if she ripped open old wounds and flooded them with salt. She only cared if the action suited her own needs.*

Annice was dead. And the woman wearing the masquerade

had murdered her.

"How are you doing this, Marguerite?" he growled. "And what the hell do you want? You're too narcissistic for a death wish, and I damn well don't need a reminder of what a sadistic bitch you are."

"Ouch, darling." Marguerite clucked her tongue and wagged one thin finger back and forth. "Now that's not nice. I'm here because I've missed you." She rose and sauntered forward, a disturbing blend of Annice's body with Marguerite's voice. She lifted her hand as if to rest it on his chest. Kenric backpedaled before she could make contact. Her eyelids narrowed as she dropped her arm to her side. Yeah. It was Annice's face, but malice leaked through her pores like venom, a stinging reminder that she was all Marguerite.

"I wanted to surprise you. Do you like your dream so far?" She caressed the curves of her borrowed image.

A fucking dream. She was inside his head and screwing with his mind. Marguerite had already taken his life and blackened his soul, but no way in hell was she going to crawl around inside his brain and infect the only part of him left that was human: his memories.

With a smug grin, she added, "I had to do something to get the master of the Enclave's attention. We've been out of touch for far too long. What has it been, three hundred years now?"

If she wanted chitchat, she had the wrong enemy. He shot her a look that said, get to the damn point.

"Don't look so grumpy, love. I wanted to remind you of how perfect we are for each other. Annice would have never been happy with you."

"Don't even go there. You defile her name," he spat. "You

didn't know a damn thing about her."

"Oh, I'm sure the pitiful *human female would have wanted children, and as you know, that's not possible. You would have made her* miserable. *Not to mention the bloodlust that would have plagued you each time you fucked her."*

She giggled. "Her sweet little heart would have never fared well with that healthy…" Her gaze dipped low, then back to his face,"…appetite of yours." She released a long sigh before continuing. "We belong together, Kenric, and you need to accept that fact."

"The only fact *that needs to be accepted here is that when I find you—" his voice dipped into a snarl,"—and I will find you—you're going to wish you'd never tasted my blood. Because I'm going to make sure Annice's death is paid for with yours." He wouldn't give her the satisfaction of a reaction to her declarations about Annice—it would only encourage her. Even if she was right. Not about the children. The bloodlust. Unlike human men, he'd been gifted or cursed, depending on how you looked at it, with the benefit of never having to worry about disease or pregnancy when he fucked. The burden he carried was much worse. Sex and bloodlust went hand in hand. He never wanted to submit any female to the cravings he'd experienced during his time as Marguerite's slave.*

Marguerite scowled and whirled. "You always were a self-righteous, holier-than-thou son of a bitch. I see a few centuries without me have done nothing to improve your personality."

His jaw ached under the pressure of his clenched teeth. She stood there, with her head held high and spine straight, as if she were the victim.

"We can see each other a little more often, now that I've

mastered my new skill. You would like that, wouldn't you?" Marguerite tilted her head, glancing at him over her shoulder. She reached out, intending once more to touch him. Kenric whipped his arm forward, knocking the vile appendage away. He couldn't stomach the thought.

"Is there any point to this?"

"Tell me, my dear. I'm dying to know…" Her eyes blazed with fury, but her lips wore a smile of seduction. She stepped closer, her words hot against his skin. "Do you enjoy seeing your precious Annice again?"

A roar erupted, and his rage unleashed. With the power of a thought, Kenric launched Marguerite into the air and against the far wall. With his mind, he held her up with her feet dangling. Every instinct rebelled at causing pain to the image of innocence reflecting back at him. It isn't her. It isn't her. The mantra looped in his head as he stalked closer.

"This is my mind, Marguerite. It would serve you well to remember that the next time you think to play in my head."

Her stunned expression shifted to a sneer, exposing her fangs. "You think you have the upper hand, love? You always were a little cocky." Her gaze dropped to his groin. She licked her lips and tongued a fang.

Kenric hit her with another blast of energy, choking off her humor. The force pressed her body and head tighter against the wall. He couldn't resist having his moment. She couldn't die here in this delusion of her creation. But he didn't give a damn. It was too sweet not to try to kill the coldhearted bitch.

"Fine, Kenric. You win. This round," she conceded, lifting her shaking hands in surrender.

He sucked in a deep breath before releasing it along

with his hold. Her body glided down until her feet met the hardwood floor.

"I can feel how much stronger you are Kenric, even as you sleep. Think about it. A master vampire, one with the potency that you possess, blended with the strength of my six centuries, plus the power I've procured—we would be a force unlike any vampire or mortal has ever seen. Nothing and no one could ever touch us."

He didn't think it was possible, but she'd grown even more insane. She spoke of power as if it were a lover, her eyes wild with lust. "What have you done, Marguerite?" Christ, what had she tapped into? "What is this procurement? Is that how you're doing this?"

"So many questions." She shook her head. "Join me, and in due time, all shall be revealed." Marguerite planted another beckoning smile on her face.

"My answer still hasn't changed, Marguerite. Never! Never again will I submit and give my mind and soul to you."

She stepped forward, squared her shoulders, and pinned him with a glare. "You're a fool, St. James. You'll regret those words."

"So be it."

Her eyes shifted from blue to green. Her face, body, and clothing reversed to their original state. Her hips rocked back and forth in invitation.

She was pure sex.

But it was difficult to be aroused when his every instinct would rather rip her apart than fuck her.

"This isn't over," she simply stated. A red ring swirled around her green irises, giving away just how pissed she really was. Good.

He seized her chin, enjoying her sharp intake of air from his sudden grasp.

"For you, Marguerite, it soon will be."

She pulled herself free and raked him with a hungry glare. Their gazes held once more in challenge before she erupted in laughter. Her image faded to mist.

Kenric gasped, lunging upright in bed. What remained of his bed linens lay tangled at the foot of his mattress. A fine sheen of sweat covered his body, chilling him to the core. The room was still, except for the sound of his rapid breaths. He scanned the darkness of his bedroom.

He was alone.

The shower door swung wide, striking the side of the glass block encasement, rattling its hinges. Even though it had been an illusion, it had felt good washing the touch of that evil bitch off his skin. Kenric stepped out onto his rippled bath mat and grabbed a towel from the bar.

The moment he dropped down on the edge of his bed, the house phone beeped. He groaned. It had to be Guerin. With the edges of the sun barely dipping below the horizon, the only person ringing this soon would be him, since he'd covered operations last night. Reaching over, Kenric pressed the speaker button.

"Yeah. What is it?"

"Damn, man. Good fucking evening to you, too," Guerin said, laughing. "Who pissed on your sheets?"

Kenric let silence hang on the line and breathed deep before he took any more of his anger out on his second-in-command. "Marguerite was here."

"Shit! How? There's no fucking way she should've been able to get through without detection. We're sealed tighter than damn Fort Knox. Do you want me to run a diagnostic on the sensors?"

"No, that's not necessary. There's nothing wrong with your sensors." Kenric ran his hands through his damp hair, pushing the unruly waves over his head, and leaned against the headboard. The antique wood frame creaked from his weight. "She was here, but not in the physical sense."

"Not in the physical sense. What do you mean? Like a ghost? What, is she dead? Could we get that lucky?"

"Shit, do you think I'd sound so pissed off if that were the case? No, in fact she's gotten stronger, and apparently, when I'm asleep, she's fucking found a way into my head. She's discovered a new talent, and now she can crawl inside my mind and pay me a visit."

Guerin whistled, long and low. "Damn, she's one sick bitch. Any idea how she's gained this new strength? If she's here messing with you, she must not have found a new male to get her hooks into."

"No. To quote you, 'I didn't get that lucky.'"

"We're going to find her. It will happen, my man. But you've got to promise me one thing."

"What's that?"

"A ringside seat when you run her through. You hear me?"

"Yeah, I hear you. And you've got it."

Guerin started detailing the previous night's watch. Kenric picked at the loose fiber in his towel, the other male's voice a distant hum in his ear. In the shower, he'd replayed every word Marguerite had uttered. There had to be a clue. She did nothing without an agenda. Marguerite was too arrogant not to have given him a hint so he'd figure out what she'd accomplished. "*Blended with the strength of my six centuries, plus the power I've procured.*" Could it be that simple? "I want you to ask Elle to research something for me," Kenric cut Guerin off.

"Oh, okay. Spill."

"I need her to find out everything she can on vampire lore from around the fifteenth and sixteenth century."

"All right," Geurin drawled. "Any particular thing she's searching for?"

"Marguerite chose her words carefully when she mentioned her new power. She brought up the fact that she's six-hundred years old and that she'd *procured* her new strength . . ."

Kenric flexed the fingers of his other hand, curling and uncurling his fist. "See if she can find any mention of ancient vampire myths pertaining to relics, or artifacts of power from that time period."

"Good idea. I'll get her on it."

"Anyway." Kenric shook his head, as if the act could erase the memory and her voice from his mind. Yeah. If only it were that easy to change his reality. Like the one where he woke every night to a dawn that consisted of shadows and moonbeams instead of UV and blue skies. If he had that kind of Etch-A-Sketch ability, he would have shaken it. "You were saying something about last night? What went down?"

"Another body's been found. A human female. Like the rest, raped and drained dry for the euphoric high by another DE-addicted vamp. That's three now in the past four nights."

"Too damn many." Kenric closed his eyes and squeezed the bridge of his nose with his thumb and forefinger. A headache hammered at the back of his eyeballs. "Where was she found?"

"The Docks. Arran found her on a side street, slumped behind a Dumpster. We took care of the remains."

"Marguerite's getting inside my head must be connected to the surge in the number of Death Euphoria-addicted vamps. She's turning innocent humans then watching them kill and fry their brains. No doubt they're her calling card to get my attention. And her presence felt too real to have been carried off telepathically from a long distance. She must be tired of playing hide-and-seek and now wants a game of tag."

Unbidden, Kenric's fingernails lengthened and curved into claws that dug into his palm. He needed to shift. The ability to shape-shift was the best part of being a vampire. If such a thing as a *good* part even existed. "Good" and "vampire" didn't quite belong in the same sentence. God, he needed to run, run until he exhausted some of his anger, before he exploded.

"Guerin, inform Arran I'll be on patrol tonight. Those murdering bastards are mine. Their cravings aren't going to give them a rest, and they won't be smart enough to find a new area for their prey. They'll be hunting tonight… And so will I."

Chapter Two

Midnight in Elizabeth Bay, South Carolina. Prime feeding time for the bloodsuckers he hunted. Despite the weight of his steel-toed boots, Kenric moved like a ghost on the cobblestoned streets. The music from a nearby pub vibrated against his chest and rang in his ears. He grimaced as a heavy-metal guitar solo ricocheted off the brick walls of the alley.

His black leather trench coat billowed behind him as the cold wind coming in off the bay funneled between the buildings, carrying with it the fish-laced, briny smell of the Atlantic. It wouldn't have been so bad if it wasn't also mixed in with the stench of rotten garbage and stale tobacco.

In a few hours, the bars along The Docks would close, emptying their drunken patrons. Most would stumble off to their vehicles, and if lucky in their state, would arrive home safely. A few wouldn't be ready for the party to be over, and they would linger, joining others who loitered after midnight on the dark corners. It was a vampire-feeding wonderland of drunks, prostitutes, the homeless, and drug addicts—a bountiful mix of easy prey.

There was only one problem: a vampire who couldn't control their urges and continued to feed until they killed their prey became addicted to Death Euphoria. From what he understood, DE was the exhilarating high received by the vampire at the moment their human prey died. DE-addicted vampires, or DEADs, were a menace to the human population, and had become an eternal pestilence for his Enclave.

Only one other thing competed with Death Euphoria for its addictive nature: the blood of an ancient or master vampire, the very thing that gave Marguerite control over her minions without the nasty side effect of turning their brain to mush like DE. He'd witnessed the effects of her ancient blood firsthand during the years he'd spent as her prisoner, watching as she used a vampire's craving for it as a tool to ensure his devotion. The vampire would become addicted to her and would do anything for Marguerite as long as he got another trip to her vein.

Voices neared the mouth of the alley. Stepping into the shadows, Kenric stilled, allowing the darkness to envelop him. Moments later, a young couple turned into the narrow corridor. They weaved into the alleyway, drunk and oblivious to his presence. Not that they would have noticed him, though, unless it was his wish.

The man wrapped his arm around the woman's waist, pulling her to him before whispering in her ear. She giggled and then kissed him, as if he held her next breath. Kenric rubbed a leather-gloved hand across his jaw. How many years had it been since he'd held and kissed a woman like that? Like he didn't know that he had slept alone for more than three centuries.

His world held no place for a woman. He had the Enclave to motivate him each evening, and vengeance against Marguerite to warm his bed each day.

It was enough.

It had to be.

The couple meandered around the corner at the end of the building. He should have been able to hear their footsteps fade, but the music's constant beat drowned out the subtle sounds.

Another gust of wind raced around the building. The chilled fingers of autumn worked their way along the exposed edges of his neckline. With a shiver, Kenric pulled his collar higher. The pungent scent of roses and musk from the woman's perfume continued to ride the night's breeze. He rubbed the back of a gloved hand across his nose and turned to leave. But a trace of a scent, hidden within the strong notes of the fragrance, sparked recognition. Anticipation kicked his heart rate into fast forward.

The heels of his boots pounded against the stone street. Rounding the corner with preternatural speed, he found two DEADs holding the young couple by their throats, their eyes and mouths wide with terror.

"You picked the wrong place to hunt for your prey tonight, boys."

Both bloodsuckers' heads jerked at the sound of his voice and they spewed a chorus of angry hisses.

Kenric slid his daggers free and twirled them around his leather-wrapped fingers. Assuming a defensive crouch, he studied them, waiting for their next move.

The vampires had an all-too-familiar look. Their faces glistened from copious amounts of smeared drool. It dripped from their chins and extended fangs. Dilated pupils swallowed up any visible whites of their eyes, turning them into something straight out of a B movie with alien vampires. Death Euphoria addiction consumed them.

He parted his lips to avoid breathing through his nose. Their bodies and clothes reeked of excrement and sweat. A classic symptom of DE addiction, it drove all but the need for the next kill from their mind, including the desire to bathe.

Kenric's gaze met the DEADs'. He dove into their minds, enthralling them, keeping the vampires' attention on him. "This is my city, and pissing me off will only get you killed," Kenric said. "Now, let them go."

Their hands opened. The humans dropped, coughing and wheezing with each breath. As soon as they hit the ground, Kenric released his control on the DEADs and thrust a hefty dose of mental influence into the couple's brains, erasing the memory of the attack and ordering them from the area.

"Fuck you!" Spittle sprayed from between one of the DEAD's overextended fangs. The nasty shit hit the street inches from the toe of Kenric's boot. If their brains had been firing on all cylinders, they'd have phased their asses away from him by now. But no. The bastards were like zombies with fangs—single-minded focus. Too juiced up to think past their bloodlust. They'd rather stand there and insult him, begging for a fight.

"Now, that's just damn rude."

With a flick of his wrist, he released a dagger. It flipped hilt over blade before sinking deep into the neck of the addict. Deep enough to hurt like hell but not far enough to end his sorry life. Yet.

The vampire shrieked in pain. His hands clawed at the dagger. Grabbing the hilt, he yanked the blade from his throat with a strangled cry. A gush of blood erupted from the open, sizzling wound. The river of red streamed down his neck and merged with the grime on the front of his *Got Milk?* T-shirt.

"You're dead, Enclave." The words, mixed with blood, gurgled from the damaged vampire's mouth.

"Promises, promises…" Kenric twirled his remaining dagger.

The vampires moved apart, circling him like vultures over road kill. Finally, they surged.

Kenric leaped, somersaulting in the air. He landed on the balls of his feet behind them. The two ground to a halt, nearly butting heads. He grabbed the forehead of the one on his right and ended his life with a swift slice of his silver-plated blade, leaving the murderer's head to dangle like an abused doll.

Ah, sweet karma.

He palmed the hilt of his dagger, enjoying the feel of its perfect balance as he rotated on his heels. The second creature reversed his step and spun, making for a quick exit. With a burst of speed, Kenric passed him, planting himself in the vamp's path. The DEAD slammed into Kenric's chest. Kenric lifted his dagger, preparing to give the rabid animal an undeserved merciful death.

But pain ripped through Kenric's right side, halting the intended path of his blade.

"What the fuck!" He whirled and found another vampire

had dropped in on the action. Another stab of pain shot through the right side of his neck. The vampire to his back had got in a lucky slice. Kenric's vision went red. He pivoted and threw a kick to the center of the vampire's gut. The DEAD crumbled to his knees, sucking hard for air.

Hot blood trailed down Kenric's side. Air sawed in and out of his lungs. His head pounded. Fury drove the blood in his veins.

Reaching out with his mind, he harnessed the power of the wind. A trick he wasn't sure every master vampire could pull off, but one he'd honed over the last century. His long coat whipped at his legs. Loose trash and sand formed a chaotic cyclone, disorienting the vampires around him. It gave him the distraction he needed.

Kenric closed his eyes. Power glowed in his mind like a white-hot orb. He coiled it tighter and tighter, compressing it, holding it as it grew. The heat of it burned inside his core for release. He shook from the increasing mental load, but he had to make sure it was enough. He would only get one shot.

Sweat ran down his face. He squeezed his eyes tighter, needing one more second…

Got it.

An invisible wave of energy exploded from his mind and body. It barreled into the newcomer and sent him flying into a brick wall. The loud *crack* of a shattered skull echoed off the stone streets. A limp and crumpled mound of vampire arms and legs slithered down the wall. He wasn't dead yet, but he was at least out of the game.

Two down, one to go.

He spun, grabbing the other DEAD's arm, and twisted.

The vampire howled in pain as the bones in his wrist snapped. The addict's knife *clinked* and bounced onto the sidewalk.

With the heel of his other hand, Kenric rammed the DEAD's forehead. The blow sent the vampire reeling back onto the concrete. Shoving his boot into the DEAD vampire's face and neck, he held him in place. The bloodsucker hissed, and his lower body squirmed in a desperate attempt to escape.

Blood soaked his shirt and clung like a warm second skin to Kenric's right side. Damn, he was losing blood too fast. Leaning over the flailing addict, he met the crazed eyes of the creature. "Like I said, pissing me off will get you killed." He plunged the blade of his silver-plated dagger deep into the vampire's heart.

Kenric yanked the dagger out and wiped the blood from his blade across the vampire's stained shirt. Smoke rose from the wound, and within seconds, the body reeked of sulfur and death, a stomach-churning aroma that smelled like a sour and rotting landfill. Loud *pops* and *crackles* sprang from the smoldering flesh. With a *whoosh*, the body swelled to twice its size and the sound of ripping seams punctuated the macabre event. Seconds later came the hissing release of implosion and decompression. Thanks to the nasty reaction of a vampire's blood to silver, Kenric didn't have to risk the hours it would take for the bodies and clothing to decompose to ash.

One stab directly into each of the two remaining DEADs' hearts, and the decomposition process was well under way. No evidence would remain of the battle for humans to find. Their blood would smoke with the rest of their bodies, leaving nothing behind. However, his own blood was making a fucking mess everywhere. He'd have to call Guerin to arrange for cleanup ASAP.

"Dammit!" He steadied himself against the wall before picking up the last scattered blade. His head spun on a perpetual carnival ride.

He edged along the wall with one hand for balance. The denim around his right leg, saturated with blood, clung with each step. The car was still four blocks away. Even as a master, there was no way in hell he'd have enough strength to phase back to the compound.

The wounds to his throat and side throbbed like a mother. The DEADs weren't organized enough to have their hands on silver-plated daggers. Good thing, because those open holes would be sending up smoke signals.

His vision clouded.

Sweat ran rivulets down the sides of his face and dripped into his eyes. The salt burned, obscuring his vision even more. Kenric leaned against the wall for support. His chest heaved. *Focus. Slow your breathing.* He reached inside his coat for his cell. *Going to need… Pickup…*

"Bloody hell!" Everything went black.

Chapter Three

"Come on… Move! It's the pedal on the right!" Emily glared through her windshield at the car with an out-of-state license plate crawling into the intersection. She twitched in her seat, her foot itching for the gas pedal. "God, I can walk faster."

Her path cleared, and she floored the accelerator of her Corolla. It sputtered, then lurched forward, building speed. She sighed in relief, amazed that something hadn't ruptured in the decade-old engine.

Track number five lit the LCD display on her CD player. Her favorite song, "Crashed" by Daughtry, filled the interior and lifted her spirits. Dialing up the volume with one hand, Emily thumped her fingers on the steering wheel with the other and hummed the melody, trying to settle her nerves.

She'd volunteered to pull the extra eight-hour shift tonight but hadn't counted on the weekend traffic clogging the main road into downtown Elizabeth Bay at this time of night. She was late, and she hated being late.

With a deep breath, Emily took the next turn, heading into the area known as The Docks. It was a seedy part of town, and she wasn't thrilled at the thought of maneuvering through there in the middle of the night. But if she kept her doors locked and kept moving, she'd be safe and shave ten minutes off her trip.

She'd been through there twice before, and each time the area had made her nervous. This trip didn't feel any less intimidating. The shortcut consisted of several turns through narrow cobblestone streets lined with bars, strip clubs, and streetwalkers.

With a death grip on the steering wheel, Emily made her third turn. This one onto Anchor, another one of the bumpy streets. Her Corolla rumbled and bounced on the uneven pavement, making her bones feel much older than their twenty-eight years.

A fine mist covered the windshield, creating murky, shadowy images. Emily tapped the wipers to clear the haze. To her right, the dark form of a man lay slumped on the sidewalk, his upper torso tilted in an awkward position, facedown. *Probably drunk out of his skull.* She shrugged but found herself slowing the car for a better look.

Emily clicked on her high beams. The wide berth of white light flooded the narrow corridor. An unmistakable trail of dark crimson ran from beneath him. She hit the brakes.

Stopping on one of these streets late at night was not the smartest move, but her internal need to help the man overrode her instinct for self-preservation. No way could she drive off and leave someone alone in the street to bleed to death. She quickly dialed 911 on her cell before grabbing her first-aid kit from her dash and exiting the vehicle.

The car's high beams cast a veil of white light around the man and her. God, there was so much blood. She placed two fingers on the side of his neck and checked for a pulse. His skin chilled her fingertips, but there was a faint thump. Shallow breathing warmed the palm she'd placed near his nose and mouth.

He was alive.

Her heart raced, each beat like a bass drum in her ears. *Hello, adrenaline rush.*

She ran to her trunk and pulled out an old wool blanket. Granted, she'd never expected to use it to cover a stranger who lay bleeding to death on the sidewalk, but hey, kudos for being prepared for anything.

First priority, she had to find the source of all the blood. After pulling on a pair of latex gloves from her emergency kit, she eased him onto his back, allowing gravity to aid her with his dead weight.

Bandage scissors made easy work of slicing up the center of his black shirt. An expanse of hard muscle brushed her knuckles as she worked. With his shirt pulled back as far as his leather coat would allow, Emily started her assessment at the top of his head, working her fingers along his scalp.

All clear.

A blast of cold wind stole her breath, reminding her of the urgent situation.

"Come on, Mister. You need to hang on for me."

Moving south, she found an open neck wound, but judging by the slow rate of seepage, no artery appeared to be nicked. It couldn't be the source of the large amount of blood. There had to be another injury.

Running her hands down his flank, her fingers slid into a

deep, penetrating wound. "Found you."

Emily ripped open a stack of gauze sponges and one by one packed them into the wound. Afterward, she covered his torso with the blanket. Satisfied she'd done all she could, Emily shuffled on her knees to recheck his pulse and respirations. With her cheek to his face, she felt for his breath on her skin and for his heartbeat with her fingertips. Warm puffs of air passed through his lips. *Thank God*. His pulse, though still weak, continued to beat.

The wail of distant sirens echoed through the narrow street.

"Not long now," she said, stroking damp raven curls off his forehead, her own breathing returning to a more natural pace. Emily traced the outline of his face down to the coarse whiskers of his chin. The fine hairs on her arms stood on end as she brushed the stiff hairs with the pads of her fingers. She shivered, blaming the cold mist.

Her thumb found the full curve of his bottom lip. Curious for the feel of the skin there, she brushed his lip with her finger. She gasped. Cool, and so very soft. Her teeth caught her own lower lip.

A blaring siren yanked Emily from her fascination. Her gaze fell back to where her fingers lingered on his lips and chin.

"What the hell am I doing?" she mumbled, snatching her hand away. God, had it been so long since she'd been with a man that she now resorted to touching one who was unconscious? Maybe her ex was right. *She* was the one in need of therapy.

The siren quieted and the emergency vehicle pulled to a stop behind her car. Two paramedics rushed from the vehicle, leaving the red and white lights to flash the dark street in dizzying strobe. Emily backed off, making way for the rescue workers to do their job.

They worked fast, assessing him while throwing questions she couldn't answer at her since she knew nothing at all about him.

With IV fluids now pouring into him and a defibrillator on hand, he had a chance. Relief swept through her on a wave of post-adrenaline rush trembles. She rubbed her arms in hopes of easing the shakes.

She breathed a long sigh of relief as they loaded him into the back of the ambulance.

"I'll follow you to the ER. I'm on duty tonight in trauma," she said.

One of the paramedics climbed into the cab behind the wheel. A silly grin lit his face as he glanced her way. "Well, looks like you got a jump start on your shift."

• • •

Someone was trying to pickax their way out of his skull.

The metallic smell of dried blood weighed heavy in the air. A wave of hunger coursed through him, tightening Kenric's stomach into an agonizing spasm. His veins burned, demanding to be fed. A thick fog clouded his mind. Where the hell was he, and what the hell had happened?

Muffled voices chattered in the distance.

The lethargy throughout his body had sealed his eyelids. Pushing through the haze muddling his brain, he assessed his surroundings. Along with blood, there was an acrid scent of antiseptic. Above his head, the repetitive sound of a mechanical heartbeat *pinged.*

Shit!

How the hell did he end up in a hospital?

Through the insistent pounding within his skull, the memory of his battle with the DEADs returned. He'd been about to call Guerin when he'd blacked out. Where the hell was his phone? He had to get out of here. The itch beneath his skin, like a fucking sundial, warned him that time was running out.

The heart monitor over his head lurched into a rapid succession of beats.

Get a grip, Kenric.

He couldn't risk drawing any unwanted attention. With a fierce hold on the gurney's rail for strength, he focused on his heart rate, slowing it to a steady pace.

Now, to find his damn phone. He searched along his left side, feeling for the lining of his coat. A cool draft floated in under the thin sheet. *Where the hell is my coat…and the rest of my damn clothes?*

Approaching footsteps and a trio of voices grabbed his attention. Taking a deep breath, he stilled his movements.

"You guys go ahead and get out of here. Can you give me a rain check on breakfast? I want to check in on our John Doe one more time before I leave."

"Come on, Emily. You've been at Memorial a year already, and you keep turning me down every time I try to get you to meet someone. Jake is really interested. I know you two would hit it off if you'd give it a chance."

"I promise I will. Soon. Just not this morning. Not yet."

"Fine," a female said with a sigh.

The sharp sound of metal rings sliding over a rod near

his head indicated one of them had entered his area.

· · ·

Emily closed the privacy curtain of the trauma treatment room. The unidentified patient she'd found earlier at The Docks lay unconscious on the hospital gurney. Bloodstained bandages covered his flank and neck.

Once the paramedics had gotten him here, the ER had been able to stabilize him with a few universal-donor transfusions. He remained in need of additional units to bring his hemoglobin into an acceptable range, though. Unfortunately, the lab was taking longer than usual to type and cross-match him. They'd found some kind of anomaly present in his blood work. There was even talk that he possibly had some form of leukemia on top of everything else, due to the extreme elevation in his white-blood-cell count.

She followed the rise and fall of his chest and couldn't help but admire the sheer will this man had to survive. And she couldn't ignore the fact that even though he lay there covered in bandages, he was the most beautiful man she'd ever seen.

His hospital gown stretched the breadth of his shoulders, while the arm openings strained to contain his biceps. The bed sheets covered the contours of his torso, but she remembered his washboard abs.

Wavy hair, a black so deep it shone under the fluorescents, was a little longer in front than back. It fell over his forehead, almost covering his eyes. The dark waves framed a regally defined face. But it wasn't perfect. In fact, a pale, thin scar ran along his right cheekbone, ending about an inch above his lip. To others, the scar may have damaged his looks. To her, it added character that accentuated his masculine features. The man was captivating, to say the least.

Her tongue traced her upper lip, and her body tingled.

Stop it, Emily! You're a professional nurse who shouldn't be ogling a patient. Just take his vital signs and get out of here.

Lifting his arm to check his blood pressure, she noticed the tattoo that wrapped around part of his right bicep. Unable to resist, she traced the outline of the connecting loops. It formed a figure eight lying on its side.

Infinity.

The symbol intersected with a dagger that pierced the center of the joining circles. Red drops of what looked to be blood dripped from the blade.

"What were you doing out there tonight?" she whispered. He was one very intriguing mystery.

Kenric lay perfectly still as the female approached him. Until he knew whom and what he was dealing with, he didn't want to give away that he was conscious. She paused at his bedside for a moment before lifting his right arm and placing a cool device under his bicep. She must be a nurse. He savored the warmth of her hands on his skin as her fingertips glided over his bicep. The nurse traced the symbol of the Enclave, and his flesh tingled.

Suddenly her touch disappeared as a cuff tightened around his arm. Her hair teased his chest, sending chills skating across his body. He drew in a long, deep inhale. The scent from her hair and skin filled his nostrils and burrowed deep inside his mind. Her fragrance reminded him of wildflowers after a spring rain. Warm, sweet, and spicy. And did nothing to quell the storm of hunger or soothe the growing need that accompanied his appetite at this state. Both threatened to unravel the edge of his control.

He clenched the fingers of his opposite hand, struggling to maintain his patience. His fist ached from keeping such a tight hold on his control. Another deep breath filled him, sparking every neuron in his brain. She was intoxicating.

Good God. The blood that remained within him surged into his groin. *Get a grip, man, before you do something you'll regret.*

He struggled to hold the vampire in check.

As if starved for her scent, he inhaled again and stifled a groan. His fangs lengthened. The drive to feed twisted in his gut.

Time had run out.

Harnessing the strength that his hunger provided, Kenric opened his eyes and reached for the woman. She swung her head around with a startled yelp. A wave of dark auburn hair fell over her shoulder.

Breathtaking.

Long, dark eyelashes framed hazel eyes specked with a hint of blue, green, and brown at the center. Her heart-shaped face held a small, upturned nose and rose-colored lips, the bottom one slightly fuller than the top. Kenric dragged his gaze away from her mouth. He needed to concentrate on holding her attention, not linger on the fantasy his mind and groin wanted to study in greater detail.

"I'm sorry," he whispered. "I didn't mean to frighten

you."

"I'm fine. Are you…okay?" Her gaze met his, giving him the opening he needed. Kenric slipped inside her mind to give her the mental nudge she'd need to accept his verbal commands.

"Don't be afraid. I need you very calm and very quiet. You are safe. Do you understand?"

"Yes."

"Good." His voice resonated, maintaining his hold. "What's your name, Wildflower?"

"Emily… Emily Ross."

"Emily, I need your help to get out of here. I want you to disconnect me from these monitors and tubes without bringing attention to us."

She didn't move. Instead, her mind pushed back, attempting to block his control.

"Now, Emily." He pushed in return, harder this time. His body trembled from the effort to maintain his presence in her mind *and* the rhythmic beat of his heart, so that the heart rate monitor kept its orderly beat. Red hair suited this female. The color matched her spirit.

As if in slow motion, her body rebelling, Emily did as he'd instructed. Her compliance took every ounce of telepathic influence and skill left at his disposal.

Once completed, she returned to his side.

He caressed the right side of her face, the warmth of her skin a heated embrace on his cool palm. With the gentle persuasion of his hand, Kenric brought her gaze back to connect with his.

"Lean closer to me, Emily."

Her eyelids narrowed, confusion written in her expression,

but she lowered her head. Kenric pulled her in, positioning her neck near his lips, and brushed a stray curl away from her neck.

"I'm sorry," he breathed against her skin. "If there was another way, I would take it. You see, you have something I'm in desperate need of." He didn't know why he felt the sudden, overwhelming desire to explain. He had to feed. And he would make sure she didn't remember when he'd finished. But something inside him needed her to understand and to not be afraid. "I'm not trying to hurt you. I promise. I will be as gentle as possible."

He savored another whiff of her sweet scent before tasting the area above her pounding pulse. She shivered, wringing a groan from his throat. He could wait no longer.

His fangs pierced her supple flesh. Tightening his hold, he held her immobile, not wanting to tear her skin. A moment later, Emily's body relaxed. He loosened his grip and gently caressed her arms, soothing her as he drank.

Her blood spilled into his mouth, a flood of hot and sweet. It filled his starved body in a tidal wave of sensation and pooled in his groin. He'd never tasted anything as luscious as the woman in his arms. And he wanted more.

Kenric reached farther around her body and lifted her onto the gurney with him. He wanted—no, needed—the feel of her whole body next to his. Her hip pressed against him. His eyes rolled in exquisite pain.

Finally, he reluctantly withdrew his fangs, licking the remaining spicy droplets of blood from the small twin holes on her neck. Pressing his tongue to the wound, he held pressure on the area for a few seconds to ensure clotting had taken hold.

"Thank you, Emily," he whispered into her ear, easing his arms from around her. She slumped.

"Shit!" He hadn't stopped in time. What the hell was wrong with him? A frantic shuffle ensued as he worked to slide out from beneath her and onto his side. Holding his breath, he checked for a pulse.

There was a strong beat.

Air rushed from his chest with relief. She'd passed out.

Good man, Kenric. This is really the way to get out of here unnoticed. He punched the pillow beneath them and silently groaned when he'd much rather have shoved his fist through a wall.

Now, not only do they have a slashed-up John Doe who will go missing, but also an unconscious nurse with bite marks on her neck.

Nice inconspicuous exit, asshole.

Kenric gripped the side rail of the gurney, pulling himself to a standing position while lowering Emily onto her back. His legs trembled under his weight, and he struggled to gain his balance. It would take a few moments to feel the full restorative effects of her blood.

Studying the auburn-haired woman in blue scrubs, he couldn't remember the last time he'd felt more alive than he had in the moments before he had fed. A physical response to do more than replenish his veins was normal, but not like that. Not to the point where he lost focus. He needed to get the hell out here, fast. *Wipe her memories and be gone.* He could take care of the mess he'd made after the fact.

With the back of her head in his palm, he closed his eyes, searching for the memories he needed to capture from her mind.

He lowered her head back to the mattress, then whirled, giving an exasperated swipe to his hair.

What the hell's wrong with you? You're not a damn fledgling.

He couldn't concentrate. Every time he found the memory he sought, it faded, slipping from his mind. It wasn't like he didn't perform this little trick at least once a week when he fed. What was it about her that had him so rattled?

Closing his eyes, he took a deep breath and slowly let it out. Back at the gurney, he held her head in his hand, searching once again for focus. This had to be done.

His mind rebelled. With a grimace, he lowered her head and threw his hands up in surrender. He couldn't do it. She didn't deserve to wake up alone, confused and sick, lying on an empty gurney. She didn't deserve to be confronted for an answer about what the hell had happened to John Doe. And maybe, he didn't want her to forget him.

Where did that *come from?*

He shook his head and huffed. He didn't need the complication of being responsible for a woman.

But cleaning up all traces of the John Doe from the hospital, with help from the inside…

He stared at his dilemma sleeping on the gurney. If he trusted this woman to help him, he would place the entire Enclave at risk. Kenric ran an impatient hand through his hair. But he couldn't, and, in truth, did not want to, leave her here like this.

"Guess there's only one way to handle this situation." He brushed an auburn lock of hair from Emily's cheek. "Wildflower, you'll be coming with me."

In a hospital bag on the counter in his room, he found

his clothes and coat. He reached in and pulled out his shirt and jeans. Sliced pieces of denim and cotton dangled from his hands. The hospital gown he had on was going to cover more of his body than the scissored mess the ER staff had made of his clothes. His phone was still in the coat pocket, though, and luckily in one piece. He pressed speed dial one for Guerin, who answered on the first ring.

"Kenric, where the hell are you, man? We've been trying to reach you all night. Arran's been out searching for you for hours."

"I'll explain when I see you. I don't have a lot of time. I need you to send a car to… Hang on." Kenric eased closer to Emily. Picking up the ID badge lying on her chest, he continued, "Elizabeth Bay Memorial."

"Elizabeth Bay Memorial! Shit, how the hell did you end up there?"

"Like I said, I don't have time for the details." Kenric's pulse thumped in his temples. "Just get me a car. Pull up outside the ER, ring my phone once you're in position, and I'll phase into the back."

"Give me about ten minutes. We found your Mercedes where you parked it. Michael's also out searching and should be near you. I'll get him to grab your car and haul ass over there. In the meantime, make yourself scarce."

Kenric snapped the cell phone closed, leaving it on vibrate to wait for the signal. Times like these, he was never more grateful to have Michael on his staff. Having a human around to venture out during daylight hours when the vampires were trapped indoors was an invaluable service.

Damn good thing they'd left his car where he'd parked it. It wouldn't take but a few minutes to get here, and with the extra tint on the windows, it would keep his ass from going crispy.

Kenric pulled back the edge of the blue-checked material surrounding his bed and scanned the area. A few distant conversations along with the clatter of equipment moved in the opposite direction. *Good, the area's clear for now.* Hopefully, it would stay that way for the next few minutes. He rubbed the stubble along his chin and sighed. With any luck, the staff would believe Emily had already left, her shift over.

Emily moaned and shifted on the gurney. Releasing the curtain, Kenric returned to her side. She was a little pale, but her pulse beat steady under his fingertips.

"Damn." He couldn't believe he'd been so reckless. His father had trained him for discipline and self-control since before he could walk. In his childhood home, those traits had either come to you naturally or you had learned them under the whip.

He *never* lost control when feeding.

The phone buzzed in his palm. The car was here. He dropped the cell into the hospital bag he held in his hand, then reached down and lifted Emily. She was a full and curvy woman, soft in all the right places, and fit perfectly in his arms. He loved the way she felt.

She whimpered and snuggled closer. Closing his eyes, Kenric fought the distraction of her body in order to focus on bringing the image of the car's interior into his mind. It would take most of the energy reserves Emily's blood had restored to phase them both the short distance.

He didn't have a choice.

It was the only option to get out of the hospital unnoticed. A passed-out nurse in his arms, and his ass flapping in the breeze while he waltzed out the front door, would not make for a subtle departure.

Slowing his heart rate, Kenric sharpened the image of the car's backseat in his mind. His body tingled. A brief falling sensation and momentary disorientation confirmed the phase. Less than a second later, he opened his eyes. They'd made it into the back of his Mercedes.

"Glad to see you're safe, sir," Michael said, turning around to toss a thick black blanket to his newly arrived passenger. Nodding his head of sandy blond waves at the woman in Kenric's arm, a slight smile curled at the corners of his mouth. "I see we'll be having a guest at the compound."

"That's correct. And we'll also be keeping this between us for now. Understood?"

"Yes, sir. However you want it." Michael faced forward.

"When we arrive at the compound, park the car near my private entrance."

"Understood, sir."

It would buy him some time. Keep her scent under wraps until he could explain—to her and to his warriors.

His skin stung even from the subdued morning light coming in through the tinted windows. Covering his face and body with the supplied blanket, and Emily as well, he eased back into the soft leather seat with Emily resting against his chest.

The car bumped and dipped, leaving the hospital parking lot. Michael revved the engine, accelerating them into the flow of traffic.

Kenric's mind raced with the upcoming task at hand: How could he convince Emily to help him erase his presence from the hospital? Not to mention, how to tell her why he needed it erased in the first place?

He was a vampire. Not just any vampire, but one who had already helped himself. He squirmed in his seat. Damn, how was she not going to be scared out of her mind? It would be scary enough for her to learn vampires were not a myth. Top that little bit of information off with the fact that she'd already been snacked on. Not good. Not good at all.

Inside the blanket, Emily's sleeping face lay pressed against his chest. He pulled her in tighter. He relished the stark contrast between the rough wool scraping at his arms and the softness of the woman contained within.

Draped in darkness, he could not escape thinking of her. Unable to resist it, he drew another intoxicating breath. He hoped working with Emily didn't take too long, because when he inhaled her scent and embraced her like this… Kenric closed his eyes. He didn't have the luxury of a distraction. Besides, any needs or desires he had for her weren't worth her dying.

Chapter Four

A hazy glow crept beneath Emily's weary eyelids. Lying on her right side, she peeked through her lashes, trying her best to make out the shapes and colors of an unfamiliar room. A lamp beside her illuminated her fuzzy environment. She blinked to clear her vision.

Where am I?

Did I get drunk last night?

She couldn't believe she would have gone out and gotten this wasted. Wait—no. She'd worked last night. Lifting the sheet covering her, she peered down at the now-wrinkled blue scrubs.

Emily performed a quick mental once-over of her body. She didn't feel like she'd been assaulted. Her head ached, and God, was she tired. If she didn't know better, she would swear she'd pulled a forty-eight-hour shift instead of an eight. Pressing her elbow into the mattress, she pushed up. The room spun, and the walls swayed with whirling, little white spots.

"Whoa, girl. Okay, well, that's not good," she mumbled on her way back down to the mattress.

With the option of pulling herself upright shelved, she tried to keep a tight-fisted hold on her growing anxiety. She looked around the bedroom. Rich browns and deep burgundies gave the large room warmth. A heavy mahogany chest of drawers with brass pulls sat across from her, resting on a dark-stained hardwood floor.

The bed appeared not only big enough for her but also one heck of a sleepover. Emily rolled onto her back. Massive, ornately carved posts stood at each corner. Her hands glided across dark and glossy burgundy sheets. *Wow, silk.* They had to be the most expensive available. *Really? Who was she kidding?* Like she would even know how cheap silk felt? But these sure were nice.

The door to her right opened. Emily closed her eyes. Whoever it was, she decided she would rather figure out their agenda before they knew she was awake.

The sound of bare feet padded around the foot of the bed. She opened her eyelids enough for a peek. A man with wavy, jet-black hair, wearing only a white towel hung low on his hips, stood with his back to her.

He didn't appear the least bit familiar. It wasn't like she needed two hands to count the number of men's bedrooms she'd been in, and there was no way she would have forgotten *that* body, even from the back.

His damp bronze skin glistened in the dim light of the room as he rummaged through a dresser drawer. Shadows formed in the valleys between the muscles flexing across his back. Tension and anxiety wound in her gut, making it difficult to remain still.

Who is he?

She glanced over to the lamp on the bedside table. The slender shape of the base would make a good handhold for a weapon. Movement in her peripheral vision captured her attention and had her gaze darting back to the man in front of her.

Without warning, the towel dropped from his hips.

"Oh, God!" Emily clamped a hand over her mouth. He must have not heard her, because he proceeded to bend over, his bare ass right in front of her. *Oh. My. God.* The finest-looking piece of male anatomy swayed against the inside of his thigh. She swallowed hard at the dry cotton lining the back of her throat and tried unsuccessfully to pull her gaze away.

He straightened and pulled on a pair of faded, snug-fitting blue jeans, up and over the tightest set of buns she'd ever seen.

He turned and lifted his hands out to his sides, displaying empty palms. "Please, don't be afraid. I'm not here to hurt you." Mr. Commando edged closer to her side of the bed. She had no idea what he had in mind, but she had no plans to hang around long enough to find out.

She bolted.

Her legs scrambled to propel her while her upper body weaved and wobbled to the other side of the bed. "Damn, damn, damn." Her feet hit the floor seconds before her legs melted. Strong arms grabbed her just before she hit the floor, face-first.

"We need to get some fluids into you." He scooped her up, holding her tight. Not like a mental patient who'd tried to escape, but rather like a fragile doll that had almost broken. The fight knocked out of her for the moment, Emily gave in and rested her head against his bare shoulder. The scent of warm sandalwood mixed with pine teased her nostrils. *Damn, he smells good.*

"No one's going to hurt you." He laid her back against the pillow.

The words sounded nice and all, but she wasn't taking them to heart until she had some answers. Like, now. "Who are you?" Emily grasped the sheet beside her and dropped it back to the bed for emphasis. "And what am I doing here?"

"To answer your first question, I'm Kenric St. James. And second, you weren't well, and I brought you here until you feel better." From the bedside table, he picked up a full glass. "Here, you need to drink. It'll help."

She recoiled. *He did not think she was going to drink that? She had no idea who he even was. He could be some ax murderer, for all she knew.*

"It's not poison, only water. Look." He tipped the glass to his lips and took a sip. His gaze never left hers as he swallowed. Emily followed the path the liquid took as it made its way down his throat and beyond. Her gaze landed on the light spray of dark hairs covering his chest. A wave of heat rolled from the tips of her toes to the top of her head in a hot rush. She'd never been what the other girls used to call "boy crazy." Had never sat and watched the way a man walked or talked. No man had ever appealed to her in that way. But *this* man. Whew! Her nipples tightened beneath her scrub top, sending a jolt of awareness between her legs. This man made drinking water a sexual act.

"See, just water," he said, handing the glass to her.

Emily crossed her arms, so he couldn't see how her body reacted to him. How embarrassing. She stared at the water, and then back at the stranger who called himself Kenric St. James. He hadn't tried to hurt her—yet, and her throat did feel like a dry lake bed. Deciding to give him the benefit of the doubt, she took his offer but immediately inched over in the bed. His presence…overwhelmed.

The cool liquid bathed her parched throat. She finished it off in three large swallows.

"Would you like another?" He raised his chin toward her empty glass. "You should drink as much as you can."

She nodded.

Kenric plucked the glass from her hand. The smell of the forest and the heady musk of testosterone radiated off him. *Very nice.* Some of the anxiety eased from her tense muscles only to gather in other places she did not want to think about.

He poured her a refill from the container on the bedside table. Still wet from a shower, his damp hair fell forward in soft ebony waves across his forehead. As he passed her the drink, his ink-black eyelashes lifted, and his gaze met hers. The color of his eyes knocked her off-kilter: azure. The same color she imagined tropical waters would appear as they rolled onto a white sandy beach on some faraway shore. Their fingers touched, and the glass wobbled in her hand. She jerked and glanced away, steadying the glass with her other hand.

He hovered at her bedside, following her every move. The way he watched her from under those lashes felt almost…possessive. *I'm not going to freak out. I'm not going to freak out. Breathe. In and out.* She inhaled through her nose and out her mouth. A parting gift from her ex left her paranoid of any man getting ideas of ownership. She had to keep a clear head. He was just making sure she was okay. At least that was what she was going to tell herself. All the way to the door.

She kept her sights trained on the tiny air bubbles in her glass and away from Mr. St. James. *What's wrong with me? I don't know this man. Yet here I am, sitting on a stranger's bed, getting all hot and bothered, instead of getting my butt up and out of here.*

"Look, I really appreciate you helping me. Really, I do. But I need to go home now. You can fill me in on what happened and how I got here on my way home. I'm sure everyone is worried sick about me," she added, glancing back up at the hard edge of his jaw. Her rational mind screamed, *Run, idiot.*

He reached for the water pitcher again. She couldn't help but follow the flexing line of muscles in his arms. Her gaze trailed along his smooth bronze skin and the cut outline of his forearm up to his defined bicep. An intricate black tattoo halfway encircled the muscle there. She reached out to touch the design. Her fingertips brushed the warmth of his skin. A sudden sense of déjà vu surrounded her, sending a shiver racing down her spine.

Emily couldn't take her eyes off the tattoo. Her stomach tightened, as if something unpleasant had joined with the ink. She'd seen this before, touched this same tattoo. Images shuttered past, frame by frame, as if she was viewing an old movie reel.

She had stood at the bedside of an injured male patient in the ER. Her fingertips had brushed the black and red pattern wrapping his bicep. The interconnecting loops had formed the infinity symbol, while a dagger, dripping blood, had penetrated its center.

The patient had woken up and gripped her arm. She'd jumped from the unexpected touch and beautiful vivid blue eyes had met hers.

Her gaze left the arm of the man beside her now and shifted to his face. Same tattoo, same beautiful blue irises, and the same scar that had graced the face of her handsome John Doe.

This isn't possible.

The patient on that gurney had had life-threatening stab wounds. She glanced to the right of Kenric's neck and saw a raised jagged pink scar. With her lungs tight and her heart in her throat, she scanned his bare chest and side.

Same story.

Impossible.

No one healed that fast.

"Who are you?" Shit, that sounded weak and shaky. Emily wanted to cringe but refrained. She hated to let anyone know she was afraid, especially a man.

"Kenric St. James, remember?"

"I know that's what you said, but you look just like my patient from the ER last night. A John Doe. A man I found stabbed and near death down at The Docks. But that's not possible, right?"

No answer.

Air sawed in and out of her chest, and with each passing moment, she inched farther across the bed and away from the man.

More memories from the previous night unreeled.

He'd asked her name, and then she'd been like a puppet on a string. She had detached the John Doe from his heart monitor and IV. Her mind had rebelled, but her arms and legs had worked against her. She had had to help him. He needed to leave. The words cycled on repeat in her head.

Next, she had sat on the gurney beside him. Per his command, she'd leaned closer. Her heart raced as the memories continued to unfold. *What had he done?* He had gripped her upper arms, urging her even closer, until his whiskers scraped her cheek. His words had whispered in her ear. He was sorry. He wasn't going to hurt her. The warmth of his breath had heated and caressed her skin.

The hairs on the back of her neck lifted and stood on end, ushering the last missing piece of the puzzle into place. Chills ran down her back, causing her to shiver.

"Oh my God!" Emily launched herself to the other side of the bed. Water sloshed in her wake from the forgotten glass, now overturned and pooling on the sheets. Sitting up on her knees with her hand at her throat, she gawked at Kenric St. James from the other side of the bed. Her fingertips brushed over two raised and tender bumps on the side of her neck.

"What did you do to me?"

He sat there, unmoving, watching her with those piercing blue eyes.

"Answer me!"

Kenric watched as Emily's hazel eyes ignited in frustration. Her reaction to what he'd done played out exactly how he'd imagined it would. He'd run this scenario a dozen times or more in his mind before she had woken up. The problem was, he wasn't any closer to knowing what to say to her at this moment than he'd been hours ago.

He'd fed on her. How does one downplay that reality? Somehow, when all was said and done, he hoped she wouldn't hate him. She could hate the vampire. He could live with that. But for some reason, it mattered that she didn't hate the man behind the monster.

Kenric backed away from the bed. He raised his hands in a nonthreatening manner. "Emily, please, I realize this sounds absurd after what you remember, and I know it must seem like these are the only words I know, but I'm not going to hurt you."

"What did you do to me? I remember you at my neck. You… It felt like… You bit me! Why would I sit there and let you do that? Why on earth *would* you do that?"

Emily slid from the bed, trying to get as far away from him as the room allowed. Holding on to the curtains for balance, she stood before a wall of covered windows. With her eyes clenched shut, she gave herself a hard pinch.

"Ouch!" She opened her eyes and grimaced when their eyes met. He couldn't resent her disappointment in his continued presence.

"You're not dreaming," he softly responded. She straightened, stood a little taller. *A woman with dignity. Pride.* He respected that, and her bravery in the face of what must feel like a nightmare. Most women would be sobbing by now and begging for mercy. This fiery redhead just got pissed. And damn if she didn't heat his blood with all that fire.

"There's a lot I need to explain. Do you think we can

talk? Can you just sit for a moment? You'll have your space. I'll sit over there." He indicated the overstuffed leather furniture in the sitting area on the other side of his bedroom. She glanced in the direction he pointed, then quickly back to him. Her guarded stance and the small clenched fist she held at her side said it all: she thought he was crazy. No doubt a part of him was, for what he was about to ask her. He had a whole lot of shit to dig out from underneath, and he had to make it smell sweet if he wanted any chance in hell of gaining her trust.

"Let me explain what happened last tonight," he said. "I give you my word. I will never touch you again without your consent."

Chapter Five

Marguerite breathed deep and pressed the combination sequence into the small square of buttons on the jeweled box sitting on her dresser. The lock released with a *click*. She opened the lid, and then pulled the deep drawer out. Inside lay a velvet sleeve covering an object the size of a large orange. Marguerite lifted it from its resting spot and slid it into her palm. She stared down at her newly procured source of power, her lips curling in a satisfied grin. This would ensure her success with Kenric.

The crimson glass vessel, formed in the size and weight of a human heart, warmed her flesh as if it still contained the live, beating essence of its former owner, Goran Madunic, not the thick sludge drained from the vampire's heart more than six-hundred-years ago. She held it up to the lamp beside her. The light shimmered off the colored glass and highlighted the dark shadow of the level remaining in the relic. Not much left—a blunt reminder of the ticking clock that hovered over her plans.

The door to Marguerite's chamber opened.

"Mistress, please excuse the interruption, but I thought you would want to…" The male's words stopped short as Marguerite jerked her head in his direction. Swinging her arm out with her palm upright, she hurled a merciless blast of energy at her intruder. It slammed into him, knocking him off his feet and into the wall behind him. A gasp of air left his lungs as he crashed into the wall and slid dazed onto the floor.

"You fool!" she shrieked. "You're lucky I don't kill you where you lie for such ignorance. The next time you *will* be dead, and I shall find a new leader for my colony."

They annoyed her at times, but she found it necessary to keep a few loyal vampires—minions—around whose minds were still intact, addicted to her and not DE. They served her sexually and were happy to handle whatever else she needed them to do, for just another sip at her vein. But that didn't make them irreplaceable.

Shaking her head, Marguerite thrust the orb back into the security of her lockbox and brought her attention back to the current matter at hand: the vamp who lay sweating on her floor.

"Forgive me, Mistress." Enrique pulled himself up off the hardwood and onto his knees. He crawled over in front of Marguerite. "I bring news of Kenric."

"What have you learned?" He remained bowed before her, his straight brown hair partially covering his face. Marguerite savored the way the candlelight glowed on the chocolate color of his naked torso, his sides flaring with each rapid breath.

"Kenric was on patrol last night. Alone, he attacked and killed three of your DEAD recruits, Mistress."

"Excellent," Marguerite replied. She could care less whether the insane bastards lived or died. All of her recruits were dispensable. What mattered most was if they'd served her purpose. And they had. "With my visit and the increase in addicts *he's* hunting now—Kenric knows I'm here." She stood, allowed her robe to fall from her shoulders and drape over her chair, leaving her naked as she moved to her bed. She stretched out across her mattress and sighed. "I do love to agitate him. He could never tolerate killing feeble humans." Rolling onto her side, she asked, "Who told you about Kenric?"

Enrique shuffled around on his knees in the direction of her voice.

"One of your addicts, present during part of the battle, gave a description of the Enclave warrior who had attacked them. It matched your Kenric St. James, Mistress."

"This vampire was not killed with the others?"

"No, Mistress. It appears he ran as the others were attacked. He went back when the fighting was over and found nothing but ashes."

"He ran?" She lunged upright onto her knees and yanked Enrique to her by the back of his neck, digging her nails into his flesh. "Does he still live?" she hissed, her face inches from his.

"Yes, Mistress. I've questioned him but kept him alive for you. I thought you may have further need of him."

"I have no use for cowards. Kill him." She jerked her palm away, and Enrique stumbled back.

He turned to leave. "Where are you going? You haven't

been dismissed, Enrique. You have a job to finish here first." Marguerite lowered herself onto her bed. With the crook of her finger, she beckoned her minion leader forth. He obeyed, crawling onto the bed and between her legs.

Twenty minutes later, Marguerite rose from her bed and glided back to her gilded Louis XIV vanity, leaving her trembling minion on the bed. She lifted her robe off the chair and slipped it on, enjoying how the cool, ivory-colored silk hardened her nipples and brought chills to her overheated flesh. The matching gilded chair, covered in her favorite ruby red velvet, sat before her mirrored dresser. She perched on the seat and selected her heavy gold hairbrush.

Her complexion glowed, thanks to the hearty meal she'd just partaken in. She brushed her hair in long, sweeping strokes and stared at the image of the sweat-drenched body of her painfully unfinished lover. Enrique moaned but lay very still. He knew better than to budge until she had dismissed him. His raging hard-on was the only thing brazen enough to move on his taut, muscled body. The wet shaft glistened and pulsed in the lamplight, as if begging its owner for relief.

She loved the power. Such a rush. After having endured seventeen years under her father's brutal hand, even though it was centuries ago, she always made sure she got what she wanted.

Always.

Never again would she allow a man to rule her, treat her as if she were less than the mud caked on their boot heels.

Her childhood years had been spent watching her so-called father shower his daughters with attention and fancy gifts. The rest of his hours had been spent taking out his anger, resentment, and disappointment on Marguerite. But her half-sisters hadn't held a candle to the body and beauty she had possessed. And she'd learned to use it. Marguerite's looks had never failed to get her what she needed from men. Her allure had even succeeded in capturing the eye of a young male vampire who, after becoming so enamored with her, shared his gift.

A gift she had been more than willing to receive.

The sound of Enrique's labored breaths filled the room. She glanced over at his trembling body. She'd almost drained him dry—just for the hell of it—before allowing him to take a small sample of her. But it only took a small amount of her ancient blood to have him soaring. She smirked in the mirror, her pulse visibly pounding at her neck at the thought. Marguerite closed her eyes, relishing in the surge of power she'd sampled from the heart-shaped orb only moments before her minion had barged into her chambers.

The small sip Enrique had stolen from her body in bed, before she'd returned the favor, would burn like a raging fire in his veins, making it near-impossible for him to maintain control. A slave to his lust.

To her.

There had been only one vampire whose mind and body she couldn't control: Kenric. That would soon change with the new source of power she'd found in Goran's blood.

God, how she wanted Kenric back. Beside her. Joined. An indestructible unit. Exactly how it had been destined.

"You can leave now, Enrique," she said offhandedly. "I'm done with you. Take care of the matter we discussed. I will not tolerate cowards in my ranks."

Enrique slid off the bed onto wobbly knees. He quickly

braced himself with the nearby bedpost while struggling to fit back into his black leather pants.

"Oh, and Enrique?" He stopped and turned. "Remember, there will be no release until you've earned my forgiveness. I don't care who you fuck. It won't matter. That aching dick is punishment for your earlier interruption."

His face gave a visible flinch. She smirked at his obvious discomfort before adding, "Don't look so worried, dear. It will go down...eventually, when my blood is finished with you. Or when you've convinced me you're truly remorseful."

Marguerite turned to face the mirror again, giving him her back as her dismissal. The door softly clicked as it closed behind him. Picking up her brush, she continued with her hair.

"It won't be long now, Kenric," she said to her reflection. "Your time away is almost over."

Chapter Six

Emily studied Kenric's expression for any sign of a hidden agenda.

He was good.

Really good.

Not a twitch.

She should run. Get the hell out of here before he could do whatever the hell he'd done to her again. But her curiosity and fatigue won the fight, and she found herself edging around the bed toward the sitting area. *God grant me the nine lives of a cat, because my curiosity could get me killed.*

Sinking into one of the large chairs, Emily wrapped herself in the sense of security the huge, soft leather arms provided.

Seconds later, Kenric was at her side.

"Take this," he said as he neared. She glanced up. He held a navy blanket out to her. "If you're cold."

"Thank you." Emily grasped his offering and draped the soft material across her before pulling a handful up to her neck. Crazy. Good-looking. And nice, too. What was she to do with that combo? Run. Get as far away from the toxic combination as possible. That was what she *should* do. She'd already done crazy more times than she'd like to admit, and had vowed to make Elizabeth Bay her fresh start. Without some guy messing up her life. She could almost hear the warning bells ringing away inside her head. So what was she doing plopped in the middle of this mad man's den? She sighed. *Listen to his story, Emily. Smile, then get out of here and forget this guy ever existed.* He may have gorgeous eyes and a six-pack any woman would give their best pair of shoes to scratch. But he was a big heaping mess of trouble. She could smell it.

He paced before her. He reminded her of a lion crossing his den. Something she might have called a bit egotistical and a turn-off with any other man, but it was different with him. She found his profound confidence…provocative.

He pulled on a snug-fitting black T-shirt before taking a seat. She couldn't help but notice how the sleeves strained around his upper arms. He massaged his neck with the palm of his large hand as he leaned back against the cushion. His T-shirt rode up, revealing his rippled abs. Her pulse quickened. She licked her lips and swallowed, trying to bring some moisture back to her throat. *Why did he have to look so damn edible?*

Finding a new position, Kenric released a long sigh, as if he couldn't get comfortable. Emily glanced at his expression and caught him rubbing his hand across his face. He looked about as nervous as she felt.

"What I'm about to tell you will probably be hard to believe. There's no easing into it. All I can do is just come out and say it." He leaned forward on the loveseat and placed his elbows on his knees. "What you've seen tonight, the speed at which my injuries have healed and what happened to you in the ER, is because"—he cleared his throat—"is because, I'm a vampire."

"A vampire?" Emily pushed herself from her seat, making sure to hold on to the corner of her blanket with one hand. Her legs wobbled. Grabbing the arm of the chair, she leaned against it and regained her balance.

"Come on," she said, rolling her eyes.

He nodded. "It's true."

"So, what you're trying to shovel my way is that you bit me, drank my blood, and that's the reason why I don't remember coming here?"

He nodded again.

"And the reason why your injuries have healed within hours, of what would normally have taken weeks of recovery time, is because you're a vampire?"

Another nod.

"Come on," she scoffed. "You can do better than that. Vampires are a myth, a scary bedtime story for children."

"We're real, Emily."

His demeanor was calm. His face a rock. He acted as if he really wanted her to believe what he was saying.

"Okay," Emily began. "Here are my two theories on the crazy story you just threw at me. Maybe you're covering up for some new genetic research that the government doesn't want us to know about. Or, maybe the biting thing is just because you're a pervert. Either of these I might have believed. They're better than the vampire story."

"Then why do you feel so tired?" He lifted one dark slash of a brow. "And why don't you remember coming home with me? Why did you help me at the hospital?" He leaned back on the love seat and propped one leg over the other. "Your memories are there. Did it not seem odd to you how you were drawn to help me, and why you did the things you did?"

"You drugged me." She shrugged. "Somehow, you drugged me."

"I was sliced open and flat on my back in a hospital gown. How would I have drugged you?"

His blue gaze turned smoky, his intensity enveloping. Her skin tingled. Not out of fear. No, she didn't sense intimidation. More like sensuality, radiating like a beacon, and she was a ship sailing into port.

Emily pushed away from the arm of the chair, tossed the blanket onto the seat, and turned her back to escape his lure. She ran her fingers through her bed-head, shaking off the need to allow him to draw her into his madness. And his seduction. She'd been down that route before, caving in to a man's charms and going against her better judgment. Never again.

She didn't know what kind of bullshit he was trying to shove down her throat, but she wasn't buying the whole vampire thing. As much as she hated to admit it, though, she didn't have a logical explanation for anything that had happened last night.

It felt good to be upright, she realized, stretching her legs. The longer she stood, the steadier she became, and she needed to feel better. Fast.

Since he obviously wasn't going to tell her the whole truth, he *was* going to tell her what he planned to do with her. She set her teeth and turned back around, ready to dig in and get some answers.

"I'm going to cut to the chase here. Answer me this: whether you're a vampire or not, why did you bring me here?" She waved around the room. "You planning on finishing me off in private?" Her voice rose when he straightened in his seat, both eyebrows shooting up. "Am I right? Don't play games."

He uncrossed his legs and leaned forward, his expression turning severe as he met her stare dead-on. She sucked in a startled breath and took a step back from his abrupt mood change. His eyes glowed with what appeared to be fire swirling around his pupils. *Okay, now that…that does* not *look human.*

"I will never feed on you again, or hurt you, Wildflower." His deep voice rolled into an accent she hadn't noticed before, catching her off guard. She clutched her abdomen. *What was it with him calling her* Wildflower*? She was not a delicate little flower to be plucked or rescued. But whatever. She had no intention of hanging around long enough to be offended by what he called her.*

"I am…truly sorry about what happened at the hospital," he added. "I was thrown into a situation that left me with no recourse but to take what I needed to survive and get out of there as quickly as possible. I do not kill humans for their sustenance."

She needed to sit down.

This could *not* be happening.

Emily lowered herself back onto the thick seat and

tucked her legs underneath her. The man before her may be a freak of nature, or some kind of alien, but she sensed he meant it when he said he wouldn't hurt her again.

Her heart rate descended from the ceiling with the revelation that she wasn't about to be the next face on a missing-person flyer. Except…who would post one? Or for that matter, who'd really miss her? She'd been lying when she'd said earlier that a lot of people would be worried about her if she didn't come home. The truth was, the only people who would miss her would be her coworkers when she didn't show up for work tomorrow night. God, wasn't she pathetic? She mentally kicked herself out of her own pity party.

"Okay, well." She nodded. "That's good to hear. And since you said you didn't bring me here to finish the job, I'd like to go home now." She rose, but Kenric got to his feet at the same time and reached out, halting her progress.

"You can't go yet."

"Why not?" She jerked her arm away from his hold. "I'm feeling better. So I'm ready to leave." Emily hit him with her best glare. "Or am I your prisoner?"

"You think you're better, but you're not. And no, you're not my prisoner." He headed over to the phone sitting on the nightstand. Kenric picked up the receiver but looked back over his shoulder before dialing. "I need to get you something to eat first."

Emily moved around to the back of the chair and observed him at the phone. If she could get a few minutes alone, maybe she could call someone for a ride. Except she didn't know where she was.

"That isn't necessary." She dug her nails into the padding

of the chair's back. "Really, it's not."

He put a hand up, silencing her protest. "Michael, I need a breakfast tray prepared for our guest." He hesitated a moment, listening. "Just prepare a sample of several different items. I'm sure she'll find something that pleases her. I'll be down to pick it up. No, that won't be necessary. I'll pick it up. Inform Guerin I'll be down momentarily."

What is he thinking? I don't care how sexy he is or what crazy things his hint of a British accent makes me want to do to him. I'm so not staying around here waiting for breakfast. Her gaze stroked Kenric's profile, her mind straying to places and parts she shouldn't be traveling. *You should be more worried about how you're getting your ass out of here, Emily Ross, rather than how firm those big biceps would feel under your hand. And how soft his hair looks, and what those dark waves would feel like when you run your fingers through them. The man just bit you, and good Lord, he told you he drank your blood! He's insane! You're not that easy or foolish, girl.*

"I can't let you leave without protein for strength and something in your system to at least bring your blood sugar back up. Besides, there's more I need to talk to you about." He moved toward his dresser. "Would you like to take a shower?"

The oh-so-handsome and thoughtful lunatic pulled out a pair of his sweats and a T-shirt from the drawer and handed them to her. She took them automatically, but her clothes were staying on.

"Like I said, I'm really not planning on staying here that long," she said, looking down at the offering.

"Take a shower. It'll make you feel better."

The pleading sound of his voice pulled her gaze back to his. It sounded as if he genuinely cared. She couldn't remember the last time she'd heard a man sound as if he cared about what happened to her, or how she felt.

"By the time you're finished," he continued, "breakfast will be here."

She considered her options, looked at the bathroom door, then back to Kenric.

"Don't worry. I won't bother you. You have my word. You can lock the bathroom door." He moved closer, his bright blue eyes a striking contrast under the dense layer of raven eyelashes. "No one will hurt you here."

He sounded so believable and sincere. And a shower did sound heavenly. On that thought, she moved with hesitant feet toward the bathroom. In the doorway, she glanced over her shoulder at the handsome, crazy man/vampire/whatever. He held his jaw tense, his body taut, but he didn't make a move. She closed the door and dropped her forehead against it with a sigh. She believed him. Down deep, at the level where a woman responded to a man. But inside her head, where the mental scars from too many bad relationships had left deep grooves, she wasn't so trusting.

Emily turned the lock. *Click.*

• • •

Laughter rolled out from behind the swinging door to the kitchen. There was no mistaking the baritone voice resonating from the other room. Guerin, his second-in-command.

Whatever had him so cranked up, more than likely, was

at Michael's expense. Guerin lived to give him a hard time. Michael could hold his own, though, and when necessary, he, too, could give as good as he got. Kenric highly suspected Michael enjoyed the bantering even more than Guerin.

Their laughter came to an abrupt halt as he stepped into the kitchen.

"Hey, man! Glad to see you're no worse for wear." Guerin sat his mug down and left his seat at the island, greeting him with a slap on the back.

Kenric murmured his thanks before heading over to the kitchen table and grabbing the seat at its head. Guerin joined him, sitting in the chair to his right.

"You *are* no worse for wear, right?"

Kenric saw Guerin's eyebrows draw down in concern as he eyed the thick, jagged scar on the side of his neck.

"Yeah, man. No worse for wear," Kenric answered with a dismissive wave of his hand, never meeting Guerin's eyes. "I'm healing fine." He palmed the still-sensitive raised flesh. Mentally…that was yet to be decided. He'd know more about how he was doing once he got past the situation he'd left showering in his bathroom, and the mess he'd left behind at Memorial. This type of screw-up wasn't like him. Bringing a female into his quarters, even with the best of intentions, wasn't like him. He couldn't afford this kind of distraction. And Emily Ross was most certainly a distraction. Kenric inhaled a deep breath and tried to pick up the thread of the current conversation. Work—that's exactly what he needed.

Heavy boots sounded in the hallway, moving in a steady procession toward the kitchen. Arran and Markus entered seconds later, one behind the other.

The temperature in the room took a nosedive at their

entrance.

They crossed the expanse of the kitchen in full patrol gear, daggers strapped on their legs.

Markus was the last one to sit at the table. As always, his long, straight black hair was bound at his neck by a leather strap. Kenric shook his head. The vampire always kept everything perfectly in its place, including his hair and his well-groomed goatee.

Neither of the two spoke as they took their seats for the evening's briefing before patrol. Nothing unusual. Social graces didn't sit at the top of their list of priorities.

An unspoken understanding existed among the group. Both possessed an aura that screamed: *keep your distance*. They seemed to prefer it that way. Regardless, when it came to trusting someone to watch your back, they didn't come any more loyal than Arran and Markus. That's why they were Enclave.

"If you two run into trouble and need any backup, Logan will be covering operations tonight along with Elle," Kenric said.

Arran and Markus lifted their chins in an affirmative reply. Arran's eyes never left his cup while he poured a dose of dark, French-roasted brew. Straight up, no cream or sugar. He two-fisted his cup, drinking with his eyes closed. His blond hair hung loose at his shoulders, shadowing his face. Arran had been the last to join his Enclave, but with a blade, the vampire could already hold his own against any of his other warriors. In fact, he was probably the best.

"Are you going to fill us in on what the hell happened last night?" Guerin stared at him, then swung his gaze wide to include the other warriors at the table.

"That's why I'm here," Kenric said, but instead of heading straight into the immediate, uncomfortable details involving the female upstairs, he turned his attention to another important matter. "How much longer until the breakfast tray is ready, Michael?"

"Give me another fifteen minutes."

"Excellent."

"A breakfast tray?" Guerin turned in his chair, glancing over at Michael, who had pulled out a silver bed tray and was stacking it with assorted pastries and a full carafe of orange juice.

Guerin returned his attention back to the table. "You know how I love me some food, but you…" he aimed an index finger at Kenric's chest, "*You* never eat. What the hell's going on?" He pinned Kenric with an unspoken *don't-shit-me* look.

"I'll be getting to that later. Right now, and more importantly, we need to discuss what went down last night, and who I feel it's all tied to."

Kenric recounted the previous night's events to his team, starting with his dream visit from Marguerite. He left out the details that involved his murdered fiancée. His warriors didn't need to know that. Only Guerin knew the full details regarding his past. With his team, Kenric was neither inclined nor felt a real need to reveal the privities of his former life. They understood Marguerite had been his sire, and that she had a destructive history. And that she relished the power of being a vampire and the superiority it gave her over humans—especially men who had the misfortune to fall in her path.

That alone made her dangerous.

That was all they needed to know.

After he gave details about Marguerite, he moved on to the attack by the three DEADs.

"We've got more of a problem than just one DE addict on our hands." He sighed. "Marguerite is apparently creating her own personal circus of bloodsuckers. I feel that last night's incident was a taste of what is to come. In my dream, she made sure I was aware of some new power source she's acquired. Guerin has Elle working on a theory to find out what we may be dealing with. That's why, from this point on, all patrols are to be carried out with a partner. No solo flights." The stronger Marguerite became, the more destruction she brought to the human and vampire realm.

He motioned to his second. "Guerin, I need you to make the necessary adjustments to the schedule." Guerin nodded. Kenric turned his attention back to the table of warriors. "We may not be able to cover as much territory, but I'd rather lose ground than lose one of you to a multiple-DEAD attack. Not saying any of you couldn't handle the fight. You're exceptional, or you wouldn't be here. You warriors at this table are all that's protecting our existence here . . . *and* the human population. But it isn't worth the risk."

Kenric pushed his chair back. He needed to move. His skin felt too tight over his bones, as if he needed to stretch. He strode over to the kitchen island. Once there, he leaned his back against it.

The cool edge of the tiled countertop brushed the backs of his arms. A nice distraction from the low-level burn that had been ignited at the ER. The etiology behind the feeling he wasn't prepared for, nor had the time, to sit back and analyze. Kenric crossed his legs at the ankles, showing his team a more relaxed posture than he felt. The rest of his report would not sit well with his Enclave.

"Now, about the food." Kenric glanced around the table. He definitely had everyone's attention. "It's for... I have a...a guest. Her name is Emily Ross."

The last swallow of coffee made its way down Arran's throat in one large gulp, choking him. Bloody hell, the looks on their faces alone were worth having her here. Had he become so predictable? Yes, he hadn't had a lover in three centuries. But he didn't realize he'd covered it so poorly.

"You have a guest?" Guerin, of course, was the first to find his tongue. "You were in the hospital last night. When did you bring someone here? You never approve of any outsider in the compound without prior notification—and she's human," he said, acknowledging the tray loaded down with food. "Why would you, master of our Enclave, take this kind of risk?"

Kenric uncrossed his ankles and squared his shoulders. "There were extenuating circumstances. I would not have taken the risk of bringing a human here unannounced without a *very* good reason. I haven't survived all these years without a semblance of intelligence."

Guerin returned Kenric's hard glare. Kenric knew his friend and advisor had a legitimate beef about the risk he'd taken with security. But if he had to do it all over again, he would make the same decision. As his second-in-command, Guerin deserved a heads-up on all decisions that could affect the Enclave. Nevertheless, something, and everything, about Emily brought out his protective instincts. He'd be damned if anyone, best friend or not, questioned him.

This time, Markus broke the silence, his deep voice

breaking the tension. "So what happened last night that earned us the privilege of a houseguest?"

Kenric swung his focus to the warrior who watched him with cold gray eyes from the opposite end of the table.

"I lost a lot of blood during the battle, and by the time I came around, I was in the ER in the grips of bloodlust. A nurse came in to check on my status, and I had to take the opportunity to feed."

Kenric let out a deep breath as he dropped back into his seat. He would rather spend a week on the battlefield, fighting and bleeding till the brink of exhaustion and death, than tell his team of his lack of self-discipline with the woman.

The faces of the warriors around him remained stoic. They waited in silence.

"She collapsed." Eyebrows lifted around the table. Dammit, he had always been the embodiment of self-control.

"I didn't kill her, for God's sake." Kenric's deep voice echoed across the expanse of stainless steel and tile. His voice was a bit harsher than he'd intended, but he needed to make sure they were clear as to what went down.

"There were already going to be too many questions regarding the John Doe who disappeared from the hospital. I couldn't leave an unconscious nurse behind with bite marks on her neck. Besides…," Kenric leaned back in his chair and surveyed the expressions of his team before finishing. "I thought she would be beneficial in cleaning up the situation with the hospital."

Guerin placed his elbows on the table. "So, this nurse, how's she handling the news that she was bitten by a vampire, and that those fangs belonged to you?" One long index finger pointed in Kenric's direction. "Or have you yet to broach that subject?"

"I've told her. She doesn't believe me. Thinks I'm crazy, or that I'm covering up some kind of military conspiracy experiment. I guess that's easier to believe than the existence of vampires." Kenric fought back the urge to smile as he recalled her stubborn defiance. He leaned forward and swiped a hand through his hair. "Don't get me wrong, she was frightened when she remembered what happened last night, but she's shown real courage. Quite impressive, actually."

Guerin nodded, a slow grin spreading across his face, showing his teeth minus the fangs.

Kenric narrowed his eyes on Guerin. "What?"

"Umm…nothing. I just haven't seen you ever talk about a woman so…fondly before. Kenric glared at Guerin. The silence screamed, *shut the hell up*.

"So…what's your plan?" Guerin said, ignoring Kenric's glare. "How would you like us to handle this?"

"Arran, Markus, you two can head out when you're ready." Their chairs scraped across the tiled floor as they left their seats. "Watch your backs."

"Always," Arran said, closing the door behind them.

"As for your question." Kenric returned his attention to Guerin. "It's business as usual. Hopefully, things will go well with Emily this evening, and I'll bring her down to work with Elle. I think she'll accept the truth and be willing to help. If not, there's always the alternative." His mind rebelled the moment the words left his lips. He hoped to hell he didn't have to go that route.

"Emily."

Hearing her name drop from Guerin's lips snagged his

attention.

"Her name. It's nice," Guerin said. "Is she as pretty as her name?"

Everything that made Kenric a master vampire roared to life. He stifled a growl. His jaw tightened with the effort to subdue his instinct to leap over the table and grab the other vampire's throat. How *dare* he even consider her attractiveness?

Kenric took a deep breath and then cleared this throat. *Tame your beast, St. James. She's not yours, and she's not going to be.*

"Yeah, I suppose." He rolled his shoulders. It did little to unknot the ball of tension riding him like a boulder—no, make that Mt. Everest—between his shoulder blades.

"You suppose…?" Guerin threw his words back with a laugh. "What does that mean? Is she pretty, or isn't she?"

Kenric squirmed for a second in his seat and then abruptly left the table, not wanting to answer or deal with all the questions he knew Guerin was on the brink of firing.

"Michael, everything ready?" After a good-to-go nod from his aide, Kenric grabbed the tray off the counter and headed out. The heat of what had to be two sets of wide-eyed stares burned into his back.

"Whoa, captain. You're not giving me any more intel on Emily than that?"

Kenric stopped.

"You're gonna leave me hanging?" Guerin added, his tone conveying his delight in Kenric's discomfort.

He turned around and gave Guerin his best dry and speculative stare before answering. "Looks like it."

Kenric backed out of the kitchen and heaved a sigh of

relief on the other side of the door. He didn't want to think about how beautiful Emily was, much less chat about it with Mr. Charisma in there.

Over the years, he had known some vampires and humans who had claimed to have found their soul mates. This was supposedly more intense for vampires due to the transfer of blood and the chemical reactions that occurred with a compatible female on a cellular level. Due to a vampire's unique physiology for utilizing and absorbing every element that comprised blood, it wasn't too alien of a concept to believe a perfect mate could exist for a male or female vampire in every way. For a master, it was thought to be an even more profound experience due to the heightened psychic abilities of the male. A master and his mate bonded mentally and physically. The unusual reaction he'd had to Emily flickered through his mind, but Kenric shook his head. That couldn't be what was happening here. He refused for that to be the case. The tight clench on his molars had his jaw aching. *Christ, not now that Marguerite is back.* As long as he kept his hands and other body parts to himself, it would not go any further than a mild attraction to a female who had served her purpose and then returned to her world. End of story.

Out of sight.

Out of mind.

On the compound's third floor, which housed his private quarters, Kenric placed the key in the lock and gave it a quick turn. With an answering *click* of the pins, he opened the door with one hand while balancing the tray with the other. A blur of movement caught his eye. He ducked as his favorite crystal water goblet whizzed by his head. It struck the door frame to his left. The sharp sound of breaking glass echoed off the hardwood floor. Kenric grabbed for the orange juice carafe heading for the floor.

"What the hell?"

Chapter Seven

"You son of a bitch! I'm not your prisoner, huh? You lied to me. And to think, I thought you were delusional as hell with all the vampire nonsense but I was actually starting to believe you," Emily said with a near-hysterical laugh. "I almost believed you when you said you weren't planning to hurt me or keep me against my will. God, I'm such an idiot!" She flung her arms in the air.

He stood there, staring at her as if *she* was the one who was crazy. *Oh, she'd show him crazy.*

She darted for the nightstand. Emily hefted the pitcher off the table, spun, and hurled it straight at Kenric's head.

Again, he ducked.

The pitcher crashed into the wall, spraying fragments and shards of crystal across the floor.

Damn! Missed again. God, could he be more infuriating? She'd lost it.

Emily liked her calm exterior. It served her well,

professionally and personally. But she had totally lost touch with her brain. This was pure, raw emotion. And so out of character for her. She abhorred violence, having lived through enough of it growing up and enduring too much of it in her last relationship.

Something inside her had snapped when she had come out of the shower, had found the bedroom door locked, and had realized she was trapped inside. All the painful memories she'd buried of her childhood and the years she'd spent with Jeff had exploded in her mind. Every bit of the fear and panic she'd experienced when her dad had locked her in the closet had swamped her. The heart-pounding rage when Jeff had sealed her in their bedroom as some form of idiotic punishment had flooded her veins.

As Dylan Thomas so penned, she would *not* go quietly into that good night. *Hell, no*. She would rage, and God help the man who tried to control or hurt her again.

With a low-pitched, frustrated scream, Emily sprinted toward the open bedroom door. Her foot crossed the threshold but a pair of strong arms grabbed her. They encircled her waist and lifted her feet from the floor.

"Let me go!" Emily beat the heels of her sneakers into Kenric's shins. It didn't have the desired effect. Like a tank with armored plating, he held her high.

Her back hit the mattress, knocking the air from her lungs. She sucked in a renewed mouthful of air as Kenric's body covered hers. His large hands pinning her wrists to the bed.

"Emily, please…whatever I've done…" She didn't want to hear his worthless excuses. He couldn't possibly understand. She tossed her head from side to side in a useless attempt to escape his words. Her struggles only succeeded in causing him to press his chest and hips firmer into hers. "I'm sorry. For whatever pain I've caused you. I'm so sorry, Wildflower." His dark and stormy voice rumbled over her like thunder mixed with lightning, quieting her. She lifted her lashes and found his full lips inches from her mouth. Their gazes locked. Was he going to kiss her? *Oh shit.* Did she want him to? She didn't know what scared her more, him kissing her, or her for considering it.

God, what was happening?

She cleared her throat and went with the best haute-bitch voice she could muster. "What do you think you're doing? You're not going to kill me, so you've decided to molest me now?" She pushed at his chest. "Bastard! Get off of me."

He lifted his hips and rolled to his side. "I was only trying to stop you, so I could explain."

She scrambled from the bed and spun. "That wasn't the only thing on your mind."

"I...I'm sorry." He groaned. "I don't know where that came from." He forced the fingers of one hand through his hair. "Damn. I swear my vocabulary does go beyond a litany of apologies." Kenric dropped his face into his palms and took a deep breath. His voice sounded strained, as if he were exhausted from the effort. "This is not at all how I'd planned to approach our discussion. And no, you're not a prisoner here."

"Really, is that so?" She crossed her arms under her breasts. "The locked door. That was for my own good, then?"

He lifted his smoky gaze back to hers. "Yes, it was," he said, his deep and rusty tone of voice returning. "My home has secure areas within and around the property. I cannot have visitors wandering around unescorted. I had hoped to arrive with your breakfast before you finished your shower." His gaze left hers and then scanned the devastation that was his bedroom. "Looks like I was a little late."

She'd taken her frustrations out on his bed and lamps.

"I don't do well locked in anywhere." She ran her fingers through her hair, avoiding his eyes. He didn't need to know the details as to why, and she didn't care to remain another second explaining. Emily started for the door. "My car, I assume, is still at the hospital's garage?"

"We need to talk first."

"Any more talking or discussions can take place in the car." She threw him a glare over her shoulder. Kenric still sat on the bed. "I want to go home. *Now.*"

He didn't move.

She whipped back around, her emotional roller-coaster ride about to derail. "What do you want from me?"

"I need your help—and that requires you to believe what I've told you about myself."

"That you're a vampire?" She grasped her lower lip between her teeth.

"Yes. That I am a vampire."

"Why is it so important to you that I believe this before I go home? What can I possibly do for you?"

The moment the question left her lips, she swore an almost animalistic hunger flashed in his eyes. Emily took a step back, but slammed on the brakes. No way was she going to allow him to see that he rattled her. She'd never seen a man look at her with such need. Her hand kneaded the edge of the T-shirt—his—that she was wearing. Her palm was sweaty. She looked away, trying to find a distraction. If not, she'd have to admit to herself that a small part of her wanted to escape, not because she was deathly afraid of him, but because if she stayed any longer, maybe she wouldn't think he was so bad. He was fascinating in a crazy, psychotic kind of way. What did that say about her? That the freakier the guy was, the more interested she became?

Surveying the room, she took in all the fine items that furnished it. "From the look of things, you're very well off, Kenric. I'm sure your money can buy you all the help you need."

"No, it can't," he sighed. "If only it were that easy. Money cannot buy trust and loyalty."

Out of the corner of her eye, she saw Kenric get off the bed. Her eyes followed his impressive build as he straightened to full height.

"It'll buy silence for a period, but eventually, it'll come back as a knife between your shoulder blades."

The distant look on his face said he spoke from personal experience. He passed by her to close the door, then turned and motioned with his hand to the leather couch. "Please, sit down."

She could feel it, the vacuum-like pull sucking her into this man's dilemma. Even worse, in her heart, she realized that she was going to help him. God, how she wished she could turn off her need to rescue others. Like the time she'd rescued the limping puppy from the side of the road on her way home from work. Her mind rolled back to that rainy night. The little guy had been so wet and dirty, shaking with fear. His curled, wiry hair had been all knotted with mud. Jeff, her ex, had been livid when she'd come in the door with him. But she hadn't cared. Emily would have taken whatever abuse he'd wanted to dole out on her if it meant giving that dog another chance. To give anyone the second chance they deserved, as she'd done for Jennie, one of the nurses she'd worked with last year. Jennie had showed up for her shift, smelling of alcohol and hung over from the night before—in no condition to work. Something like that should never happen. Not when a nurse is responsible for the safety of others. Jennie was young and possessed so much potential, but a bad breakup with her boyfriend had skewed her judgment that morning. Emily had sent her home, agreed to pull her shift, and to keep the incident to herself as long as Jennie promised to pull herself together.

Whether it was a stray, a coworker, or a man who believed he was a vampire, it seemed she couldn't fight her basic instinct to help someone in need. Emily sat down and Kenric sat beside her. He faced her with a somber expression.

"When I was in the ER, I imagine blood tests were performed on me. Am I right?"

She nodded. "Of course. You were close to death when they brought you in. You were given several units of blood right away, and then labs were drawn to type your blood for additional transfusions."

"That's what I was afraid of."

"From what I remember, they were running into some problems with matching your blood type," she said. "The blood bank ran the specimen a few times but ended up asking us to redraw your blood." He watched her, as if hanging on her every word, making her nervous. She rubbed her damp palms across her thighs before continuing.

"They thought it might have been contaminated, since

they couldn't isolate your type, and because there were multiple antigens present on your red blood cells." Kenric's eyebrows shot up, but he didn't say a word. "The emergency physician thought you had some form of leukemia, due to the elevation in your white blood cell count. He ordered a consult with a specialist."

Kenric tossed his head back against the couch cushion. "Shit!"

She jumped. "This is the problem you've been referring to? The fact that the hospital has your blood, and that the results were brought to more than one doctor's attention?" *What am I supposed to do about that?*

"They couldn't type my blood because I'm no longer human." He rubbed both hands across his face and then turned to face her. "I cannot allow this information to go public. If it does, it would spell disaster for my kind."

"You're nuts." She shook her head. "You really expect me to believe the reason they couldn't type your blood is because you're not human? That you're some kind of…undead… creature-of-the-night? Kenric, I'm looking at a human male. I've…felt you. And you felt pretty human to me." Heat flashed into her cheeks, as well as a vivid recollection of exactly how incredibly human he looked and felt.

A sexy little grin curled his lips. He reached out and brushed a stray lock of hair behind her ear. Small electric tingles trailed wherever his skin touched hers. She closed her eyes.

"What can I do to convince you, Emily?" he whispered. "Tell me what it would take for you to believe that what I'm telling you is the truth. You've already experienced me feeding. What else do you need?"

She shivered. His words were like pure seduction. The memory of his teeth at her neck should freak her out, but instead her nipples stiffened into hard peaks and a tingle arrowed straight to her core.

Emily opened her eyes and rose from the couch. She darted to the foot of the bed. Distance. Yes, she needed distance. He was way too dangerous. Too much raw sexuality poured from him for her sanity to survive.

"Okay, I'll play along." She turned and faced him. "Since you're insistent that I believe this."

"Finally."

"I guess for me to really comprehend all this, I'll need you to give me a brief education on vampires. We can call it Vampire 101. Like, what does a vampire do, other than drink blood?" She wrinkled her nose at the thought. "For starters, I see you don't sleep in a coffin." Her hand patted and then rubbed along the carved, dark wood of the footboard.

"That's correct—pure myth." He raised one arm and rested it along the top of the couch. "What else do you want to know?"

"What about sunlight? Is it true you can only come out at night, or you're toast?"

"That one is true, even more so for a younger vampire. Although if I've shape-shifted, I can tolerate the sun's rays for a short duration."

"Shape-shifted? Are you saying *that* myth is true, that you can turn into a bat?" She gave him a skeptical stare.

"For me, not a bat. But yes, most vampires can assume at least one other form, usually a wolf. Over the years, I've gained the ability to become several alternate shapes."

"Prove it." She lifted her eyebrows and couldn't help the

smug smile she knew curled her lips. "You wanted to know what it would take for me to truly believe you are a vampire. Show me."

He got up from the couch. A slow and deliberate rise. Her heart stuttered as he moved closer. He leaned in, his breath a gentle caress to her ear.

"Is that really what you want to see, Wildflower?"

She nodded, her throat suddenly too dry for words.

"Think you can handle it?"

She tilted her head back and met his eyes. His gaze held a hint of a challenge. *Bam!* He hit her weak spot. She could never refuse a challenge.

"I said, prove it."

Kenric stepped back a few inches and grasped the tail of his T-shirt. Up and over his head, he pulled it off before dropping it on the coffee table behind him.

"What are you doing?" Her voice sounded a little panicky, but she couldn't help it. She hadn't anticipated a striptease.

"What you asked me to do. If I'm going to change shape, I need to take my clothes off. Or didn't you think about that when you asked? We can talk about showing you proof another way, if you can't handle me naked."

His eyes challenged her again. *Ooh, he is so irritating!* She wanted to stomp her foot, but she wouldn't dare give him the satisfaction. Instead, she cocked an eyebrow. Hell if she was backing down now.

"Oh, I can handle it," she said, proud of the confidence ringing in her voice. "I am a nurse, remember."

A slow grin spread across his face as he went for his zipper.

So pleased with his damn self.

There wasn't much she hadn't already seen in her three years as a nurse, and it wasn't like she hadn't seen most of him anyway while he had been her patient. Not to mention earlier, when he'd been wearing only a towel. So why would this be any different?

"I thought I would share my wolf with you," he said. "It's my favorite alternate form. But I want you to remember one thing after I've changed." His playful expression suddenly grew serious. His eyes narrowed. "I would never harm you. Don't be afraid."

She swallowed back the lump in her throat that had grown out of nowhere. No one had ever made her feel so off balance. He made her want to run for safety, yet at the same time, he tugged on just the right strings to make her want to stay and save him.

"Emily. Did you hear what I said?"

"Yes." She ran trembling fingers through her hair and straightened her shoulders. "I won't."

He seemed satisfied with her answer and proceeded to push his jeans to the floor and kick them to the side.

Oh. My. God. Her heart did that flip-flop thing in her chest. Oh yeah, this was very different. She'd thought the earlier rear view had been sweet. But Lord, the front view—it ought to be a crime. Emily tried maintaining a clinical expression while staring at close to six and a half feet of a naked and fully aroused man. *Instead of a wolf's form, he should go for a stallion.* He certainly had the parts. His erection dipped, in what looked like mocking approval of her continued inspection. She licked her lips, stifled a groan, and dragged her gaze away from the incredible piece of endowment standing at attention between his legs. She needed to *try* to look at his face.

"Well," she said. "Go ahead, or do you need me to say abracadabra or something?"

He tossed his head back and laughed. The jovial shift in his mood was no doubt a direct response to her squirming in her pants… Or her panties.

"All right." She waved her hands. "You've had your fun. Stop laughing. Now, let's see a wolf."

He scrubbed his hand across his mouth as if wiping his chuckle away and then winked before closing his eyes. No, he did *not* just wink at her. She bet he'd charmed the pants off numerous women with his sexy little wink and charm. Well, he would be getting a quick reality check if he thought she would be dropping her panties.

Her stomach clenched in anxious anticipation as a shimmer raced over his body from his head to his feet. It could have been her imagination, it happened so fast. Then his entire body collapsed before her eyes. She shrieked and leaped up on the bed.

A large black and silver wolf stood in Kenric's exact spot.

"Oh, my God! You weren't freaking kidding!"

Kenric padded over to the edge of the bed where Emily sat trembling. His front paws went up on the mattress, and he nudged her leg with his nose.

"I can't believe it." She turned to face him with a look of wonder and awe in her eyes. "You…did it. You turned into a wolf." Her hand shook as she reached for him. Tilting his head to the side, he met her palm and nuzzled it. Emily sighed as she ran her fingers through his dense fur.

With her immediate fright dissipated, he climbed the rest of the way onto the bed and lay down beside her.

"Wow," she whispered, lifting his muzzle. "Interesting… Your eyes look the same as they do when you're human. They're that same beautiful azure color. I've never seen a wolf up close before, but as wolves go, I would have to say you *do* make a handsome one." She threaded her fingers through his fur and scratched behind his ears.

He could have lain there all night and let her stroke his fur. It seemed as if she was more comfortable touching and talking to the wolf than the human. However, fantasy playtime had to cease. He needed her assistance.

His human shape unfolded within Kenric's mind, ushering his form back to its original state. He stretched his legs and lifted his head to Emily. She jumped and shrieked again.

"Why don't you warn a person before you do that?"

"Sorry, I can't talk when I'm a wolf. You know, with the muzzle and no human vocal cords." He grinned.

"Ha-ha, you're so funny. You can put some clothes on now, too." She pointed to his bare chest and waved her finger at the rest of him.

"Yes, ma'am."

Kenric rolled from the bed and grabbed his jeans from the floor. The heat of her gaze warmed him as he sauntered over to the coffee table to grab his T-shirt. It felt nice having all her interest focused on him. Regrettably, he could not allow himself to become involved—with any woman. His life consisted of nothing but violence and death, especially with Marguerite around again. That situation, though, he intended on handling personally. Very soon.

"Any more questions?" Kenric slipped his jeans back on. "Or other demonstrations needed? I take it by your reaction to my wolf form that you now believe I *am* a vampire?"

He pulled his shirt over his head and found Emily standing before him.

"One last thing," she said. Her soft request skated over his skin and lifted the hairs on his arms. Whatever she wanted, it was hers. He clenched both fists.

"Yes?"

"Show me your fangs."

"What? Why? The wolf wasn't convincing enough?"

"I don't know why I want to see them." She shrugged. "I just do. Somehow, I think it'll make it all the more real for me."

"If that's what you need, let's do it." He brushed past her and sat in the chair. "Come here, Wildflower." He patted the coffee table in front of him. "Sit here, facing me."

"Okay." She eased closer and placed herself on the table between his knees. "I've been meaning to ask you something else that's been bugging me. The nickname, Wildflower. Why do you insist on calling me that? Believe me, I'm no delicate flower."

Kenric held her gaze for a brief moment, then reached out as if to touch her hair but instead curled his fingers away. "Of that, I'm sure." A hint of a smile played at the corner of his lips. "The answer to why is another lesson in your Vampire 101. We have an enhanced sense of smell," he said. "May I hold your hand?" Emily chewed her lip, as if assessing the danger in the contact. "You just watched me turn into a wolf, and I didn't eat you. How lethal can it be to hold my hand?"

With an exasperated huff, she slipped her fingers into his palm.

He brought the inside of her hand up to his lips and nose. From under his lashes, he studied her beautiful hazel eyes. He closed his eyes and inhaled, bringing the sweetness of her underlying fragrance deep into his lungs. His lips brushed the inside of her wrist. Gooseflesh lifted on her skin before she jerked her arm back.

He opened his eyes. "It's how you smell to me. Like a field of wildflowers blooming right after a spring rain. Very sweet and fresh."

"Oh," she said, tucking a stray auburn curl behind her ear. She glanced away and rubbed her palms across the cotton of the sweatpants. "I was just wondering." Her casual shrug and the tone of her voice said bored, but the flush of color in her cheeks and the sound of her increased heart rate said quite the opposite.

She had the same effect on his pulse, driving the blood south and creating an uncomfortable fit in his jeans. He needed to get her home before he did something else he would regret.

"You still want to see my fangs?"

"Yes. I do."

He closed his eyes, centering his focus on his recessed fangs and the need for them to lengthen. They would naturally extend on their own during periods of hunger, anger, or sex. But without the emotional or physical stimulus, it took a conscious effort to will them into place. His gums tingled in response, and the fullness in his mouth signaled their arrival.

"I'll ask you again." The words held the slightest lisp as he spoke. He opened his eyes. "Are you sure this is what you want to see?"

"I'm sure," she said. Her throat worked on a visible swallow of apprehension.

He leaned forward, hesitantly opening his mouth wide enough for her to see. His upper lip peeled back, sliding against the warm length of his fully exposed fangs.

A sharp intake of air rasped from Emily. Her eyes widened, and the wild thump of her heart drummed in his ears.

Damn! Why the hell had he agreed to this? He started to put an end to the demonstration, but she lifted her hand.

"May I touch one of them?"

Shit! He clamped his mouth shut and jerked his head back. "What?"

"I'm sorry." She yanked back her hand.

"You've felt them enough, I should think." *What was she thinking, wanting to touch the damn things? Wasn't it bad enough that he'd stuck them in her neck?*

"I didn't realize I had crossed a boundary." She rubbed her palms against her thighs. "I was caught up in the moment."

"I've agreed to all your demonstrations. After last night in the ER, I wouldn't have thought this one necessary." He jumped up, leaving her at the coffee table. He needed something to do. She still hadn't eaten, so he busied himself with salvaging the remains of the breakfast tray.

"I see. You're right, of course. It isn't necessary for you to remind me of our close encounter. I have the holes in my neck to do that."

Kenric straightened his shoulders. The decorative handles

of the tray dug into his palms. *Touché*. He glanced at Emily. Her fingertips stroked the marks on her throat. *His mark.*

Hands off, vampire. That can never happen again.

For her sake.

For her very life. He had to keep his hands off.

"Yes, you do." He swung his gaze back to the food and returned to laying out her breakfast on one end of the coffee table.

He'd been a vampire for more than three hundred years and had quit apologizing for who he was long before the last two centuries. Coming to terms, or so he'd thought, with his existence. It hadn't been his choice to live the rest of eternity as a predator, but he couldn't change that fact. He'd never embraced the life of a vampire, but he had learned to live with it.

He didn't kill for his needs.

In fact, he did his best to protect humanity from the part of his race that couldn't control their impulses. So why did he want to claw his insides out for having fed from Emily? *No*. It wasn't because he'd taken her blood. What grated his insides was how poorly he'd controlled the instincts of the beast. He'd scared the hell out of her.

It made him sick.

And mad as hell.

"Okay. School's out," he said. "Let's get some food into you."

Her stomach growled as he uncovered the plate containing a large ham and cheese omelet and hash browns.

"Wow." She laughed, pressing her hand over her stomach. "There's no point in pretending I'm not hungry. That looks delicious." She slid off the coffee table and onto the sofa to dig in.

"I'm glad to see you have an appetite. Eat as much as you can, and when you're done, I want to talk to you about your help with removing the evidence of my visit to the ER."

She stopped chewing, and both eyebrows shot up.

"You don't have to worry about getting into any trouble or losing your job. No one will ever know. I need your expertise and knowledge of the lab reports and Elizabeth Bay Memorial's computer systems."

She went back to work on her meal. Nevertheless, her expression didn't give a hint as to what she thought of his agenda.

"If you are okay with all this, I want to take you downstairs to meet some of the members of the Enclave. I would like you to share with them what you remember about the tests performed on me. With your skill, and their expertise, we should be able to fix this."

"The Enclave?" Emily mumbled around her breakfast, one cheek bulging from the forkful of omelet she'd placed in her mouth. Then she swallowed. "What or who are they?"

Chapter Eight

On patrol at The Docks, Arran and Markus weaved through the never-ending onslaught of humans after their next score, drink, or fuck.

Saturday nights usually packed the streets, making Arran jumpy as shit. The rush of a good fight? Hell, yes—he thrived on it. But crowds—*shit*. He hated them. He rolled his shoulders and glanced at Markus. The grimace on his partner's face told the same horror story: weekends were hell.

Especially tonight.

The warm temperature, unusual for this late in November, had people out in droves. In turn, a multitude of humans brought out the DEADs. Sometimes you had to look for the positive. He would get to kill an addict or two.

He indicated with a tilt of his head for Markus to turn into the alley on his right. It was only eleven, and experience told him the crowds wouldn't let up for another hour or two.

"Damn, I had to get off that street," Arran said, rounding the corner.

Markus grunted in agreement.

The humid air swamped his nostrils with the greasy smell of fried seafood and stale beer. That, he expected for the area, but not the other metallic scent triggering his vampire senses.

Arran glanced in his partner's direction.

Markus gave a slight nod. "Blood."

Both knew each other's next move from years spent together as part of the Enclave. Without a ripple in their wake, they shifted from civilians out for a walk to predators on the hunt.

Farther into the darkened corridor they moved without a sound, a convenient trick for vampires. That way, the prey never hears the predator until it's too late.

A few feet in, both came to a halt.

Markus lifted his chin and motioned with a subtle nod toward the back. Muffled and wet growling noises emanated from the end of the alley. Arran tilted his head and glanced at the rooftop of the building beside him, then back to Markus with a grin. His partner raised an eyebrow, a slow smile forming. It seemed the idea of going topside for an aerial approach pleased him as well. The roof would provide an excellent vantage point, since it ran parallel to the street perpendicular to the alley.

A small wrought-iron balcony extended from the second-story window, making the leap effortless. Arran followed Markus's silent approach to the rooftop. More than likely, they could have made the leap to the third story, but no need to risk a misstep when there were straightforward footholds for each level.

They made it in mere seconds and then moved quickly across the black-tarred surface. As they neared the edge, the noises grew louder and more vicious, as if a pack of wolves snapped and growled, fighting each other over their latest kill.

At the edge of the roof, both warriors crouched and peered over the side. The wind rode the wall of the four-story dwelling, driving straight up and into their face and nostrils. The scent alone told the gruesome story of what had already played out beneath them. The air reeked of semen and blood.

Four DEADs fought over the leftovers of one mangled woman, a macabre scene of clawing and biting. A half-naked, blonde female lay slumped against the building's brick exterior. She'd been repeatedly raped and bitten. A fucking nightmare of an end for the human female who'd had the misfortune to walk down this alley. Vampires in the violent throes of DE bloodlust had lain in wait for her arrival.

Arran gave Markus a brief glance and a nod: time to make like a bat and fly. In unison, both stood and took one step, dropping directly behind the creatures. No sweat. No broken bones. He loved the badass superhero part of being a vampire.

The warriors' boots struck the pavement. The frenzied vampires jerked their heads from their meal, then hissed and leaped to their feet.

"Get the fuck out of here, Enclave!" One of the crazed addicts pointed a long and dirty finger toward Arran and Markus. His lips peeled back, exposing his two long fangs in a contorted look of rage.

"Make me." Arran emitted a low rumble from his chest

for added effect.

The warriors pulled their daggers in one smooth move.

The DEADs attacked. But they were unarmed, unless one counted their long-ass fangs and razor-sharp claws.

Two lunged into the air at him, one from each side. Their wide eyes glowed with the insanity of DE. The others dove in his partner's direction. Markus cursed before tossing out a sadistic laugh as he fought off the DE duo.

All at once, Arran's crazies slammed into him, knocking the air from his lungs. He dropped and rolled, elbowing one bloodsucker in the face. The other took an unlucky swan dive onto his dagger, taking the full measure of the blade into its chest. The DEAD howled as Arran pushed him over and pulled his dagger free. Smoke billowed off the dying carcass.

The other addict shook off the blow to his face and sailed at him again. Arran raised his arm in time to block the impact. The crazed vampire hit but didn't deflect. Instead, he bit down and ground his fangs and teeth deep into Arran's arm. The DEAD writhed and growled, attempting to rip flesh from bone.

"Son of a bitch! You're about to piss me off."

Reaching down with his free arm, Arran sheathed his dagger. Inside his boot, he had a nice fix for a rabid vampire. The crazed bloodsucker slobbered and growled on his arm while his teeth made mincemeat of Arran's flesh. Arran wrapped his hand around a custom, nine-inch curved blade.

One second, a blood-crazed vampire gnawed at his arm—the next, a headless torso dropped to the street.

Problem solved.

"Sick bastard," he mumbled.

The vampire's head hung on Arran's arm as he worked at freeing the embedded teeth. After a few seconds of rocking the jaw, the head finally gave way and dropped with a *thud* onto the asphalt.

Arran quickly tore off a piece of his shirt and wrapped it around his bleeding arm. He had a job to finish, and he'd heal soon enough. Blocking the burning pain from his mind, he decomped the remains. The silver, as usual, worked its magic, turning the remains to ash, though the detached head would decompose rather fast even without the silver.

Arran looked around. Where the hell had Markus gone? The surrounding area had grown quiet, except for the usual sounds of traffic. The last thing he remembered seeing was Markus taking off after one of the filthy bastards.

After half an hour of going through every nearby side street searching for his partner, he'd come up with a couple of ash piles but no sign of his fellow warrior. Back in the area where their battle had begun, Arran grabbed his cell and punched speed dial two for Markus. After six rings, it flipped to voice mail.

"Shit!" He snapped his cell shut. *What the fuck?*

Kneeling beside the DEADs' latest victim, Arran did his best to drape her lower body with what was left of her leather miniskirt. Unfortunately, nothing could help the young female. A bloodied cross, attached to a broken gold chain, dropped from her torn sequined shirt as he covered her mangled torso. Pity that the sentimental trinket couldn't save her. Picking it up, Arran noted an inscription carved into its back. Using his thumb, he wiped enough of the blood away to read the writing. *To Heather, I love you. Mom.*

"I'm sorry, Heather," Arran whispered. "So sorry we

didn't get here sooner."

He was going to have to call for cleanup and then continue his search for Markus on two wheels.

Flipping open his cell, he hit speed dial for Ted at Memorial Gardens Crematorium. After a couple of rings, Ted answered with his typical chipper tone. Strange, considering what he did for a living.

"Good evening, Enclave. What can I do for you this fine night?"

A sharp pain targeted the crease right between Arran's eyes at Mr. Sunshine's cheerful greeting.

"We have a situation that needs cleanup. Second alleyway off of Seventh Street, in the rear."

"Second alley off Seventh Street, in the rear. Got it. The usual?"

Arran sighed. *Such a fucking waste of life.* He hated how the families of these victims never received closure. But there was no other way. Evidence like this could not be left behind for the police.

"The usual. Nothing remains." Arran closed his phone. Ted was a pro at what he handled for them. As a vampire himself, he had added incentive to be thorough.

Arran made his way back to where they'd parked their motorcycles. Markus's red ride hadn't moved.

He swung a leather-clad leg up and over and straddled his black Ducati. Slipping on his matching helmet, he cranked the machine. He gave the engine a couple of hard revs before burning out. The crowd had thinned, allowing him to cover more ground with greater speed on his bike.

• • •

Emily waited behind Kenric as he punched a code into a digital keypad before placing his hand on a blue screen. A high-pitched *beep* sounded before a massive steel door, like something from the next century, opened and slid into the wall on a whisper of air.

Enclave central command.

Seemed very high tech and James Bond. He even had the accent and looks to complete the picture.

Her head swam not just from their three-story elevator ride down, but also with all the information she'd learned upstairs. Kenric had filled her in on things she thought could only exist on the big screen: vampires, Death Euphoria, DEADs—*oh my*. Like Dorothy in *The Wizard of Oz*, she definitely felt like she "wasn't in Kansas anymore."

He'd brought her downstairs, intending for her to meet some of his Enclave—a volunteer group of vampires that had slowly grown over the last century to a team of six, he'd informed her, after he and his second-in-command had first partnered to control the DEADs that had been preying on the human population in the city.

Kenric called his team Warriors. The term conjured up images in her head of giant men with armor and swords. One gorgeous six and a half foot vampire pushing her buttons was enough, though. If they were all like him, she didn't know if her nervous system could withstand it.

She followed Kenric into an enormous underground complex. No interior walls blocked the view from one end to the other. It appeared to run the entire length of the house. Emily soaked up the view and tried to keep up with Kenric at the same time. An entertainment section with a big flat-screen TV, a stereo, and a couple of pinball machines filled one end. A glass conference table took up the center—six black leather executive chairs surrounded it.

Seated together at the end, opposite all the fun and games, were two men and one woman. The men flanked the brown-haired woman, who was busy tapping away at a keyboard on a multilevel desk. The brunette's gaze tracked her work on two wall-mounted computer monitors. All eyes turned their way as they approached.

The female of the group must have sensed her unease right away and gave Emily a warm, encouraging smile.

"Guerin, Logan, Gabrielle, I would like you to meet Emily Ross," Kenric said, pointing out each member of the team with one hand as he placed his other palm at her lower back.

"Hi, Emily. Nice to meet you," Gabrielle said, the first to break the ice as she held out her hand for a polite shake. "You can call me Elle," she added with another warm smile.

Logan, standing maybe an inch taller than Kenric, moved forward next. His deep brown hair shone with natural gold highlights. He'd gathered it at his nape into a ponytail, which hung to his waist. Even with his hair bound, she couldn't miss the sprinkles of gold.

"Very nice to meet you," he said with a slight brogue. His rough hand, almost double the size of hers, swallowed her palm as he shook her hand.

"Scottish, I take it?" Emily's gaze met his emerald green irises.

"Guilty as charged, lass," he answered with a smile that would have singed the hairs right off a girl's arm. Man, he was impressive.

Well, almost as impressive as the man who stood beside

her. She dropped Logan's hand and gave Kenric a sideways glance.

The man Kenric introduced as Guerin stepped up next, looking very Mediterranean with his dark olive complexion and wavy mahogany hair. He nudged Logan out of his way.

"*Ciao, bella*," he breathed with a seductive smile on his lips. *What a charmer.* Too bad he didn't do a thing for her.

He gently took her hand, all the while holding her gaze with his deep brown bedroom eyes. He lowered his head and placed a kiss to the back of her hand.

As Guerin's lips touched her hand, she felt, more than heard, a vibrating growl come from behind her. Guerin's head popped back up at that exact moment, his gaze darting to Kenric. Emily glanced over her shoulder. Kenric was sneering, his glare aimed straight for Guerin's throat.

Guerin's hand released hers. The vibrations ceased as quickly as they'd started. "Nice to meet you, Emily," he added with a slight smile.

How bizarre was that? She slipped her hands into the pockets of her borrowed sweats. Kenric's palm pressed a little more firmly into the small of her back, making small circles against her skin through the fabric. She smiled, enjoying the comforting warm presence as she met the room of vampire warriors. Instinctively, Emily leaned into the protective weight of his hand.

"Let's get down to why we're here, shall we?" Kenric broke the tension hanging in the air. Pulling up an extra chair, he placed it beside Elle and motioned for Emily to take a seat.

"Emily," he said, then dropped a hand onto Gabrielle's shoulder. "Elle is our resident computer guru." Emily's gaze fixated at the point where Kenric's hand rested. The deep sound of his voice continued to fill the room, but she didn't have the power to pry her gaze away from where his hand touched the other woman's body.

Why is it necessary for him to touch her the whole time he's standing there? Maybe she's his lover? Emily's stomach churned at the thought of Kenric naked and lying next to Elle. She clenched her teeth and gripped the arms of her chair. It took everything she had not to jump up and snatch his hand off her.

I've lost my mind. That has to be it. Emily shook her head. Where were these lunatic thoughts coming from? Besides, he was way too overbearing for her taste. The last thing she needed, or wanted, was to fight her way out of another possessive, dominating relationship.

"Emily… Emily? Did you hear anything I said?" Kenric's voice rang through, shaking her out of her daydream.

"Yes, I'm hearing you." She nodded her head. "You were saying something about me talking to Elle about the hospital computers."

His eyes narrowed into a pay-attention glare. She must have lost a part of the conversation. Emily brushed her hair back and lifted her chin. She stared back at him with a silent, *I'm listening—see?*

He cocked a brow, and a corner of his lips curled into a smile. With a shake of his head, he went back to work.

"Elle, this is what I need done," he said. "Use whatever information Emily can provide about Memorial to help you get into that system. I need you to do whatever it takes to scrub those records on John Doe. Discreetly, of course. We don't need any more attention brought to us than my visit has already generated."

"Consider it done," Gabrielle said with a nod.

"Emily, see if you can recall the name of the doctor who was consulted on my case. We'll need to pay him a visit."

"Okay, but if I can't remember, once Elle cracks into the system, I can pull your records and get his name for you. If you don't mind my asking, though, what will you do once you find him? You said the Enclave doesn't kill humans. They already know about your blood. It's not only in their files. So, how do you plan to handle this?" She shrugged her shoulders and laughed. "Give them amnesia or something?"

"That's exactly what I plan to do."

"You can do that? Really? Actually tap into someone's mind and take their memories? Oh my God... No wonder you've been able to stay undetected for so long. If you're exposed, you simply make us forget we ever knew you. How...very convenient for you," she added with a pissed-off glare at Kenric.

The idea that he could do that to her, and probably would, made her madder than hell. What had she done? She had been minding her own business, doing her job, and yet somehow, she'd managed to get involved with a man who had the ability to control her life on a level she couldn't even imagine.

"You must understand... I don't take pleasure in manipulating another person's mind. It's what I have to do, if we're to survive." Kenric paused, as if searching for the right words, then glanced over to Guerin and Logan and back to her. Both warriors had grown tense, but they remained silent while keeping their eyes on her and her reaction to Kenric.

"I explained before we came downstairs that every one

of us here has taken an oath to give our lives, if necessary, to protect humanity from those of our kind who've succumbed to Death Euphoria. However, we do have to feed. As you have experienced." Kenric's voice lowered, and his eyes darted from hers for a split second, as if uncomfortable discussing their encounter in front of the others.

"And when we do," he continued, "we use what powers we have to erase the memory of our presence. If we didn't, with the frequency that we need to feed, we would be discovered and exterminated."

Nausea bloomed in her stomach at the word *exterminated*. It sounded so horrific, but history clearly demonstrated the expected human reaction would be fear, followed by a cry for genocide. Hadn't fear and ignorance always driven humans to perform horrendous acts of cruelty? What little remained of the Native American population was a prime example of a civilized nation's response to something they didn't completely understand.

"We also use what we term compulsion, or psychic influence, to help the humans experience as little pain as possible while we feed. The process doesn't have to be painful or cruel." He eased closer. His gaze almost a physical touch.

He studied her as if trying to ascertain how well she'd digested his latest revelation. "Please, come with me." He reached out and clasped her arm, moving her toward the other side of the room. "Give us a moment," Kenric ordered without looking back at his team.

"Where are we going?" She slapped at his hold on her arm, her feet doing their best to keep up with him.

"I'm finishing our conversation."

"We could have finished where we were." He slammed

to a halt as quickly as they'd begun. "I'm not some dog on a leash you can just up and decide when it's my time to heel," she bit out through clenched teeth.

Kenric placed her back against the wall and blocked the others' view. Reaching down, he took her hand in his. With his other, he lifted her chin with his fingertips, bringing them face-to-face. Or as close as her five-feet-four to his six-feet-six would allow. "No. You're most certainly not a dog."

He stepped closer, warming her with the heat of his body. She squirmed under his overwhelming presence. Their hips almost touched. A flash of disappointment washed over her, dousing a bit of her anger. Not that she was ready to let him know that.

"I need to explain something to you. And I didn't want to do it with an audience." This time, the sound of his words grew deeper, smoother. "If a vampire wishes, when he feeds, the process can be quite...pleasurable for the human." He squeezed her hand gently and gave her the most erotic smile. It carried from his lips all the way to his eyes. The passion reflected there sent shivers of lightning racing down her spine.

It dawned on her that she'd stopped breathing. Her breath hitched, and she used the interruption to drop her gaze. Kenric stepped back, as if he'd suddenly remembered they weren't alone. She rubbed the palms of her hands against her arms at the chill that had gripped her the moment he'd moved away.

"Sometimes it's not pretty or pleasant, but it's what we have to do to survive. Nevertheless, it's who I am. It's who *we* are." He indicated with the tilt of his head to the group waiting patiently behind him. "Is this something you can live with?"

He asked the question with an expression devoid of emotion. Those dazzling blue irises bore into her soul as he waited for her response. No evidence of begging or pleading ever entered his gaze. Clearly, the decision was hers and hers alone.

She stood on the precipice of a monumental decision, the ramifications of which could change her life forever.

Even with what had transpired last night, deep inside, she'd already become more attracted to him than she'd like to admit. But it was there. No sense denying it.

He hadn't really hurt her. In fact, he'd taken good care of her. Scared her? In the beginning, hell yeah. But not now. She didn't fear him physically. Emotionally—she hadn't quite decided.

Emily had to go with her gut. It told her this man lived as noble a life as possible with the cards he'd been dealt. Nobody had the right to judge him.

She could live with it. He did. But they would have to talk about his amnesia magic trick. No way was he going to mess with her mind.

That would never be a part of the deal.

Chapter Nine

Marguerite stared at the image she'd removed from the hidden bottom of her drawer. Gently, she traced the outline with the pads of her finger. "One day you'll understand." She nodded. "Once I make things right, you'll be happy and see why I had to do the things that I did. Everyone will." Her fangs lengthened and she snarled. "And they'll bow, trembling before us."

She breathed deep, regaining her composure before slipping the photo back into its protective sleeve and tucking it away. With a shove, Marguerite closed the compartment tight and tapped her high-heeled foot on the wooden floorboard, growing more impatient for Enrique's return with each passing second. She lunged from the seat at her dresser, flew to the door of her master suite, and flung it wide open with a *bang*.

"What's taking so long?" she shouted, startling her servants in the hall. Marguerite marched down the corridor, into the den, and over to her chaise longue. She parted the translucent gold panels of fabric and lay back on the crushed velvet of the seat. The sheer material of her emerald gown clung to her body, leaving little to the imagination.

Everything had been going exactly as planned since her arrival three months ago to South Carolina. She had never liked trusting a male with anything of importance. The chance for failure and disappointment was too high for her liking. But the risk was too great to take care of it herself. This time.

Enrique had better not screw up.

If he wanted to live.

Annoyed with her wait, she needed entertainment. A distraction. Marguerite motioned for the tall, blond, muscle-bound minion who stood against the wall. The vampire came forward and knelt before her. He pulled his shirt over his head and bared his chest, then dropped his head back, exposing the full length of his neck. A gift of his throat.

She wasn't hungry. But waiting was so tedious, and the minion did look delectable. It had been a while since she had last tasted him. Marguerite pulled him closer and, without pretense, stabbed her fangs into his throat. He flinched, then let out a groan as she took her fill. As expected of her lovers, his hands roamed her body and pinched her hardened nipples. Lower still, he searched between the slit in her gown to her mound below. He found her core, and she thrust her pelvis into his palm.

His fingers worked through her slickened folds and into her heat as she continued to suckle at his neck. He thrust in time to each hard draw at his neck, driving deeper into her clenching depths, bringing her to a swift climax. Her orgasm gripped her, forcing her to release him. She rode the spasms until the waves of pleasure lulled her to a satisfied bliss.

"Very nice." Marguerite licked at the trail of blood seeping from his wounds. "You're in luck tonight. I'm in a giving mood."

The minion jerked his head up. His eyes glowed with excitement. The tips of his already descended fangs glistened from underneath his upper lip. Marguerite lifted her arm and handed her wrist to the slave for his reward. The moment he reached for her, she drew back her offer and grabbed his head. She wrenched his face to meet her glare.

"You will stop when you're instructed, or I *will* kill you," she said then thrust her wrist back in his face.

He clutched her arm with both hands and quickly brought her offering to his mouth. His fangs sank into her flesh, but she didn't flinch, her flesh and veins accustomed to centuries of this practice. He drank in large, greedy mouthfuls.

Marguerite dropped her head to the chaise's arm and her mind flashed back more than three hundred years to a time when another young vampire had once hungrily fed from her vein. *Kenric.*

She vividly remembered the feel of his lips as they pulled at her flesh. The way his wavy ebony hair would brush against her skin. Her clitoris throbbed once again. She crossed her legs and clenched her thighs. The ache wasn't for the vampire at her side but for the one who would not kneel. The one who would not willingly come to her bed or to her vein.

"Enough!"

The minion dropped her wrist with an agonized groan,

then tore at the zipper of his pants. Marguerite grinned as his erection sprang free from its constraints. He reared his head back, and with a guttural cry, gave in to his release.

A prolonged squeak echoed through the large room, distracting her from the moans of her minion. Aged hinges complained under the weight of the double doors to her receiving parlor, announcing someone's arrival. She'd taken up residence within an old colonial house shortly after her arrival to the area. The home, located in an isolated area southwest of Elizabeth Bay, provided exactly what she needed to continue in her endeavors. The sprawling mansion proved large enough to hold the number of servants she required, while the layout of the grounds provided security for her growing army of vampires. With only one road accessing the property and the immediate perimeter cleared around the house, no one approached undetected.

Marguerite slid from her chaise, delighted to see Enrique had not returned empty-handed.

"Mistress, I present to you what you've requested." Enrique bowed before her and tossed a barely conscious male at her feet.

The offering collapsed to the floor before struggling to push to his knees, unable to stand. Glazed eyes looked up as she glided forward. The man's face held bruises and lacerations, no doubt from the hard battle with her DE-addicted vampires. He weaved, even on his knees, under the influence of the ketamine-filled darts Enrique had acquired.

Marguerite grabbed the swaying male by his long black hair and yanked his head back. His blank gray eyes stared at her with large, dilated pupils.

"You are a handsome one," she said with a smile,

stroking the short black goatee at his chin. "I shall enjoy you immensely."

She laughed, then reached for the neck of his sweater and ripped the soft material from his body. He fell forward as the material gave way, his palms slapping the wooden floor from the weight of his impact. His bare back glared with the exact prize she'd hoped to find. An infinity symbol with a bloodied dagger piercing its center covered his left shoulder blade.

Marguerite smiled and bent forward. "Welcome to my home, Enclave Warrior," she whispered into his ear.

• • •

"So, what's the verdict, Wildflower? Can you live with what you know about who I am?" Layers of conflicting emotions flickered across Emily's face as Kenric waited for her decision. She'd been pissed at his assertive tactics to maneuver her to a more private area. He wasn't pleased about that. But he had had to get her alone. The woman had a way of turning him inside out and chipping away at the hard edge of his control. The look in her eyes had killed him. In that moment of his confession, everything had registered for her—he saw it in her eyes and in the accusing look she gave him.

She'd understood how far-reaching his powers as a vampire extended.

Even though what she'd experienced in the ER had not been consensual, he'd wanted her to know feeding could also be a very intimate experience. It didn't have to be an act of violence. He didn't take pleasure in abusing his power.

He did what he had to, for survival.

Not sadistic pleasure.

He would run himself through before he ever became like Marguerite.

Kenric ground his back teeth, waiting for her answer. An even-bigger question loomed in the back of his mind. The one he kept trying his damnedest to avoid.

Was he prepared for what he needed to do if her answer was no?

He'd held her in his arms, imprinted her scent and taste. Could he remove her memories, walk away, and never look back? Only twenty-four hours had passed, and it annoyed the hell out of him that he didn't like the idea of having to let her go. But there would be no other choice, if she said no.

After what felt like an eternity had passed, she parted her lips and spoke, "Yes, I think I can live with it."

"Good." Kenric dropped her hand and turned, hiding his sigh of relief, his stomach unwinding from its knotted state.

"Whoa, wait one minute there." She grabbed his arm. He pivoted back around. "I said I could live with it, but that didn't mean everything was settled, just like that." Emily snapped her fingers. "We still need to talk about what this means."

"What else is there to discuss?" Kenric's voice dropped an octave as he leaned against the wall, his hand resting beside her head.

"Hey! Are we still planning to put our heads together over here and get this situation handled?" Guerin called out from the other side of the room.

Kenric glared over his shoulder. "Yeah, that's the plan. Why? You got somewhere to be, Romeo?"

"No, nowhere to be, my man." Guerin shook his head. "Just itching to get started, that's all."

"We can talk more later," Kenric said, returning to Emily, his voice barely above a whisper. "I needed to confirm once more that you were on board with all this." He brushed his knuckles along the delicate surface of her cheek. So very smooth. Her eyelids shuttered under his caress. Kenric yanked his thoughts and hand back from the road they were headed down. He needed to handle his present situation.

"It's either black or white with me," he said. "Either you can handle this, or you can't. I've already said this upstairs, but I have to be sure you completely understand. I'll be entrusting you not only with my own existence but with my entire Enclave's." He reached to brush her cheek once more but fisted his hand instead and dropped his arm to his side. "You've said you can handle this. Please be very sure, Wildflower. If you give me your word, it will be all I ever need to hear."

Emily chewed her lower lip and searched his face, and her heart, one more time before she answered. "You have my word," she breathed.

Kenric leaned in as if to kiss her but, at the last second, froze. Instead of the feel of his lips, two fingertips trailed down her cheek, then dropped. She gasped. Damn him. He continued to hover above her lips, his breathing harsh. At least *he* was breathing. The air felt locked inside her chest, waiting for his next move.

And then it came.

He closed the distance, but a second before his lips touched hers, he diverted his path, brushing the rough texture of his five o'clock shadow along her cheek. The warmth of his breath at her ear heated her core.

"Good. Because I wasn't ready to let you go." He turned without another word and headed back to his team. Her knees wobbled as she returned to the group and took her seat. Emily tried to ignore the stares that burned into the side of her head as the team waited to hear from their leader.

Kenric moved to stand beside her. This time, he placed his hand on her shoulder before he spoke. She pinched her lips tight, hiding the satisfied smile.

"We will proceed as planned," he said. "Emily will be assisting us in whatever way she can. To put everyone's mind at ease, she is fully aware of what might happen if others find out what she's learned today. I've placed my trust in her. As you know, that is not something I do lightly, since she'll be aiding not only me but the entire Enclave. Emily is now considered under my protection. Therefore, she is under the protection of the Enclave. Understood?"

The weight of his words crashed on her shoulders. *He trusted her completely*. She would have never guessed how heavy it felt to carry the load of someone's faith in you. It was damn hefty.

Emily held her breath as two of the team's warriors approached her.

"It will be my honor." Logan knelt before her, taking her hand in his. He lifted her hand, placing it near his lips. Was he going to kiss her? She braced herself.

Only he inhaled instead.

The air slid from her lungs. It didn't feel intimate, like

when Kenric had done something similar upstairs. That had made her heart skip a beat. This was more like a simple handshake. All very formal and ceremonial.

Next, Guerin came and proceeded in the same manner. "It will be my honor as well." Placing her hand close to his face, he breathed deep.

Emily glanced up at Kenric, about to ask about all the smelling, but he beat her to it.

"Each warrior has taken your scent, because you are now under their protection. They have imprinted you in their minds. Should the need ever arise, if you're near, they will find you.

"Impressive," she mumbled, staring at the back of her hand.

"Two of the Enclave's warriors are still on patrol. When they return, both will take the same vow to keep you safe. You are important to me, therefore, you are important to them."

Over the next few hours, Emily worked with Elle reviewing the records she'd been able to crack within the hospital's system. Instead of deleting the files which showed anomalous results, they entered bogus, normalized ones. Too many of the staff involved in Kenric's case would remember the John Doe admitted on the thirteenth of November. For the record to disappear entirely would raise even more suspicion on top of his vanishing act.

Alongside her and Elle, Kenric examined every detail. Emily couldn't help noticing the camaraderie that existed between Elle and Kenric. She wondered how long they'd known each other and how exactly Elle had come to be part of the Enclave. Had there ever been more to their relationship? God, she wanted to groan from the green and ugly monster stirring her insides each time Kenric glanced at Gabrielle. But nothing about their interaction suggested more than a common bond. She shouldn't feel anything at all about a man she'd only met yesterday. When this was over, she had to make an appointment with her ob-gyn. Maybe her estrogen levels were out of whack.

"How about tomorrow night?"

"What?" Emily dropped her pen and glanced up in Kenric's direction. "What about tomorrow night?"

"If you're working tomorrow night, I'll meet you there. Together, we can make sure all my blood samples do a disappearing act."

"Yeah, sure. Tomorrow night sounds good."

"Perfect," he said. "With all of the samples gone, they won't be able to reconfirm or deny the changes in the results. Good job, ladies." Kenric lowered his gaze to Emily. She cleared her throat and quickly turned her attention back to her notes, trying to hide her smile. He didn't need any more encouragement.

With the complete names of the consulting specialist and emergency physician obtained from John Doe's record, Logan and Guerin volunteered to pay them a visit and alter a few select memories. Elle deleted the request for the consult, since the blood work no longer indicated a problem. Everything from files to thoughts needed to match.

At last, Kenric spoke the words she'd waited for all evening. "Let's get you home." He turned back to Elle. "I'd like to discuss the other matter with you that Guerin asked you to work on when I get back."

Elle nodded. "Okay. I have some stuff bookmarked for you to check out." Kenric gave an affirmative lift of his chin, then returned his attention to Emily.

Emily gathered her work clothes, and Kenric escorted her to the garage.

He opened the door of a shiny black convertible sports car. It sat between a BMW and what looked like a Bentley.

"Is this a Lamborghini?" Emily swung a glance over her shoulder at Kenric before her rear came into contact with the most buttery-soft leather she'd ever sat on.

Kenric climbed into the driver's seat and cranked the sleek speed machine. "Yes, it is."

"What is it that you do, anyway, other than kill really bad vampires and drive very fast cars?"

"Let's just say it doesn't hurt to be in possession of a great deal of very old money. And a damn good stockbroker."

"Ah, I see." Emily stroked the rich feel of the leather bracing her thighs. Her butt was in cushioned heaven.

"Actually, this is a Murciélago LP 640 Roadster, to be exact."

"Ooh la la. Sounds like it was built for speed," she said.

He chuckled, and the black roadster rumbled forward like a predator on a leash, begging for release.

"*Murciélago* is Spanish for bat," he said.

Emily glanced his way. A devilish grin sat on his lips.

"Oh, you would have a car named bat, vampire." She laughed, and it felt good.

"Buckle up, Wildflower." Kenric shifted and punched the accelerator, laying her back against the seat with the force of the acceleration.

Hot damn.

"You like that, don't you?" Kenric's azure eyes sparkled in the moonlight that beamed in through the open top.

She just smiled in answer to his question, allowing her head to plop against the headrest. Closing her eyes for a moment, she enjoyed the feel of the wind in her hair.

Relaxed, Emily lifted her lashes and rolled her head to the left. The breeze smoothed Kenric's raven hair away from his face, accentuating the sharp and sophisticated lines.

He was beautiful, the scar on his right cheek the only imperfection she could find. Truly, it wasn't a flaw at all. It reminded her of how much man lay beneath. Emily rubbed her palm over her breastbone as if she could calm the sudden jump in her pulse. Her hand dropped to her stomach, trying to calm the nervous flutters. She wished she could blame it on the intensity of the ride, but she knew they came from the man sitting next to her at the wheel.

As they neared Elizabeth Bay, she picked a star and made a silent wish toward the heavens for the drive to last a little longer. Because for right now, she liked how safe, happy, and free he made her feel.

But all too soon, it was over.

Kenric pulled into the hospital's parking garage, and Emily directed him to the fourth level, where she'd parked her car the previous night. He pulled up into the vacant space beside her vehicle and cut the engine. She grabbed her things and made her exit.

Emily tossed her clothes into her car and performed a quick check that her wallet and cell phone were still in her glove box. She straightened and smoothed her shirt with sweaty palms. Could anything feel more awkward? This hadn't been a date. It had been more like a kidnapping. But her captor hadn't been human, and she'd somehow allowed herself to be pulled into his world and was about to help him commit a crime. She felt like she'd been strapped to a monster of a roller coaster, mad as hell for permitting herself to climb on board, but loving every minute of the ride.

"Do you want me to call you tomorrow evening so that we can coordinate when and where to meet? I'll give you my number, and I would like yours as well…after I follow you home and make sure you're safe," he said.

"Oh, no. That's not necessary." Emily shook her head. She didn't need this guy to know where she lived.

"I think it is. You're under my protection now." Kenric got out of his car, sauntered over, and, with a molten look, lifted a lock of her hair from her shoulder and gently pushed it back.

How could something as simple as a touch to her hair send electricity running through her insides? She opened her mouth again to say it wasn't necessary, but ended up groaning in frustration instead. The firm set of his jaw declared he would see her home. What little she already knew of him told her he did what he wanted, permission or not.

"Fine. You win. This time." Emily dropped into the seat of her very used Corolla, then glanced over her shoulder. "But don't get used to it."

One corner of his mouth lifted as if he found her humorous. "Warning noted," he said.

"I live on Magnolia Island." She closed her door, the action a little harder than necessary but still pretty darn satisfying. Rolling down her window, Emily looked up and met his gaze. "Try to keep up if you can."

"I'll do my best."

Chapter Ten

Two hours later, and Arran had yet to find any sign of Markus. He rolled his Ducati to a stop, snatched his helmet off, and pulled his cell phone out of his pocket.

"Damn, voice mail again." He clenched and unclenched his fist, waiting for the beep. "Markus, where the hell are you, man?" he growled out, wishing he had an addict's head to pound his fist into and exorcise some of his frustration. "Call me when you get this, you bastard, and let me know you're alive. If you don't, I'm going to kill your ass and feed you to those fucking bloodsuckers." With that said, he punched End Call on a snarl.

Only a few more hours remained before he would have to go in. "Fuck!"

He punched speed dial for the compound. Maybe they'd heard from Markus. If not, Kenric and Guerin needed to know he'd gone missing.

"Arran?" Gabrielle answered on the second ring, her

voice urgent but soft and warm. "Are you okay?"

His pulse surged. She probably thought he must be close to death. He never called in.

"Yeah, I'm fine." He tried to sound calm and indifferent. A difficult feat, considering what had gone down with his partner tonight and the beautiful woman on the other end of the line that kept him tied in knots. "Markus and I took on a few DEADs. We got separated. Has he checked in within the last few hours?"

"No, he hasn't." Her words were hesitant. Probably from shock. He'd probably spoken more to her in the last minute than in the previous five years she'd lived on the estate.

"Inform Guerin and Kenric that Markus has gone missing, and I'll be out searching until sunrise. Notify me immediately if you hear *anything* from him."

"Will do."

"Good."

"Arran?"

"Yeah."

"Be safe," she whispered.

Arran closed the phone and rolled his shoulders. He didn't need attachments. She especially didn't need to attach herself to him. One *big* mistake he wouldn't allow her to make. After what Gabrielle had been through, he definitely was *not* what she needed.

He cranked his bike and yanked his helmet into place. Twisting the throttle, he burned out, leaving a boiling cloud of white smoke in his wake. He hoped like hell that if he didn't locate Markus before dawn, his partner found cover from the rising sun—before it found him.

. . .

Emily shoved the key into the deadbolt for her unit. The heavy fall of boots on the wooden steps behind her told her that Kenric was right on her heels. She wondered what he thought of her meager accommodations. Her gaze wandered to the complex's faded brown paneling. It had seen better days. The constant salty spray coming off the ocean played havoc on any dwelling. Everything in the area appeared much older than its actual years. Her mom's thirty-year-old condominium complex looked closer to sixty. Mom had loved it here, and Emily loved the memories—the ones before her dad had lost his battle with the bottle.

"Come on in—if you must," she said, flipping the light switch to the right of the door.

Emily strode through the living area toward her bedroom, talking as she went. "Make yourself at home. I'm going to change my clothes. I won't be long." She glanced back and pointed in the direction of the small galley kitchen. "There should be something to drink in the fridge. Oh." She halted and then turned. "That's if you drink anything other than— well—you know." She shrugged, knowing her smile had to look uncomfortable.

"I can drink other things on occasion. If I wish. But I don't necessarily get thirsty."

He'd parked himself inside the closed front door, leaning against it in that casual, I-have-no-idea-how-sexy-I-look kind of way. The leather jacket he'd slipped on before they'd left and all that midnight wavy hair added to his bad-boy aura.

"Okay. Well, if you would like something tonight, there should be sweet tea and soda in there." She backpedaled a couple of steps, then spun and headed down the hall.

Entering her room, she noticed the red light from the answering machine was blinking. She strode over to the table and groaned, knowing the callers were probably the people she despised most in the world. Bill collectors, or Jeff, her ex-fiancé. The thought of either made her want to hurl. Both hounded her constantly for money. She braced herself and pressed Play.

Yup, collectors. Including one call from the bank holding the lien on the condo. If they didn't have her payment soon, she risked foreclosure. Why she had allowed Jeff Monroe to convince her to borrow so much money, she'd never understand. She took a deep breath and released it, blowing the bangs out of her eyes.

The next three messages mimicked the first. *Payment due immediately*. Then she came to Jeff's. Of course he'd called. Why the hell would he even think of giving her more than a seventy-two-hour break from his bullshit? His deep voice, scratchy from years of smoking, filled the bedroom. "You owe me. Pay up, bitch, or I'll make sure you wish you did." The call ended. It was always the same threat.

What had she ever seen in him? She'd been too young and too desperate for attention. So eager to jump into the arms of the first man who acted as if he wanted to take care of her. Never again. She slammed her finger down on the delete button.

Emily changed into a pair of her own cotton sweats and a matching T-shirt. She brushed her teeth and ran a brush through her hair. Kenric had already seen her without makeup, so no sense in going there. Turning off the bathroom light, she grabbed the door frame and took a deep, calming breath.

He wasn't in the living room when she returned. Ice clinked against glass in the kitchen. Maybe tonight, he had a taste for something…cold.

"Thirsty tonight?" Emily nodded at the drink in his hand. He stood in the open door of her avocado green refrigerator, pouring a glass of sweet tea.

"No. Actually, I made it for you. You still need to drink a lot of fluids."

"Thanks. By the way, here's my cell number." Emily held out a slip of paper. She'd jotted it down before leaving the bedroom. Kenric silently moved toward her over the black-and-white tiles.

"How do you do that?"

"Do what?" He stopped in his tracks.

"Move like that?" She pointed to his boots. "Without a sound. It's spooky. It's like you're not really here. I'm looking at you walking toward me, but I can't hear you."

"Sorry, I didn't realize I was doing it." Suddenly, the sound of his boots returned. The hard soles thumped the floor as he took the final two steps to hand her the tea.

"Thanks for the tea. That was very thoughtful," she said, reaching for the glass. Her fingers brushed his. He didn't let go. She glanced up, and for a moment, she found herself captured by his gaze. Long dark eyelashes overshadowed striking blue eyes. A faint smile lifted his lips. She hoped her T-shirt and bra were thick enough to hide the effect he had on her nervous system.

"It was my pleasure," he said and handed her the glass

before he took the piece of paper and slipped it into his pocket.

"So, what didn't you realize you were doing?" Emily crossed her arms over her chest and headed into the living room.

"I imagine I do it without thinking anymore." Kenric's deep voice followed her. "We're able to silence our movements. It's essential when we need to feed, and when we hunt the ones who enjoy killing. We have the ability to levitate and move without striking the surface. In effect, we glide."

"Incredible," Emily said as she took a seat on her overstuffed, brown-and-white-checkered couch. "I can see where that would come in handy." The ice cubes twirled in her tea while she fidgeted with the glass. She glanced up and smiled. "I have to say, though, it's still spooky."

He laughed, then added a warm smile. He crossed his arms and leaned against the wall beside the sofa.

"You are so refreshing."

Man, he curled her toes with the sultry sound of his voice. "Gabrielle seemed nice," she said, covering up her reaction. *Real smooth transition there, girl. You're not obvious at all.*

"Yes, she is."

She cleared her throat and stared at the ice in her drink. "I noticed she didn't make the same pledge as Logan and Guerin. She is part of the Enclave, right?"

"Elle is human. She works with us, but she's not an Enclave warrior. She's been with us and under my protection for five years now and is an invaluable part of our team."

"She's human? I didn't realize. She's under your protection, too—like me." *Wonder how many beautiful women he thought needed his private security services?*

"Are you two close?" She chanced a glance from under her lashes. He stared back at her, a slight grin lifting his lips.

"What? Why are you grinning at me like that?" She had to resist the urge to kick him in the shin and knock that smile right off his mug.

"Are you jealous, Wildflower?" He moved away from the wall and came closer. With the tips of his fingers, he lifted her chin. "She's family. Like a sister whom I care a great deal for. But that's all there is. And in case it's the next question coming, you are the only woman whom I've placed under my protection outside of the Enclave."

Emily pulled her chin free. "Well, it's nice to hear that you care so much about each other. And just so that we're clear here…," She hesitated a second to make sure she had his complete attention, "…I'm not jealous, and like I've said before, I'm not yours or anyone else's wildflower."

She leaned forward to set her tea on the coffee table—and missed. The glass hit the floor and shattered. Tea and shards of glass flew in all directions across the pale hardwood floor.

"Oh, my God!" Emily jumped to her feet and bolted into the kitchen. After snatching a towel from the counter, she hurried back to the wet mess, forgetting she was barefoot.

"Ouch!" *Damn.*

"Be careful." Kenric grabbed hold of her while she hobbled on one foot. "Here, let me help," he said, tugging at the dish towel.

"I've got it." She yanked the rag free and dropped to the floor, mopping at the sticky mess. "If I'm capable of creating this mess, I think I can clean it up." God, she was so embarrassed.

"Damn." Emily jerked her hand from the soaked towel.

She peered at the center of her palm.

"Let me see." Kenric knelt down beside her and wrapped his hand around her wrist.

"I'm the nurse here. I'm all right." Emily tried to pull free from his grasp.

"Let me *help* you. You're shaking—it's okay." He held her hand steady.

How did he do it? Make everything better with his gentle words and the touch of his hand? She quit her struggles and allowed him to help. She peered over his shoulder as he worked the glass free from her palm. He ran the pad of his finger across the surface. A small drop of blood formed in the center of her hand. Before she could react, he lowered his head.

His lips touched the sensitive center. She gasped. The warmth of his tongue brushed across the wound. She nearly came unglued. Christ, how could something so simple feel so erotic? From under his lashes, his blue eyes met hers. Without words, his gaze alone told her he enjoyed her taste.

"Let me take care of you," he said, lowering her hand. He reached for her foot.

She opened her mouth to protest, but no sound emerged.

He pulled the shard free, and then his warm lips met the sole of her foot. A whimper came out of nowhere. That had to be her. His tongue moved to her ankle, and a moan filled the room. Oh yeah, that was her.

No. no. no. Too much, too fast. What was she thinking? Emily jumped up. She grabbed the towel and limped toward the kitchen. "Uh…I'll be right back."

• • •

Kenric couldn't fight back the growl that rolled from his own throat. She'd tasted like sin, and he'd lost his soul to her flavor. He'd healed her foot, and now he wanted more. Much more. The sound of her pleasure-filled moan, and her passionate gaze, had blasted the lock off his control. Thank God she'd jerked away when she had. He couldn't have borne another minute without touching more of her.

Emily stepped back into the room, another glass of tea in her hand. Kenric moved to one end of the couch and took a seat. Without a word, she eased down onto the opposite side. He didn't have to be a vampire with supernatural senses to detect the thick wall of tension growing between them.

"Listen…," Emily cleared her throat. She glanced in his direction then stared off at some invisible spot on the far wall. "I think I should make it clear that I'm not ready or looking for a man, of any kind, in my life." She traced the edge of her glass, then turned and this time met his gaze. "I agreed to help you get what you need from the hospital, and I'll keep my word. But after that…"

"That's all I ask…" Kenric inhaled deeply. "Nothing more."

"Good." She nodded, then took a sip of her beverage.

"Good."

She leaned forward and placed her glass on the table. "I'm glad we agree."

"We do."

"You're so not my type anyway."

"I'm not your type…?" The hairs on the back of his neck prickled. "Because of what I am?"

"Could you blame me if it was? The first time we met, you bit me." She shifted in her seat and met him head-on.

"But that's not the whole issue. You're a bit of a control freak. Good Lord, you even have your own Enclave." Emily shook her head. "Vampire or not, you would drive me crazy wanting to control my life. Been there, done that. Got the T-shirt, memories, and bruises from the trip. Not going back."

Another growl exploded up from his chest, but he choked it back. He'd overwhelmed her enough.

Bruises?

"Who hurt you?" His gums tingled from the threat of his fangs. It was all he could do to keep them in check. *Hold it together, vampire.*

Emily stood. "Bad word choice." She dismissed his question with the wave of her hand and moved toward the kitchen, giving him her back. "No one hurt me. I don't know why I said that."

He didn't plan what happened next. Instinct claimed his brain and his limbs, and before he could think better of the action, he was in front of her. She gasped and stopped in her tracks.

"You're lying."

Her eyes narrowed. "You don't know that." She lifted her chin, her jaw tight.

"There. Right there." Kenric lifted his hand, and with one finger, traced the delicate outline of her chin. "I can see the tension." He dropped his arm. "You're lying."

"I don't appreciate being called a liar, and my past is none of your business." The green flecks in her irises sparkled.

"I didn't say you were a liar, only that you're lying now. I don't like the idea that someone hurt you."

"This is what I'm talking about." Her hands went to her hips, and her voice lowered to a near rumble. "I tell you nothing happened, but you won't let it go." She shoved at his chest. "You can just kiss my—"

Kenric claimed her mouth, breathing in her gasp. The thought of someone else touching her, hurting her, made him scream inside. He wanted to protect her. Mark her.

She moaned and gripped his biceps. Not pushing him away, but holding on for more. She opened her lips, and the sweetness of her desire flowed from her lips and tongue. Emily was fire and ice. A blistering mixture that burned him to his core.

But he'd die before he'd allow her to be hurt again, or worse, hauled into a war that wasn't hers. A war that could cause her much more than pain.

It could kill her.

That was the very reason why he hadn't taken a lover in centuries, and his aversion to the heightened lust for blood associated with sex. All gifts from his years spent as Marguerite's slave.

So who was the bigger monster here? The bastard who'd bruised her? Made her fear another relationship? Or the selfish male who would risk her life to have her in his? He groaned. Torn between his rational mind and his desires. But there really was no choice.

This could go no further. The night would end exactly as it should.

With him leaving.

His cell phone chimed.

Perfect timing.

Kenric reached deep inside and tore himself away. Emily stumbled back but quickly gained her balance. After putting some distance between them, he pressed the answer key.

"Kenric."

"There's a problem," Elle's soft voice replied. "It's Markus. Arran called and said they'd had a run-in with a few DEADs. He's missing."

"How long?" His grip bore down on the phone. The hard plastic case popped under the pressure.

"He didn't say. Just said to tell you and Guerin he'll be out searching until dawn."

"I'm on my way back. Have Guerin contact Arran and find out where he's searched so far. The night is almost gone, and we need to make efficient use of what's left."

He jabbed End Call as Emily came up behind him. He didn't need to see her to know she was there. Her warmth slid over his body, wrapping him like a hot blanket on a cold night. Closing his eyes, he inhaled deeply through his nostrils. The sweet floral scent that was uniquely Emily rode the air, laced with the hint of her lingering arousal. Her very presence heated his blood and calmed his soul. Opening his eyes, he glanced over his shoulder.

"What's happened?" She crossed her arms under her breasts.

"I'm sorry. I have to leave," he said, reaching for the keys in his pocket. "One of my warriors is missing. I'll call you tomorrow evening as planned."

Kenric paused long enough to place his card on the table near the front door. "If you need me, my number is right here."

Mid-step over the threshold, he stopped and turned, knowing she stood inches behind him. "Goodnight, Wildflower."

Chapter Eleven

Making tracks down the hallway toward the kitchen, Kenric kept pace behind Arran.

Dawn had arrived.

The UV light forced the warriors to find shelter inside. And to leave one of their own behind. Frustration rolled off the team, swirling and surrounding them like a dense fog. The air pulsed with its intensity.

Arran's fist slammed into the kitchen's swinging door, knocking it open and into the opposite wall with a loud *bang*. Sitting at the center island, Michael jumped, sloshing coffee down the front of his shirt. He cursed and frantically grabbed for a towel.

With a *click* and a *hum*, the electronic darkening system went to work on the bank of windows in the kitchen and throughout the compound.

Guerin and Logan strode into the room, abusing the wood of the door with equal venom.

"I'll take to the sky again at dusk," Kenric said, the consolation directed at Arran, who stood with his hands braced on the back of a kitchen chair, his back in a defeated hunch and his blond head hanging. The muscles in his forearms flexed as he white-knuckled the wood. Kenric swung his gaze to Guerin before adding, "Getting an earlier start in my raven form, I'll have a better chance at finding a clue. Hopefully, the storm won't damage whatever trail might be left behind." As if on cue, thunder rumbled on the other side of the shutters.

"True," Guerin said, running his fingers through his rain-slicked hair, then turned his head toward Arran. "Arran…"

With a roar, Arran hurled the chair into the wall, silencing whatever Guerin had started to say. It broke apart, multiple pieces flying in every direction. The sound of splintering wood reverberated off the tiled floors and steel appliances.

The last piece struck the floor, leaving nothing but pained silence.

All eyes fixed on the vampire wrestling with his rage. He paced the floor, sucking air into his lungs as if it were fuel for his anger.

Minutes passed, though it seemed more like an hour, before Arran regained enough control for speech.

"I fucking hate being trapped!" His fist hammered a single blow onto the top of the island.

"We all do. But we don't take it out on the damn furniture," Logan said disdainfully from across the room.

"Fuck you!" Arran spun on his heels. He lunged toward Logan with fangs bared.

Kenric stepped between them.

Arran's fierce glare met his, giving Kenric all the opening

he needed. He dived in, grabbed Arran's mind, and seized control.

"For the record, I don't give a shit about the chair," Kenric said with a firm grip inside Arran's head. "But I do give a shit about my warriors tearing each other apart." He released his mental hold.

Arran staggered. His eyes narrowed on Kenric for a moment before he recessed his fangs. Kenric rotated on his heels and faced Logan, making sure he, too, got the signal to back down.

"We're all just a little on edge, Kenric. Sorry, man." Logan glanced in Arran's direction. "We're cool. Right, Arran?"

"Ice." Arran wheeled, giving Logan his back.

The frigid display confirmed Kenric's suspicion. Something more churned beneath the surface between these two. Their actions spoke of two males who had an ax to grind—or a grudge to settle. When Arran had joined the Enclave ten years ago, Kenric had asked them whether they'd known each other during their early years spent in the Highlands. Both had denied it.

Getting a wolf to heel was easier than trying to get Arran to talk about his past. And all Kenric could pry out of Logan was that he'd met Arran about a century ago up north when they were both part of another colony of vampires. Logan had summarized his opinion of Arran with one simple statement: he hadn't liked the bastard back then, and he was on the fence now.

Arran was loyal, though. Kenric had sensed that the moment he'd met him. Or he'd have never brought him on board. He couldn't figure out what the hell had gone down between them. Neither would talk. But both men, Kenric knew, would give their lives for the Enclave.

Dropping into a chair, Kenric threaded his fingers through his hair. This was not going to work. He'd have to keep those two from killing each other long enough to figure out how to resolve the situation. He needed all his warriors fighting for the same team.

Not with each other.

"At sundown, we'll pick up where we left off," Kenric said. "And every sundown after that until we find Markus. It's frustrating as hell. But we've done all that we can do for now." He understood that each minute that passed without a word or a sign from Markus ate away at their hope like acid.

Markus was his responsibility.

He would search for the rest of time until he found something—anything—that could tell him what had happened to his warrior.

"Get out of here and get your asses some rest." Kenric dismissed them with a wave. "And try not to kill each other in the meantime." His gaze purposefully flicked between the Highlanders.

Before the last word left Kenric's mouth, Arran was already out of the room. Logan and Guerin dispersed, grumbling something about hating this fucking shit.

"Anything I can get for you?" Michael stopped at the table with a broom and garbage bag in hand.

"No." Kenric shook his head. "Thanks."

"No sign of Markus?"

"Not a damn thing."

"What do you think happened?"

Kenric glanced at Michael. Lines of worry etched his face.

"I don't know. But you can be damn sure I won't rest until I find out."

• • •

Ten minutes later, Kenric fell naked onto his mattress and pulled a sheet over himself, exhausted from the events of the last two nights. A loud clap of thunder rumbled behind the closed shutters, while driving wind and rain pelted the windowpanes.

Hunger unfurled its claws in his gut. His fangs dropped into place. He hissed and pushed the demand to feed into submission and his fangs back into his jaw.

He should have fed while out, but he didn't desire the anonymous taste of a stranger to ease the burn inside.

Emily's flavor haunted him.

Unconsciously, he'd dismissed the opportunities for blood. Tonight he would have to feed, whether he wanted to or not.

His body stirred, remembering their evening together, the flavor of her kiss on his tongue. Reaching under the sheet, he wrapped his hand around his cock. He moaned, stroking himself with the memory of her scent, the taste of her skin.

Shit. He couldn't remember being so turned on by a woman—ever. Riding the arch of his erection with his fingers, he stroked the sensitive underside of his cock's head. A clap of thunder rattled the walls of his bedroom. He closed his eyes and lifted his hips, slowly pumping into the air. The raging storm outside matched the fierceness of his need for release.

Hunger burned like a twisting, raging fire, wrenching him back from the edge.

Kenric opened his eyes to a darkened cell, flat on his back with his wrists shackled to a wall behind his head. He shifted his legs, only to find he couldn't move them more than an inch or two. Large cuffs held his ankles down at opposite sides of his cot.

He roared.

"Fuck!" His fangs caused the word to come out with a lisp.

His arms trembled from the time spent suspended over his head, combined with the agony in his gut for blood. He'd wither and die before he'd ever drink her blood. The putrid, hot residue of her on his tongue lingered from the last time she'd forced it down his throat.

He'd awakened in the midst of ferocious hunger, clawing at the stone behind his head. She'd slashed open her wrist and used her powers, forcing him to accept it as she jammed it into his mouth. Her psychic influence had combined with his body's own demand for blood, and he'd swallowed.

That had been at least five days ago.

If he were older and stronger, he could try to phase the fuck out of this place. He had seen it done before. Marguerite had used that trick when she'd snatched him from the battlefield about three years ago. But she kept him starved, kept him weak, and he was as trapped now as he'd been when he was human.

She'd left him alone again to slowly build the hunger in hopes this time would be different. Marguerite wanted him hungry enough not only to feed but also to mate.

The bitch was insane.

Marguerite had apparently grown bored of him as her personal human blood supply. The night of his turning, she'd declared that his impressive mental endurance would make him the perfect vampire. A master. Stronger, more powerful mentally and physically than other males.

Hers.

She wanted him to take her as his mate.

After his transition, she'd explained that mating required the male to submit to the female. Blood, body, and soul. Once completed, the mated female would have access to her mate's thoughts and emotions, and *she would share his power.*

Kenric had had no idea what he would be capable of in his new form, but he did understand that if the queen bitch wanted him this badly, no way in fucking hell would he ever let it happen.

"Sounds like someone missed me." Marguerite's voice echoed off the stone walls from the other side of the cell. The rattle of a key and the groan of the iron cell door announced another round.

"I heard your roar, darling. Are you hungry?" She trailed one long fingernail up the length of his leg and then a lazy scratch along his abdomen and chest.

She placed the lone finger into her mouth and sucked. Her eyes lingered on him through half-shuttered lids. For a moment, she appeared to savor his flavor. Then suddenly, she bit down.

Blood oozed from her mouth. A deep crimson trail flowed over her lips, down her chin, and dripped onto his chest. The ravenous beast within him writhed in agony.

Drop after drop of the hot red beads coalesced and pooled between the ridges of his abdomen. Shackled and stretched out on his back like a sacrificial offering, all he could do was grip the chains above his head in an effort to control his body's response. His arms burned and ached under the tension. Sweat dripped from his forehead, stinging his eyes.

He'd chew his own fucking arm off before he'd beg to be fed or take her vein.

She eased the finger from her bloodied mouth. A spasm coiled in his stomach. Above his navel, Marguerite dipped into the puddle of red. She swirled two fingertips in the thickening pool. Mesmerized, his gaze followed as she lifted her hand and brought his stare to her face.

Her compulsion seized him.

In horror, he could only watch as her blood-coated fingers slid between his lips. His heart raced, jackhammering in his chest. The taste of her blood exploded across his tongue.

No! He didn't want this. Why didn't she just kill him?

She bit her wrist and forced it to his mouth. A wave of fresh blood spilled down his throat, choking him. He swallowed, even as his mind rebelled. His body quaked from the effects of her blood scorching his veins. His contortions rattled the chains above his head and at his feet.

Marguerite yanked her wrist from his mouth and released him from her mind. He sucked in a breath and spat. The mixture of saliva and blood landed on the lace bodice of her gown. She hissed as her hand flew from her side and landed against his cheek. The sound of the skin-on-skin contact rang off the cell walls.

"You are an ungrateful bastard, Kenric St. James. Do you know how many kill for a taste of me?"

It wasn't a slip of the tongue. They did kill for her. Her minions battled before her to be the next male to share her *bed and drink from her vein.*

Slowly, he rolled his head up and faced her. He licked his lip, removing the flavor of his blood from where his fang had nicked him. Bile welled in his throat from the lust-filled, satisfied smile on Marguerite's face.

He didn't need to look. He knew his body betrayed him from the effects of her blood.

"Marguerite, it will never happen. You can leave me in here for an eternity to starve and rot. It won't change a damn thing. I will never become so deranged that your blood—and you fucking me—will ever make me want to be your mate."

Undeterred, she crawled onto his cot and straddled his thighs.

Kenric wrenched on his chains, attempting to pull himself from her, but there was nowhere to run. Her hand reached for his erection. Disgust assailed him for what seemed like the millionth time. He squeezed his eyes tight and braced for the shudder of revulsion that always came from her touch.

"Kenric, if only you'd relax and enjoy what I'm offering you, it would be so easy and so much pleasure for both of us. We're perfect for each other. All you have to do is give yourself to me and let me walk you through the mating. All the hunger and pain would simply..." Her hand flitted in the air, "...go away."

Like a serpent, her voice licked incessantly inside his head.

A vision of a beautiful, auburn-haired woman with hazel eyes came out of nowhere and flashed before his mind. He knew her...

This woman warmed and calmed his body. The scent of wildflowers invaded his nostrils, jarring him back to the present. Marguerite was in his fucking head again.

He flung open his eyelids.

Rage erased the lust-filled gaze on Marguerite's face. She'd glimpsed Emily in his thoughts.

"Who is she?" she roared and levitated from his body, hovering above him.

Her hair and gown whirled in an illusion of wind.

"None of your damn business." He growled, and the shackles binding him dropped from his wrists and ankles. He blasted from his cot into the air, snagging Marguerite's shoulders. With one hand securely around her neck and another on her arm, he slammed her back against the bars of the cell. His hand slid from her throat to her face. His finger dug into her flesh as he held her gaze. A low growl continued to resonate from his chest.

"You never learn, do you, Marguerite? Whether we're in reality or your demented version of a dream, I still don't want you. It doesn't matter how many centuries pass. I didn't submit to you then, and I won't submit to you now."

"You must need a reminder of Annice's fate." Marguerite's eyes burned with fury. "I will find out who she is. Of that, you can be assured."

"Get the fuck out of my mind!" Kenric bellowed, squeezing hard at the flesh under his hands.

Kenric bolted naked from his bed. His chest heaved as he wiped the sweat from his face, then ran a hand through his damp hair.

"You'll never have Emily, Marguerite. Of that, *you* can well be assured."

Damn the sun. He wanted to haul his ass back over there and check on Emily—to see her face again.

He picked up his cell and the small piece of paper she'd given him.

"Hello?" The voice that answered sounded weak and sleepy.

"Emily, it's Kenric. Did I wake you?"

"Oh. No, you didn't wake me. I was just getting up from a nap before work. What are you doing awake? I thought vampires slept during the day."

"They do. I happened to wake up early today." Silence hung for a few seconds between them while he searched for a good reason for his call. The fact that she now had a more than six-hundred-year-old vampire bitch gunning for her wouldn't be the best conversation opener. Finally, he went with, "How are you feeling?"

"I'm good. A little nervous about our joint endeavor tonight."

"You have nothing to worry about. No one will remember seeing you there, or me for that matter. I'll call you later and let you know when I've arrived."

"Okay. I'll talk to you later, then."

"Emily… It'll be nice to see you again." He wanted to groan with how sappy he sounded. His heart swelled behind his sternum to an almost painful fullness. *Dammit*. It had been so long since he'd allowed himself to feel anything, and he barely knew what to do with the resurgence. For so long, the only "feelings" Kenric had been concerned with he could label on one hand. And anger and bitterness had headed the top of the list. But he never expected this. This overwhelming desire to grab on to Emily and never let her go. Christ, for the first time in more years than he cared to remember, he craved something else—someone else—more than his need for vengeance. And it was unsettling.

Silence permeated the line for a few telling seconds. "Emily, are you still there?"

"Yes, I'm here. It'll be nice to see you again, too." He could hear the smile in her voice. How could he have allowed this to happen? Emily was the personification of compassion, beauty, honor, and…light. Things that didn't belong in his world. Things he had no right to want, because he would only bring her the darkness. Yet for some reason he couldn't stop his tumble down the slippery slope into her life. He'd never believed in the whole "soul mate" theory before. But whether he was ready to admit it to himself or not, Emily made him feel—made him yearn again. And it was good. Too good.

"Until then," he said and ended the call.

No way in hell would history repeat itself. He would die before Marguerite could touch Emily.

Chapter Twelve

Stretching over to her nightstand, Emily tapped the end button and dropped her cell back onto the wood.

She kicked back the covers and swung her legs over the side of the bed. Her conversation with Kenric ran through her mind, playing havoc with her stomach.

"*It would be nice to see you again*," he'd said. On her way to the shower, she giggled like a teenage girl. Then warning bells rang in her mind, and her toes hung off the edge of a crumbling cliff. Her smile disappeared.

Don't do it, Emily Ross!

Emily had to put the brakes on. She could not fall for this man.

Man?

He wasn't even human. *Girl, you really know how to pick 'em.*

She reached in and turned on the shower. Kenric was… more everything than any other man she'd ever dated, and it scared the hell out of her. If she had any common sense, she would run like hell. God only knew why she hadn't already started sprinting . . .

With her hair washed, Emily worked up a lather inside her washcloth. Memories of last night replayed in her mind. The way Kenric had made her feel... Her pulse raced. When he'd touched her palm... Her heart stuttered. Kissed her... Emily's head swam, making her grasp the tile for support. He'd smelled so good, like pine and cinnamon spice. She took a couple of deep breaths and tried to cool herself down. This wasn't good. From the very moment they'd met, the guy had triggered every reactive cell in her body. Was it purely physical? *Yes.* At least a part of it was. But if her response to him was only sexual in nature, she could turn it off. That was the problem, she realized. Her reaction to Kenric was based on more than his good looks and their chemistry. It was the man underneath the alpha exterior that had gotten under her skin. His heart. The way he cared about others— his team and the human race. His mission, and...the way he needed her. Turning into the shower spray, she cranked up the cold water, allowing it to rain over her face and breasts.

She shivered, chilled from the cold water—or maybe from the fear that a part of her might need him just a little, too.

What would she do about Kenric St. James?

An hour later, Emily hurried into the ER, running her fingers through her hair to unlock the still-damp curls. She couldn't blame the traffic, and no way would she tell anyone about her fantasies of a certain dark and sexy vampire and how they'd kept her from leaving the house on time.

"Emily!" Shawna's voice called out from the front desk

of the nurse's station. "You've got a phone call."

"Sorry I'm so late," Emily said, reaching the desk and breathing hard after her trot from the parking deck.

Her friend waved the phone's receiver in her hand. "I've got Jeff on hold. This has to be the third time he's called in the past fifteen minutes, girl." Shawna rolled her eyes and shook her head. As she did so, a few of her blonde locks escaped her braid to sway around the petite features of her face. "You really need to get a restraining order."

"Been there, done that. Doesn't faze him."

Shawna moved from her chair and passed the phone over to Emily.

"I'm just worried about you, hon. From what you've told me, the man's a nutcase. If you ever need a place to stay or just hide out for a while, you know where I live."

Since the first day Emily had arrived at Memorial, she and Shawna had hit it off. Shawna always had her back, covering for her whenever she was late or offering her help whenever things were tight. One day, Emily hoped to be able to return the favor.

"That means a lot, Shawna. It really does. Thank you." Emily settled into the vacated chair.

"You know you're like my little sister. And I mean it. Anytime, okay?" Her hand brushed Emily's shoulder.

Emily nodded. "I know you do."

Shawna turned and headed toward triage.

With the phone at her ear, Emily sighed, then pressed the Hold button.

"Leave me alone, Jeff. You can't keep calling me here, or I'm going to lose my job. And if I don't have any income, you'll be left without a reason to harass me." She kept her voice low but firm. Enough to get her point across without drawing attention.

"Damn, you're bitchy tonight. Sounds like you need a good fuck to calm you down. You sure you're not missing me just a little bit?"

She gripped the edge of the desk. Deep breath. She needed this job. The temporary satisfaction of cursing him out would only succeed in making things worse in the end.

"Bitter much, Jeff?"

"I'm bitter about my damn money."

"I don't owe you anything," she spat. "I put *myself* through school. You didn't cough up one red cent."

"You lived in *my* house, and I fed your ass for four years. If it weren't for me, you would've been out on the street. It's time I was compensated."

"It's not about that at all, and you know it." She cupped her hand around her chin and the receiver. "I'm not giving you any more money to pay off your gambling debts."

"I'm warning you, bitch, if I don't see some green within the next twenty-four hours, I'm coming to find you."

With a *click*, the line went dead.

Emily hung up the phone. Suddenly chilled, she rubbed her upper arms vigorously for a couple of seconds, then she reached in the pocket of her scrub top. She pulled out a hair clip, brushed her fingers through her hair, and pinned her curls into a ponytail. If only she could pull the rest of her life together so easily.

It was blackmail—pure and simple.

She knew better than to give in. Jeff would never stop if she gave him money. But God, it would be so easy if she had a way to give him enough so he'd disappear.

"Hey, girl." Shawna came up beside her and plopped down in one of the black task chairs. "Are you okay? You look pale. Was Jeff threatening you again?"

"Really?" Emily placed her palms on her cheeks. "I feel okay." She managed to get the words out in a steady voice that even surprised her to hear. "It's probably just that time of the month. You know how it gets. I'm a little anemic." She cringed at the bald-faced lie that had come out of her mouth. Well, not all of it was a lie. She was a little low on red blood cells. "I'll go get some juice and I'll be fine."

Emily left her chair for the break room with Shawna following on her heels. She waved her ID badge over the door's security sensor, and the lock gave a soft *click*. Pushing open the door, she fanned her hand in front of her nose. The enclosed small space of their employee refuge reeked of old tuna sandwiches and overheated Lean Cuisines. She skirted between the tired and tattered navy blue couch and the round white dinette table with its vented plastic chairs, making her way to the refrigerator.

"He was just going on as usual about money. What's new?" Emily grabbed an individual Minute Maid off the fridge shelf and twisted the cap off.

"You know what you need?"

Emily lifted her eyebrows, giving her a nonverbal "what's that?" look, while taking a long swallow of the cold juice.

"You need some fun in your life—a little excitement. A tall, dark, and handsome man to whisk you away to his mansion and take your mind off your troubles. You need a man who knows how to treat a woman right."

Emily choked. Orange juice sprayed from her lips and all over the front of her top.

"Oh, my God! Are you all right?" Shawna snatched some paper towels from beside the sink and handed them to her. "I didn't think my idea sounded that crazy."

"It *is* crazy," Emily said between coughs. "Besides, how many tall, dark, and handsome men with mansions have you seen around here?" She hated lying to her best friend. Though, technically, it wasn't a lie. He was a vampire, not a man. Either way, she could never tell Shawna what had happened to her or what she'd learned.

"Good point." Shawna laughed. "I'd have already tried to snag one for myself."

"Believe me, the last thing I need is a man to whisk me off my feet and take control of my life." Emily tossed the rest of her OJ in the trash and headed back to work.

. . .

Pulling on a pair of black leather gloves, Kenric made his way down the stairs from his private level, a dagger strapped to each thigh.

The day had passed like an eternity. With Marguerite knowing about Emily and thus threatening her, he needed to find Markus as soon as possible. Then he needed to get Emily into safekeeping.

And no place would be safer than here—with him.

The aroma of freshly brewed coffee wafted into the hallway as he made his way toward the kitchen.

Kenric opened the door and flinched. He slammed his eyes shut from the sudden burst of harsh fluorescents. Opening his eyes a crack, he spotted Michael at the island working on his next experimental concoction.

"Is all this really necessary?" he growled before pulling out a pair of dark shades.

"If I plan on being able to see while I cook, it is." Michael glanced up briefly from his project. "Your eyes will adjust."

Kenric leaned over the island, resting his weight on one large hand. "Some days, I question why I ever saved your sarcastic ass."

"Because of my winning personality, and because I'm a damn good cook." Michael lifted his head and grinned.

Michael would have a home here for the rest of his life, and he knew it. He'd become like the son Kenric would never have. It was Marguerite who had coldly informed him, after he'd been turned, that he had nothing left to offer any human woman. A fact that she'd gloated over again just a couple of nights ago. Sadly, he'd seen no births in all his years to contradict her statement.

"A damn good cook—you wish." Kenric pushed back from the island.

"You just resent the fact that my pot roast makes you salivate even though you haven't needed to eat in centuries."

"You have a point there." Kenric smiled. "That it does." He turned on his heels and headed toward the somber group at the table.

Guerin sat at one end with Arran, Elle in the middle, while Logan propped himself at the opposite end. Kenric grabbed the closest chair and eased into the seat across from Arran.

"I've some things for you to look at," Elle said and handed him several sheets of paper. "I got a few hits on the subject, but the one that grabbed my attention the most, I placed on top." She tapped the sheet. "I think you'll find it interesting."

In bold, the title read, *LEGEND OF THE VAMPIRE, GORAN MADUNIC.* The article said that Goran was one of the earliest recorded vampires. He'd been a brutal man, bloodthirsty. The legend went on to say that he'd killed hundreds of men and women in Croatia during his rampages. He had had an army of fellow creatures—loyal servants who hunted and fought with him. At the time of Madunic's demise, the myth stated that according to his wishes, his minions were to remove the heart from his headless body and drain the organ of its contents, sealing the blood inside a glass vessel. His army supposedly hid this essence, awaiting the next master vampire. The successor would then drink from the relic, merging the former leader's power and consciousness with his own. Goran had believed that his power was so great that he could live on through the next master who consumed his blood.

Kenric eased back in his chair and dragged a weary palm across his face. "If this is what she's unearthed...," He glanced around the table, meeting his fellow warrior's grim faces. "We've got a big problem on our hands."

"Elle showed me what she printed out," Guerin said before lifting his mug for a gulp. "You think that vessel would still be around after all Croatia has been through?"

"It fits the clues Marguerite dropped. The time period, and the new surge in her power." Kenric leaned forward, resting his forearms on the table. "And if we're right, and she's drinking this shit..." He shook his head. "The ancient vampire DNA will be concentrated—off the charts, and Goran was correct about one thing: his essence will affect the vampire who absorbs him. His consciousness is long gone, but the potent genetic material left behind will prey on her mind."

"How do you propose we find out what she has?"

He cocked his head in Guerin's direction. "I ask her. She'll be back, to screw with my mind, and if I'm right, Marguerite won't be able to resist admitting it was Madunic's blood she's found." Kenric looked over to Arran and Elle. "Even if we stop Marguerite, we have to find that vessel. It's too much of a threat to allow it to fall into the hands of a power-hungry vampire like her." He swung his gaze back to Guerin. "It must be destroyed."

Kenric dragged his hands through his hair, his mind drifting back to the early years of his turning and the implications if the insane female had found that vessel.

During the three years he'd spent with Marguerite, she had already eradicated the last drop of empathy she may have once had for the human race—and that was three centuries ago. Now... Now God only knew what lurked in the dark void where her soul used to reside. Yes, he'd wondered more than once, while watching her torture then drain the life from her victims, if there had ever been a time when Marguerite Devonshire had cared about someone other than herself. For most, to have lost their grip and fallen so far over the edge meant at some point they had possessed something to hold onto. Some small nugget of sanity. But the look of pleasure she wore when inflicting pain made him question if her ability to feel compassion had ever existed. If it had, she'd made sure to excise it from her heart. And if she was consuming the blood of Goran...

Michael passed behind them, opening the interior shutters for the night, when the door to the kitchen swung wide.

The entire table jumped to their feet, transfixed on the figure in the doorway.

"Son of a bitch!" Arran voiced the exact words that had crossed Kenric's mind.

"Miss me?" Markus stood before them in the kitchen, his clothes dirty and torn, his lip bloodied, but very much… alive.

"Where the fuck have you been?" Arran rounded the table.

"I got back as fast as I could. I couldn't call you, man." He pulled out what was left of his cell and held it up to Arran. "One of the filthy bloodsuckers crushed it when it fell out of my pocket. That, and I've been holed up in a damn warehouse for I don't know how many hours, waiting for the sun to go down. No phones."

Markus trudged over to the table and slumped into a chair, his straight black hair falling across his face. After sweeping it back, he scrubbed an open palm over his shadow of a beard.

"Shit. What happened?" Kenric shook his head, relief spreading through his limbs. The SOB was alive.

Arran moved back to the other side of the table as the rest of the team took their seats, everyone eager to hear what had happened.

"After I finished off the motherfucker who broke my phone, I went after another one I'd seen running toward The Docks." Markus tilted back in his chair. "Once I got down there, I caught sight of him slipping behind one of the warehouses. He saw me and took off. You know how that area is around the shipyards—it's like a fucking maze.

Bloodsucker knew the place way too well. He maneuvered it like it was his playground."

He turned his gaze in Kenric's direction, his gray eyes shadowed with intensity. "There had to be a lair somewhere nearby. I wasn't going to lose him." His focus returned to the rest of his team.

"I followed him into one of the warehouses. Shipping containers filled the place from one end to the other, stacked almost to the damn ceiling. After, I don't know…" He shrugged, "…twenty minutes or so, I spotted him again. I ran after him before he leaped off one of the crates to a window and got out." He slammed the table with his fist.

"Damn. I was so fucking pissed. I jumped up onto a section of crates to follow him. The next thing I knew, I was under a mountain of the damn things and it was dawn."

"Shit. No wonder we couldn't find you," Arran muttered.

"The only thing I could do was wait out the sun in one of those fucking crates."

"Glad you're alive, and that you made it back," Kenric said. Then with a nod, "Now, go get cleaned up. You reek." The team chuckled, and Markus displayed a rare grin. The relief around the table was palpable.

Kenric rose, following Arran and Markus from the kitchen.

"Arran," he called. Both warriors paused in the hallway and reeled about. "I'm going to need you at Elizabeth Bay Memorial tonight in case there's trouble."

"What's going down?"

"I'll be meeting the woman you both heard about yesterday to take care of the lab evidence I left behind."

Arran nodded. "You got it."

"I haven't had a chance to talk to everyone yet, but I have reason to believe the woman, Emily, may be in danger."

"What do you mean?" Markus stepped in closer. "What makes you think she's in danger?"

"Marguerite made a threat against her life. Last night, I announced placing Emily under the Enclave's protection. Under *my* protection. Marguerite will *not* touch her." Kenric hit both men with a glare. "Is that clear?"

"Understood," Arran said, nodding his head in affirmation along with Markus. "We have your back."

Kenric whipped around and headed out for a drive to clear his head before his meeting with Emily.

"By the way…" He stopped and glanced over his shoulder at the two silent warriors behind him. "I'll discuss it with the rest of the team later, but I'll be bringing her back to the compound. For her safety."

"Of course," both replied in unison.

Chapter Thirteen

Emily jumped at the sudden tap on her shoulder, breaking her hypnotic gaze on the computer screen.

"Have you heard anything I've said?"

"What?" Emily reeled around in her task chair, faced Shawna, and gave her tired eyes a rub with both hands. "No. I'm sorry. I guess I'm a little distracted." In reality, she grew crazier with each passing minute, waiting for Kenric's call.

"It's okay. I know that sorry ex of yours keeps you on edge." Shawna eased into the chair beside her. "Hey, and what about your John Doe from the other night disappearing like that? That was so weird. Security didn't have a trace of him at any of the exits on video. It was like he just *poofed* out of here." She dramatized the Houdini action with her hands.

Absently rubbing her midsection, Emily whirled back around to the computer. This was so much harder than she'd thought. Her head pounded, and her stomach ached. If he would just call... The firm reassurance of his voice would help steady her nerves.

"Oh, about what I was saying earlier," Shawna went on, oblivious to Emily's abdominal distress. "It's twelve thirty, and I need to start those antibiotics on bed A. I've already tried twice to get a line in him. Would you mind seeing if you can start one for me?"

Pushing back from the computer station, Emily plastered a smile on her face before accepting the IV supplies from her friend's hand. "Sure. I need to occupy my mind with something else."

They'd almost made it to bed A when Emily's phone buzzed against her thigh. With her heart a pounding lump in her throat, she pulled her cell free. The caller ID displayed *Private*.

It had to be him.

"Shawna, I'm sorry, but I have to take this call." Emily glanced left, then right, searching for a replacement who could help Shawna out. "Would you mind getting Sylvia? She's right over there." Emily pointed to the dark-haired nurse in pink scrubs. "She's new, but I've heard she's excellent with IVs." She gave Shawna her best reassuring smile. "I just have to take this call. Please cover for me for a few minutes. I owe you one." Before Shawna could reply, she tumbled the supplies back into her hands, spun on her heels, and headed away from the ER, down the back corridor.

A quick glance up and down the hall assured her she was alone. Good, she had a few seconds of privacy.

She hit the talk button.

"Hello," she whispered.

"Hi. It's me. Are you ready?"

She bit back a groan. *Why did his voice have to be so damn sexy?* "Um… Yeah." She switched hands, wiping the dampness from her other palm onto her pants leg. "I've got someone covering, but not for long. What do you need me to do?" Emily's footsteps echoed off the walls in the empty hallway, the hollow sound chipping away at her already frayed nerves.

"I need you by the lab," he instructed.

She slowed to a stop and closed her eyes, steadying herself for what was to come.

"Be sure you're alone," Kenric added. "Let me know when you're there, and I'll be in."

"How will you know where I am—where the lab is?" She could hear the nervous edge in her own voice no matter how hard she tried to control her jitters. "Have you somehow placed a GPS on my rear?" Emily opened her eyes and started moving again. She wasn't far from where they were to meet.

"Think of it as vampire GPS."

"Oh. I take it that's another lesson in your abilities you haven't filled me in on yet?" She rounded the corner and stopped a few feet from the laboratory's doorway. "Okay, I'm here," she whispered and leaned her hip against the cool surface of the wall.

"Good."

A few seconds passed without another sound. "Kenric…?" Had he hung up? A hand landed on her shoulder.

"I'm right here."

Emily fumbled the phone, but managed to catch it before it fell. She whipped around and shoved at Kenric's arm. "Good Lord. Don't do that." She gave her shoulders a shake and stuffed her cell in her pocket. "Damn, it's unsettling."

"Sorry I startled you." Kenric brushed his palm down her arm, creating a rippling warmth in its wake.

Reflex begged her to lean in and absorb the sensation, but this wasn't the time or the place. As if there could ever be such a thing as the *right* moment with a vampire. She stepped back, placing a little more distance between them.

"You okay?" He curled his fingers away, and his gaze shifted to the hospital corridor, surveying for any unexpected company. "Any fallout from my disappearance?"

"I'm fine, and no fallout. Apparently, no one's connected me with your vanishing act." She followed his lead and watched the hallway. "But you certainly are the talk of the nurses' station with how you disappeared without a blip on the security cameras." She poked him in the arm with her finger. "You gonna tell me how you located me like that?"

He dropped his gaze back to hers and rubbed his arm. "Hey, watch it with that finger, Wildflower. You could hurt someone."

She snorted. "Come on. How did you zero in on me?"

Kenric lifted her chin with two fingers, locking their gazes. Emily stared back at him, refusing to be the one to blink first. He grinned as if he enjoyed their little contest. Then he spoke.

"Because a part of you remains in me." He closed the distance, then the sudden realization struck of what he'd meant by those words. Her blood. That was what he meant, and it still flowed in his veins. Her breath hitched at the thought. Kenric froze and stepped back, rubbing a hand across his mouth and chin. "We need to finish what we came here to do," he stated.

Emily watched as a complete transformation rolled across his face and body. The vivid blue eyes that had greeted her seconds ago turned to ice. The ease of his posture hardened. This was the master vampire of the Enclave. Powerful. Frightening.

Sexy as hell.

"Take me to the lab," he said.

Take me to your bed, her body screamed.

"You'll go in, find the sample, and I'll take care of the rest."

Emily nodded. The lab entrance loomed a few feet away.

The lack of cameras and offices made their previous location ideal for Kenric's arrival. This area would prove more difficult to maneuver.

Adam worked the night shift in serology. He'd been hounding her for a date ever since she had started working at Elizabeth Bay, making him more likely to hand her the samples without a lot of questions.

Poking her head around the corner, she gave a relieved sigh. Thank God.

Adam was alone.

Glancing back, she held up her hand, signaling for Kenric to hold back.

"Hey, Adam." Emily leaned against the doorway to the lab. Adam's red head popped up from his superfluity of tubes and vials on the stainless-steel counter.

"Hey back at you, beautiful. What brings you to these parts?" He gave her a big toothy grin.

A low growl emitted from beside her. She waved her arm at Kenric behind the door, hoping he got the message to keep it down.

"I was wondering if you could help me with something." She eased farther in and up to the counter.

"Sure. What you got?" Adam pushed back from the counter and made his way over to her. He dropped his gloves in the trash and shoved his safety glasses to the top of his head. Stopping in front of her, he leaned against the table.

"Would you mind checking to see how many samples you have of that John Doe's blood we had in from two nights ago? Dr. Castle is in tonight on a consult and asked if I would check on it." She brushed her fingers through a few of her loose curls and tilted her head. "Even though the patient went AMA, he's still interested in additional testing for study purposes. I know I could have called, but I needed a break." Emily flashed him her sweetest Southern smile.

Bull's-eye.

His grin went off the charts. He crossed the room to his computer and pulled out the keyboard. "Do you have the medical record number?" He glanced over his shoulder.

She pulled out the sticky she'd jotted the information on from her pocket, and called out the numbers.

"We should have two samples in storage," Adam said before moving over to open the large refrigerated storage unit. He pulled out a wire shelf and, after a couple of seconds, lifted two serum-filled vials. "Yup, here they are."

Before Emily could open her mouth to reply, something blurred across the room. She wasn't sure she had actually seen anything until Adam's body went limp, collapsing into Kenric's arms.

"Is he okay?" Emily darted around the counter and crouched beside Adam's body, checking for a pulse.

"He'll be fine. I only stunned him with a psychic wave. It momentarily interrupts the conscious mind. It'll give me just enough time to grab these…" He placed the two vials into his pockets, "…and get out of here."

He knelt beside Adam, his shoulder and thigh brushing against hers. The pine and spice scent of him drifted to her nostrils, heightening her awareness of his presence. She wanted to lean over and rub herself against him, purring like a cat in heat.

He glanced her way. "I need you to go and keep a look out. I have to plant new memories for the last few minutes."

"Oh, okay." Emily got to her feet, dusting off her pants as she hurried to the door. Checking the hallway for traffic first, she stepped into the empty corridor. The night shift, most of the time, left the halls sparse. *Thank God.*

She kept an eye on Kenric through the door, not wanting to miss what he did to Adam. His hand slid once across Adam's forehead and eyes. The tech's eyelids flickered. Slowly, he sat upright and rose to his feet. Kenric placed his palm to the back of Adam's head and held his gaze. Kenric's lips moved, but the words were too soft for her to hear.

It only took a few seconds for Kenric to complete whatever he'd said before Adam moved away from his hold, returning to his workstation. He slid his goggles into place and his hands into a pair of clean gloves. Adam returned to his work, as if a strange man in black leather didn't fill up the room.

Like nothing had happened.

Emily shifted back and forth on her feet. She'd heard them talk about abilities at the compound. Heck, she'd even experienced his powers of compulsion firsthand. But to watch it unfold before her eyes made her stomach rebel. Dear God, what was she doing with this man—vampire? Why didn't she listen to her instincts, instead of her heart?

Kenric strode around the corner and touched her arm, leading them at a brisk pace back to where he'd first arrived. Emily increased her pace and slid from his hold. She couldn't help it. At the moment, she didn't want to enjoy the feel of his touch. What he could do with those hands disturbed her.

Kenric dropped his arm to his side in resignation. He may not have had a woman in his life for centuries, but he understood exactly what her body language said: *Don't touch me.*

What the hell happened? He'd felt her gaze as he'd worked with Adam. Had what she'd witnessed affected her this way? God, he would never hurt her. She had to know that.

The waves of her ponytail bounced with each sway of her hips. He wanted to reach out, smooth the loose curls at the back of her neck, and tell her everything would be fine. That in fact, he'd die before he'd let anyone harm her.

At the end of the hall, Emily stopped and whirled, facing him with her back against the wall. She lifted her chin, but her gaze touched everything except him.

"So, what all did you do to him back there?"

He placed a palm on the cool wall beside her head, leaning in before answering in a quiet voice. "I did a sort of...reset...on his memory. Took him back to before you were ever there. He won't remember anything about our visit tonight. You won't have anything to worry about."

A shiver raced over her.

"It had to be done, Wildflower."

"I realize that," she snapped.

"Then why are you so angry? You won't even look at me."

Her gaze locked with his. Defiant hazel eyes held him in a silent pissing contest. No woman, including Annice, would have ever challenged him in such a way. So why in the hell did he have a raging hard-on right now?

"There." She arched one delicate red brow. "I'm looking at you."

"Well." He lowered his face and deepened his voice. "I don't know if I would call that looking. More like throwing daggers."

She shoved at his chest and maneuvered around him. "I've got to get back to work. What else do you need from me?"

Everything.

This had not gone as planned. Somehow, he had to get this feisty woman back to the compound for her own safety. He could tell this wouldn't be an easy task.

"I need to get into security and make sure our images are erased from our stop at the lab. You head there first to minimize the number of times the cameras capture me. Make sure the coast is clear, give me a call, and I'll phase to your location just like before."

"Fine." Emily left without looking back.

Kenric groaned and scrubbed a hand over his face. Damn, she was a frustrating woman. She made him want to fuck her until he couldn't move and, at the same time, spank her ass. Well, that wasn't such a bad idea. He leaned against the same warmed section of wall Emily had vacated, a grin begging to be formed on his lips.

The second half of the mission went off without a hitch. He got into security, removed the recordings from the lab monitors, and replaced them with blank DVDs. The guard wouldn't remember anything, and with nothing to rouse their suspicions, no one would have any reason to notice a few hours of recording were missing. If they did, it would appear like the recordings had not started until later in the night.

With the hospital handled, he could focus on getting the redhead next to him to safety and putting an end to Marguerite's hold on his life.

He'd lay it all out there for her, exactly what she had to do. She would come to the compound in the morning and stay until he felt it was safe for her to return to her life. With the mood she was in, it would be best if he didn't leave it up to discussion.

"Since we're finished, I've got to get back to work before they fire me." Emily spun and started to leave, but Kenric grabbed her arm.

"Wait a minute. Before you go, I have to talk to you about something." He loosened his grip on her forearm. "I have reason to believe your life may be in danger."

Emily turned, her hazel eyes wide.

"What did you just say?" She stepped forward. "I thought this was it. Wasn't it you who said, 'help me with this and there won't be anything to worry about?'"

"It has nothing to do with tonight. But I can't get into it here. That's why, before I arrived, I arranged for my driver to be here in the morning when you get off work. You'll be returning to the compound until I can be assured you're safe."

A flash of red raced to her cheeks, and her eyes widened even more. "I *will* be returning to the compound." Both hands went to her hips. "*You* decided?"

She narrowed her eyes and closed in on him with that dangerous forefinger raised, and dug it into his chest. "Listen up, *Dracula*, I don't need you coming into my life and telling me what *you've* decided without a second thought about what *I* want. You can just take your driver and your decisions and shove them where the sun don't shine." She stabbed her finger into his chest with each word for emphasis. "Oh, excuse me. I guess that euphemism is lost on you, Mr. Vampire."

Well…shit. Guess the direct, don't-leave-it-up-to-discussion approach was a bad idea. At least she hadn't lost her sense of humor.

"You don't know what you're dealing with here. You need to listen to me. My compound is the only place where I know you will be safe."

Her body shook as if she didn't know whether to slap him or run.

"I'm a big girl, and I can take care of myself. I've fought for too long and way too hard for my freedom. I'm not moving in with you and letting you control my life. No way."

She whipped around and practically ran down the hall.

"*Emily!*" he called to her in her mind, using his powers of projection. "*Don't go like this.*"

She came to a halt a few feet away, grabbing her head with both hands.

Glancing back, she braced one hand against the wall.

"Leave me alone, Kenric," she cried out. "I'm not going with you." Tears glistened in her eyes before she shook her head and hurried down the hall—and away from him.

. . .

Emily slumped into a task chair at the nurses' station. Her chest hurt. It was as if someone had wrapped a vise grip around her heart, attempting to squeeze the very life out of her. How in the world did she let it get this far?

For sure, the man was crazy. Who the hell did he think he was, telling her *he'd decided* where she would live? She'd had her fill of dominating men, and she didn't need Kenric St. James joining her list of bad mistakes.

"Emily, where have you been?" Shawna's voice yanked her back to the present.

"I'm sorry. That phone call was an emergency. I didn't mean for it take so long." Emily grabbed her lime green stethoscope she'd left on the desk earlier and rose, meeting her friend coming into the station.

"I'm just glad you're back. We have a trauma coming in five. An MVA. I need you to help prepare the trauma room."

"Sure. I'm on it." Thank God for the diversion. A trauma would keep her busy the rest of the night and her mind off one dark and sexy, overbearing man. She had to get him out of her head, because he could *not* be a permanent fixture in her life.

Emily grabbed an armload of supplies and started prepping the room. At the counter, she pulled the essential lab materials together for all the blood work she anticipated they'd need.

She moved a box of four-by-four gauzes to the side, placing the various vacuum collection tubes in a metal holder, when she spotted a vial of blood lying on its side against the wall. Picking it up, she read the name and date scribbled in her own handwriting: *John Doe ER 11/13/13.*

Holy crap!

How in the world had this gotten overlooked? It must have rolled to the back of the counter and gotten covered up during all the chaos the other night. Reflex had her aiming the vial straight for the biohazard container on the wall, but she stopped before letting it drop. An ugly thought loomed in her mind. She palmed the cool tube in her hand.

She could never do that.

Could she?

The moment he'd opened his eyes, Kenric had taken what he needed from her without a second thought. In a flash, he'd barged into her life, commanded her, and then confined her. Now he wanted to do it all over again. Take control of her every move. So what if she took from him a little of what she needed? She could hold the reins for once. Emily glanced down at the simple sleek vial. So much power contained within a benign tube of blood.

The nasty taste of bile surged to the back of her throat. Never in her life had she deliberately betrayed another soul. The thought sickened her. So many of her problems would vanish if she could find the right buyer for the evidence this would provide. She'd vowed not to reveal their secret. Her gut twisted. This would be playing dirty. She paced the room.

But how many times did she have to be the victim before she learned to seize an opportunity that presented itself, for herself? The lien on her home paid. Jeff out of her life. Peace of mind from the debt bloodhounds. . .

She groaned, slipping the tube into her scrub pocket. The blood was near forty-eight hours old, but with the preservative present in the tube, it was still viable.

They spoke of extermination if their existence became public. Yet Kenric and the Enclave had plenty of money at their disposal. With enough of the right people hired and in place, the Enclave surely had enough power to make it all go away at some point.

Emily chewed her bottom lip. With his money, he'd be okay.

He would never forgive her. But he'd survive.

The question was, would she ever forgive herself?

Chapter Fourteen

Gearing down his motorcycle, Markus rolled to a stop in front of the weatherworn, aged Victorian mansion. With the kickstand in place, he slung his leg over his bike and dismounted.

He rubbed a palm against his midsection. His gut ached. With each step toward the front door, the misery eating away at his insides became more urgent.

The pain. This place. It drew him like a tether to a ball.

Markus lifted the rusted metal door hammer and rapped twice. The porch groaned under the weight of his shifting feet. He glanced back down the isolated, dirt driveway. It was all familiar somehow.

But when? And why the hell had he been here before?

The massive door with its peeling paint opened, creaking loudly. Candlelight glowed from within. A large, dark-skinned man dressed in only a pair of black leathers filled the door frame.

"Welcome, warrior," he beckoned in a thick Spanish accent. "Our mistress has been waiting for your return and report." He backed away from the opening and, with a swing of his head, indicated Marcus should enter.

He took a step and a stabbing pain, much worse than before, tore through his abdomen. Markus let out a loud hiss and doubled over. "What the fuck!" he managed to mutter when the pain decided to give him some air, but not before he broke out in a cold sweat.

A hard and icy hand grabbed his arm and dragged him over the threshold. "Our mistress has just what you need."

The need to quench the fire in his gut dueled with his turbulent impulse to get the hell out. But still, he followed the stranger, his feet moving like leaden weights beneath him.

The musky odor of mothballs and decay assaulted his senses, but even through the murkiness that was his brain, he knew the other scent riding the air all too well. The stranger before him was a vampire, and from the smell of things, he wasn't the only one.

Why did I come here?

"*You know why*," a voice in his head murmured.

"No. No, I don't," he mumbled. Bile scorched a path inside his chest. He swallowed, forcing the acid back into his stomach.

The large, leather-clad vampire came to a halt before a set of heavy wooden double doors. They protested as he pushed them open. Markus squinted from the onslaught of the hundreds of candles that set the cavernous room ablaze.

Compelled to see and understand what drove him to this place, he forced his gaze to lift.

A woman with long, flowing black hair lay draped across a red chaise elevated on a dais. She turned her head as he entered the room, inserted a slim finger into a red vessel, then lifted it out and licked the dark thick coating from her flesh. He didn't miss the satisfied gleam as she sealed the container and passed the item to a male at her side, before rising. *Marguerite?* He'd never actually seen her face, only Kenric's recount of her description. But what other female held this much power?

She called to him. Not with her voice, but within his head.

The slide of her voice inside his mind—his chest seized. He gasped for air.

"Breathe, my warrior. Come." She reached out and summoned him with her hand.

Air filled his lungs once again. Not sure why, but he responded and crossed the great room. At the base of her dais, he dropped to his knees.

Not because he wanted to. He had no choice.

His hands fell to the floor, and his gaze followed. Beads of sweat riddled his forearms, making his palms slick against the smooth planked floor.

The air stirred as she neared. An erotic scent of musk, sex, and blood filled his nostrils. It shot straight to his groin, filling his cock to a painful rigidity. He growled, neurons firing in remembrance.

"Marguerite." He tilted his head back and bared his fangs.

"Yes, warrior. Welcome home."

His gaze homed in on her wrist and the crimson drops falling from the open wound. Another slice of agony twisted his insides. He hissed a curse, dropping his head.

"When do you plan on sharing? Or is my suffering your entertainment for tonight, Marguerite?" A sudden wrench at his hair yanked his head back.

"That's *mistress* to you, minion," she spat. "And I'd be careful with that mouth of yours if you plan to taste me ever again." She released his head with a jerk.

"Yes, mistress," Markus forced out.

She stepped before him and lowered her wrist to his mouth. Grasping her forearm with both hands, he brought it to his lips. He slipped his tongue out and licked once at the puncture. He glanced up from under his eyelids. Her pupils grew large, leaving only a thin ring of green surrounding the black.

Fuck. His cock jerked. Yeah…fuck.

Markus groaned and sank his fangs in.

She cried out. Hungrily, he drank the hot, thick, intoxicating liquid. It soothed the knives in his gut and electrified his veins. *Yes!* God, how had he ever survived without her taste?

Without warning, she pulled his head back and tugged her arm free.

"No!" he bellowed. "Not yet." He fell forward. His heart galloped in his chest, muscles spasming in his arms and legs, begging for action.

So alive.

How and why did Kenric ever resist her? To hell with protecting the human race. Every fiber of his being wanted to fuck her.

"Pick yourself up, minion."

Her voice, a command to his limbs, jerked him to his

knees.

"There will be more where that came from. But first, you must give me your report."

Green and ruby silks shimmered around her as she draped herself on her chaise. Her gaze, the color of a lush tropical forest, held him transfixed.

"Now, minion, were you convincing at your homecoming?" She gave him a smug grin.

"Yes, mistress. No one questioned the story of my disappearance."

"Excellent." Marguerite leaned forward with an excited gleam in her expression. "Tell me what you have learned about Kenric's new woman."

"Her name is Emily. She works as a nurse at Elizabeth Bay Memorial, where Kenric ended up a few nights ago after being injured. Arran and Kenric are meeting with her tonight. She's helping him dispose of the evidence that remains of his ER visit."

Marguerite leaped to her feet and waved a silencing hand. "Enough of that babbling garbage. I want to know if he cares for her. Is he protective?"

Markus tilted his head and met her glare. Rings of red swirled like fire around her green irises. A startling effect.

"Yes, mistress. He placed her under his personal protection and the Enclave's."

A shriek ricocheted off the hollow chamber walls. Marguerite whirled, pulling at her hair. She descended the steps in a blur of color.

Markus jumped to his feet and backed away, but not fast enough. Her hand gripped his throat, bringing his retreat to a suffocating end.

"You will kill her for me, slave."

Markus shuddered, the pressure in his skull climbing to a screaming peak. How the hell was he supposed to do something so heinous and traitorous? The force of her compulsion, combined with the unrelenting hand at his throat, pushed him near the brink of implosion. *Shit, shit, shit.*

"Kenric's destiny was sealed the night I made him. He is mine." Her grip loosened. "This temporary fascination of his will not ruin my plans."

Markus stumbled back. He drew in a coughing, ragged breath. The crawling warmth of blood returned to his face and head along with the incessant push of her will inside his mind.

"You will see this done for me."

"Yes, mistress," Markus croaked out. "Consider it done." And he knew without a doubt he would. For her. A nagging itch inside his chest said acting on her order to kill the female should bother him. *Betraying Kenric—the Enclave—shouldn't it prove harder to bear?* Markus searched inside, reluctantly seeking what had once been his blemished and serrated moral compass. But instead of finding a treacherous knife carving out his gut, a block of ice sat in its place. Hard, cold, and unmoving. *Perfect.*

A moment in Marguerite's darkness was all it had taken to freeze his soul, and like a vortex of evil, she'd sucked him into her frigid hell. The potent elixir of her blood and sex, mixed with the intensity of her resolve, had reanimated the monster he'd fought so hard to keep buried in his past. It seemed no matter how many years or miles one placed between themselves and their sins, somehow they find you.

Kharma truly was a bitch.

A slow, satisfied smile that promised great rewards bloomed on her face. His cock twitched, painfully filling the confines of his jeans.

Oh, yes. But he would enjoy his reward.

Chapter Fifteen

"Oh God, make it shut up!" Emily lifted her head up from the pillow, groping on her nightstand for the cell phone that wouldn't stop its incessant ringing. "Hello." She didn't attempt to hide her less-than-enthusiastic tone.

"Emily? I was about to come over there. I've been calling for almost an hour. Are you okay?"

"Shawna?" She rubbed her eyes and tried to bring the clock into focus. Five in the evening. *Good.* The sleeping pill she'd taken had done its trick. She'd slept nine hours straight without any dreams about Kenric.

"Yeah, it's me. I was worried about you. After your break last night, you barely spoke to anyone, and you left without a word. Did I do something to make you angry?"

"No. No, it has nothing to do with you."

"It was that phone call, wasn't it? You said there was an emergency. Are you okay?"

"I'm okay. You know what they say, this too shall pass,"

Emily said, massaging her chest where a dull ache throbbed beneath her breastbone.

"It's a man, isn't it? Only one thing would have a woman like this: a man."

"No. God, no. It's not a man." Emily bit her lip and slung her legs over the side of the bed. It really wasn't. She wasn't lying. He certainly had all the right body parts. However, technically, he wasn't a human male.

"I think someone doth protest too much."

She could almost see Shawna's ear-to-ear grin and her eyebrows dancing on her forehead in excitement.

"Let it go, Shawna. There's no man."

"All right, all right. Call me when you're ready to talk. And when you're ready for me to meet him. Can't wait. Bye, now."

"Shawna... Arghh!" That woman defined tenacious.

After brushing her teeth and a quick shower, she felt more awake. The hot water had done nothing for the dull pain in her chest, though. It had started right after her blowup at Kenric and hadn't left her alone since, except for the few hours she'd managed to sleep. Damn...she missed him. It had been less than twenty-four hours, but the sting of his absence went soul-deep. And as much as it chapped her rear to acknowledge the fact, she'd liked having him around. His presence filled a room even in the silence. Although that attribute could be overwhelming at times, Emily had quickly grown to take comfort in its intensity. He drew her like oxygen to a flame. But it was that same heat, the inferno brewing just beneath the surface, that scared the hell out of her, because she didn't want to get burned.

Dressed in her favorite blue jeans and a loose T-shirt,

she headed toward the kitchen, when a sudden pounding on the front door froze her in her tracks. She ran to her bedroom, grabbed the baseball bat she kept beside her bed, and crept in the direction of the living room.

Kenric's premonition of danger looped like a scratched record in her head. Her pulse thumped wildly in her ears.

Another pound on the door vibrated through her. She swallowed hard and raised the bat to her shoulder. Tightening her grip, she stopped five feet from the door and yelled, "Who is it?"

"It's Kenric." His deep voice rumbled from the other side.

Dropping the bat at her side, she mumbled a curse before turning the dead bolt and yanking the door open. "What the hell are you pounding for? I live in a condo, not the White House. A simple knock would've been fine."

"Just making sure you answered the door. We have to talk." Kenric stood with both gloved hands bracing the door frame. The collar of his leather jacket stood straight up around his neckline and black sunglasses covered his eyes. The sun had barely sunk below the horizon, leaving bright pink and red fingers of color streaking the sky and glowing across her doorstep. He rubbed the dark shadow of stubble on his chin. "You gonna let me in, or do I get to simmer on your front porch?"

She swung the door wide, not concealing the annoyance on her face. He eased across her threshold, all hard muscles in blue jeans and leather.

"You've got five minutes." Emily pivoted in his direction as Kenric slipped his sunglasses into his pocket. White rings, matching the outline of his shades, circled his eyes, revealing a red flush to the remainder of his face.

"Dear Lord! Are you burned?" She rushed forward and placed a palm to his cheek. He flinched from her touch. "Your face is on fire. You weren't kidding when you said you were simmering on my porch. Just how early did you come out?"

"It doesn't matter." He shrugged. "What matters is that I need you to understand how serious I am when I say you're in danger. The only place where I know you'll be safe is with me."

"We've already had this discussion." She brushed past him, heading to the kitchen, but Kenric was on her heels. Emily spun back around. He reached out and pulled her to him. She gasped. More from his sudden overwhelming presence than surprise.

"Wildflower, please." Kenric released her and captured her cheeks between his palms. "Talk to me. Why do you keep running from me?"

She pushed against his chest. His scent and touch clouded her mind. "I'm not running."

"What do you call it, then, when you keep moving in the opposite direction from the person who's trying to protect you?"

"I call it taking of care myself. By myself." A shiver worked its way over her upper arms. The compassionate look on his face proved too much to look at. She wheeled around, desperate to focus on something else. Anything else but him. Her ficus needed watering. She tried to swallow, but her throat had gone dry.

"I respect that, but you need to understand you're not dealing with a normal *human* situation here. There is a certain vampire…"

He grew silent. She glanced over her shoulder. The dark expression on his face quickened her pulse. She turned and took a step toward him, compelled to offer comfort, but stopped. He didn't need her help. She needed to let him go.

He cleared his throat and started again. "She is a very ancient vampire. One who is determined to destroy anyone I care for. And right now, her focus is you." He moved closer. The warmth of his presence enveloped her.

"She. You said she." Emily backpedaled until she bumped into the solid wall of the den.

"Yes." He nodded. "My creator. Three hundred years ago, a vampire named Marguerite Devonshire took my life and turned me against my will."

"You never wanted this?"

A flash of red ignited and swirled in his eyes. He lowered his lashes, as if he didn't want her to see the rage, but she knew it seethed there.

"No." His voiced deepened, becoming something close to a growl of an answer. "I never wanted this. Nevertheless, it is what I am." He lifted his lids, the blue of his eyes once again as clear as a summer's sky. His roughened fingertips slid the length of her cheek and jaw before tipping her chin. "She's found me and is more powerful than ever. Marguerite has gained the ability to visit me in my dreams." He groaned, tossed his head back as if in pain, then slowly rocked his head forward, capturing her gaze. "She's seen you. Inside my head, she's seen your face. Knows you're important to me." He bared his teeth, chewing out the next few words. "She *will* kill you if she gets the chance."

He made it impossible to maintain her convictions when

he got this close. The room tilted on its axis. Her head spun.

She would not do this: succumb to the desire to let him rescue her.

Not with a man this powerful and dominating. He'd lock her in a cage. And she couldn't handle that.

Maybe, if she went far enough away, got the heck out of town, his presence wouldn't affect her so, and all this—these feelings—would diminish. She slipped from his grasp, but he caught her hand. "Let me go!"

"What are you doing?" He tried to pull her back into his embrace. "Did you not hear anything I just said?"

"I have to leave." Emily tugged at his grip. "If I get away from you, she'll leave me alone. You won't have to worry about protecting me." She clutched his bicep and met his gaze, searching for an inkling of understanding. "Please, just let me—You have to let me go." Her voice cracked.

His expression shifted from shock to anger. He tugged her to him and proceeded to back her up against the wall. Emily squeezed her eyes shut. If she didn't look at him, maybe she could stay strong. But damn, with her eyes closed, his cinnamon and pine scent, along with the hard feel of his body, drove her to the edge of the cliff known as restraint.

"Look at me," he growled.

She didn't want to see.

"Look. At. Me."

Her eyelids fluttered open. A passion-filled gaze crashed into hers, sending a wave of weakness to her legs.

"You want to leave? Is that *really* what you want?"

She parted her lips, forced a weak "yes," and dropped her gaze.

"Really?"

"Yes. Damn you!" She pushed and squirmed without success against the unmovable mountain holding her. "What exactly do you drink, blood laced with cement?"

"Why?"

"Why, what?" she snapped.

"Why do want away from me so badly?"

"Because I have to."

"Not good enough. Why?"

Why wouldn't he just shut up and leave her alone?

"Will you just let it go? Please!" She shimmied against him again. He didn't budge. Her sensitized nipples hardened against the hard, leather-clad wall of his chest.

"Not until you give me a good-enough answer."

Emily sucked in two panic-filled gulps of air and blurted out the words that refused to stay buried. "Because I want you too damn much, and it scares the shit out of me!"

His body stilled. Silence filled the room, except for the ragged breaths leaving her lungs. The hardened ridge pressed against her hips told her he wanted her, too.

She couldn't bring herself to look at him, yet the tingling heat lifting the hairs on her arms let her know his gaze hadn't moved. His warm palms rode up into her hair as he tilted her face to his. Her breath hitched. So much pain and desire.

"Wildflower." His hand drifted to her chin where his thumb traced her lower lip. "Believe me when I say, I would die before I brought you harm." He closed the distance between their lips but stopped a breath away, as if asking permission.

She licked her lips and pulled the lower one in, holding it with her teeth. She didn't know what else to do with him so close. She would not kiss him. That would be a terrible mistake.

Wouldn't it?

Her jaw trembled under the tension. Hell, make that her whole body. Unable to resist, she buried her hands in the silkiness of his dark waves. She moaned. *Damn*. He had to be the dark angel of temptation, because she didn't want to live another second, another breath, without tasting him.

Grasping two handfuls of hair, she pulled him in to her starved mouth. The heat of his kiss shot straight to her core, warming and swelling her with desire. She lapped at the sweetened spice of his mouth. The short overnight growth of his beard scraped at her face. Every sensation against her flesh heightened her awareness. Her need for him.

A growl vibrated from the back of his throat. Their tongues thrust in rhythm to the rocking of their hips. Getting him inside her possessed her. This man took her to a place where she didn't recognize herself anymore.

Emily cried out and broke away from him. "What the hell am I doing? I can't do this."

She ran the short distance to her bedroom. Tears swelled and threatened to spill. Blindly, she grabbed her travel bag from under the bed and tossed it onto the mattress. She pulled random shirts and pants from her closet and tossed them into her weathered blue carry-all. Out of the corner of her eye, a dark outline filled her doorway.

Kenric watched as Emily jammed her clothes into her satchel. "You're running again." She shot him a drop-dead look but continued to pack without breaking her stride. "I know you believe me when I say I would never harm you. I can feel it. So what is it? Why are you jumping like a scared rabbit?"

Her hands stilled. She turned from the bed, her cheeks a rosy pink, her auburn curls a chaotic mass around her face.

She'd never looked more beautiful. Her gaze met his, swimming in a pool of unshed tears. A sharp pain tore through his chest. He gripped the door frame to keep from closing the distance between them, pulling her into his arms, and not letting go.

"You. Okay? You wanted to know so damn bad. Well, it's you."

He tightened his hold on the wood, her words stinging like a strike across his face.

"You overwhelm me. Everything about you. Your power. The things you can do to a human being." Emily's head dropped, and she absently worked to fold a shirt.

His didn't think his heart would withstand another moment of seeing her in so much pain. Pain that he had caused.

"It's the way I feel when I'm around you. It's like I'm not in control of myself." Her head popped up, and her expression held a grimace. "I hate it. I hate not being in control. I've been hurt too many times when I've let someone in like that."

Enough. He couldn't stand there and watch the anger and frustration rack her body. Crossing the room in three strides, he gripped her shoulders and turned her to him. His hands roamed up into her hair and around to her cheeks. Her pain hadn't begun when he'd entered her life. Someone else had hurt this beautiful woman. And they would pay.

"Who hurt you like this?"

"Let it go." The tears crested and fell one by one like hot rain onto his fingertips. Her body shook under his palms. "Let *me* go. It would be better for both of us. Without me here, she would have no reason to hurt me or you."

"It wouldn't work."

"Why not?" Emily tossed her head and sniffled. "Why would she look for me if I was out of your life?"

"It wouldn't work, because I would have to stop caring about you." He stroked her hair and traced her full bottom lip with his index finger. "And that is something I don't believe I'll be able to do."

Her sudden inhale breezed across his fingertip and had his cock pulsing. But taking her pain away took priority.

"Kenric, you're tearing my heart in two and making it hard to walk away." Another tear escaped and rolled down her cheek.

"Then don't go," he whispered. "I tell you what. If you'll stay, I'll back off on trying to get you to come with me. Give you some room to think." Relief washed over her in a visible wave, releasing the tension in her body. "But…" She sniffed and straightened her back.

"Of course there's a condition. Here it comes…"

Kenric lifted the corner of his mouth at the thick dose of sarcasm. Here was the Emily he knew.

"I stay here."

"What?" Emily backed up two steps, bumping against the bed frame.

"You won't come with me, then I have to stay here. On the couch, of course." He glanced toward the room door.

"Oh my God." She shook her head. "You make me dizzy,

Kenric St. James."

"I'll take that as a compliment."

She rolled her eyes. "Of course you would." Emily pivoted, facing the mound of clothes half in and half out her suitcase. "Fine," she said, sighing. "But stay out of my way."

• • •

Emily didn't think one evening could crawl by any slower. But Kenric had kept his word and had stayed out of her way. Completely nonintrusive like he'd promised. That was half the problem. He'd stayed quiet, sitting in a chair in the corner of her living room, watching her. He didn't eat. Didn't drink. And it was driving her bonkers. Every so often he'd case the place, looking for anything out of the ordinary, and then check in with the Enclave. It was like having a giant watchdog caged in the room, waiting for the perfect opportunity to bite something. Or somebody.

She rolled over and tried to sleep for what felt like the hundredth time. Knowing he was on the other side of the door, not sleeping, uncomfortable, protecting her, felt so wrong. But he did normally sleep during the day, so that didn't make her a complete bitch. Emily flopped to her back, eyes wide. She should have never taken that sleeping pill when she'd come home from work.

Kicking off the covers, she slung her legs over the side of the bed. If he was going to stay all day, he might as well have the guest room and not the couch.

Emily headed across the hall to the other bedroom and went to the windows. She pulled the blinds and loosened the heavy drapes for added UV protection. The bed had clean sheets already, so in preparation for morning, she turned back the comforter and fluffed the pillows.

"Everything okay?"

"Just getting your room ready," she said and turned toward Kenric.

"My room?" One dark brow lifted.

"If you're going to spend the night, you might as well have something more comfortable and safe at sunrise." She jutted a thumb at the covered windows. "I thought the confined room would keep the sun out better."

"Thank you." He nodded. "With everything I've put you through, that was very thoughtful."

"You're welcome." She cleared her throat and darted under the arm he'd placed up on the door jam. "I'm… I'm going back to bed. Make yourself at home." Emily slipped through her bedroom door, not waiting for a reply. She leaned her back against the wood. He kept her so mixed up. One minute he was the dominating lethal creature of the night that every instinct cried out for her to leave alone, then the next he was a gentle tortured soul that screamed for her to hold him and take away his pain. She blew out a puff of air, lifting the fall of hair from her brow. Too much to figure out in one night. Her temples throbbed. She rubbed the spot beside her right eye and made her way back to bed. Emily plopped onto the mattress and eased under her covers. Maybe answers to her dilemma would rise with the sun while he was out of sight. Good luck with out of mind.

$\cdots$

"Get out!" A loud bang followed the shout, yanking Emily

awake and from her bed. Her heart rate jackhammered. Soft light peeked through her blinds, littering just enough daylight across her floor to keep her from breaking her neck as she scrambled for her bedroom door. Oh God, was the vampire bitch in her house?

Emily flung her door wide and searched the shadows of the hall and room beyond. Nothing.

"Nooo…"

The sound came from the other side of the guest room door: Kenric. Gently she placed her palm to the door and breathed deep.

"Kenric," she called out. Emily pressed in close, listening. A low growl rumbled through the wood. A lump formed in her throat. What was going on in there?

"Get off me." His words came out as if strangled from his throat. *Oh shit, he's in trouble.*

Emily fisted the doorknob, twisted, and pushed inside. The sight that greeted her sent her veins into a deep freeze. Kenric lay nude, except for a pair of black boxer-briefs, his arms over his head, fists gripping the headboard. His comforter had been kicked to the floor, and the bedside lamp had crashed to the floor beside the mound of cotton.

Dear God. Every vein along his forearms and his neck was distended. His jaw clenched as if he were in agony.

"Kenric!" Emily darted to his bedside. Sweat covered his body in a fine sheen. No response. He flung his head from side to side. "God, Kenric," she called out. "Wake up!"

A loud groan tore from his throat, and his body arched, but it was as if his wrists and ankles were chained to the bed. His spine collapsed to the mattress and his head flung back. Emily kneeled on the bed, leaned in, and with a trembling hand, reached out and brushed the hair from his eyes.

"Kenric?" She touched his cheek. So cold. "Can you hear me?" He didn't move. "Kenric!" Louder this time. Still nothing. He didn't budge. That's when it dawned on her: nothing moved. He wasn't breathing. "Oh, God! Oh, God!"

Emily grabbed him by the shoulders and shook him hard. "Kenric! It's Emily. Open your eyes!" His eyelids sprang open.

"Oh, thank God…"

His lips curled back over long fangs with a hiss, and she jumped.

"Fuck with me all you want, Marguerite," he said, his voice hoarse while staring into the emptiness of the room. "Kill me over and over, if you wish. But you can't have her, even if your gut is filled with Goran's blood."

What the hell? Her? Is he talking about me? Emily glanced around the room. Nothing seemed out of the ordinary. She dropped her gaze back to Kenric. He'd mentioned Marguerite had found a way to get inside his head, but this was unlike any dream or sleepwalking episode she'd ever witnessed.

"I knew you'd never deny its possession." Kenric sneered, then flinched, his head darting from side to side. "I'd rather starve, he spat.

What was she doing to him? "Kenric!" Emily cried again. She had to get him awake. Had to get him away from her. The look on his face. The strain in his body. Marguerite was torturing him, and the sight of it was like a knife through Emily's heart. She bent over and clasped his cheeks, forcing his face in her direction. "Kenric, it's Emily." His eyes were glazed, pupils dilated, staring at some point beyond her.

"You have to hear me. Come back to me." Her voice choked. "She's not here. Marguerite is in your head." Emily gritted her teeth then cried out, "Let him go!" She had no idea if the woman could even hear her, but she had to try.

She shuffled closer, placing them face to face. "Kenric!" His fangs were extended, touching his bottom lip. The sight of the sharp points should have freaked her out, but at that point, all she could see was the man. A man in pain. The man who had placed her life before his own.

"Emily?" he mumbled, and his brow wrinkled.

Her heart raced. "Yes, yes. It's me." She ran her fingers through his hair. "Look at me. Focus on me."

"Get out of here!" He shook his head as if trying to break her hold and back away.

"Kenric," Emily said, her tone dropping to an, I'm-a-woman-who-won't-be-moved level. "Focus on me. Get her out of your head."

His eyelids slammed shut, then he blinked, and his gaze bore into hers. Seeing her for the first time. "I said get out of here," he growled. "I can't…I can't promise you I'm in control." He sucked in a deep breath. "Leave me." His attention shifted to something in the distance. "Need you," he began, the words fighting for birth from his throat. "Need you safe."

"Oh, hell no!" Like she could live with herself if she walked out that door. The very thought had her gasping for air. His head slipped from her grasp, and his eyelids fluttered. His eyes rolled back in their sockets. The bed jerked and his body stiffened. "Kenric?" Emily lunged forward, nearly on top of him. "Kenric," she shouted and grabbed his head, rocking his face forward. "Don't you die on me," she uttered, her voice fierce. "You put me in the middle of this, and I need you to stay with me. You hear me?" she asked, her lips next to his. "Come back to me."

Emily pressed her mouth against his, willing him back to reality. To her. There was a lot about Kenric that scared the hell out of her, but she realized suddenly that the thought of him not being in her life frightened her even more.

At first there was no response. Only her lips moving across his. She choked on a sob, then poured herself back into action. He jerked, and then his palms were on her upper arms, air filling his lungs. Kenric pushed her back.

"What are you doing?" His eyes narrowed, the pupils no longer human, obscuring almost all the white. "You have to get away from me."

Emily shook her head. "I'm not leaving you like this. She's trying to kill you." She reached out and gripped his face. "Because of me," she whispered.

"You don't understand…," he began, his voice hoarse, as if he'd emerged from a long desert journey.

"I understand you need me. That's all I need to know."

• • •

Kenric closed his eyes, and a shudder wracked his body. Her words slicing into the last hold he had on his restraint. He lifted his eyelids, meeting her gaze. "Are you sure, Wildflower? Please be sure, because I don't know…. If we go any further—I can't promise I can—"

Emily clamped her mouth onto his, swallowing whatever else he was about to say. His brain short-circuited and he groaned, meeting her passion, devouring all that she had to give. Every cell in his body cried out for her.

More of her.

To have her.

His head soared under the influence.

He reached up, sank his hands into her hair, and held on. The effect—Emily—grounded him. The feel of her in his palms reminded him this was his Wildflower. He would not be the monster who only took like the last time he held her. She deserved so much more. He dug deep, clamoring for purchase on some small shred of control.

Kenric released her, leaned back, and lifted the hem of her T-shirt. He pulled it over her head, revealing full breasts that gently rocked with each inhale.

"Sweet, sweet Wildflower. You are so beautiful." Reverently, he lowered his head and placed a kiss to the top of each areola, then moved lower. The sight of her creamy flesh and dark red nipples had his mouth watering. With his tongue, he gave one lazy circle to a rosy bud before drawing it in and ravishing the sensitive tip. The taste of her skin was a sweet indulgence to his senses. A startled gasp and then a pleasure-filled moan urged him on. He longed to suckle the other, but first, he had to see—and touch—the rest of her.

He tugged at her sweats and panties, and she lifted, helping him to yank them free before tossing them to the floor.

Emily brushed her fingertips across his chest. His chest heaved, and he trembled as she explored. Her touch excited every nerve under his skin, and he couldn't hold back the groan. It was as if his flesh had never been awake until her touch. He watched as she followed the narrow width of his chest hair until it disappeared beneath his waistband. His cock jerked, straining, with her only inches away.

"Show me," she breathed, and he nearly came unglued. Kenric clenched a fist, released, then moved her gently to the side and shoved his underwear down. The heat of her gaze had every hair on his body lifting in acute awareness.

His erection sprang free and up onto his lower abdomen as he pulled Emily close. He palmed the hard length, stroking his throbbing shaft once, then twice, enjoying the way her eyes followed his hand, as if they were envious.

"I want to taste every inch of you." Kenric released his cock and scooped her into his arms, rolling them until he'd maneuvered her onto her stomach. As badly as he wanted his shaft inside her, he had to get his mouth on her. Her breath left her lungs with the sudden shift in position. He straddled her calves. "I'm dying to know if you taste as good as you smell." A soft whimper left her with each lick and kiss he placed behind her knees and to the back of her thighs.

So soft, sweet, and salty. Heaven.

Lifting her hips, he placed her knees underneath her to gain better access to the prize before him.

"Kenric…?" Her voice quivered as she glanced over her shoulder.

"You're okay, love. I want you to do something for me."
"What?"
"Grab the headboard."
"Why?"

He slid one finger through her swollen folds, stopping at the engorged bundle of nerves at the tip of her sex. She arched her back and gasped.

"Grab the headboard and hold on. Don't let go."

She glanced over her shoulder then reached for the

spindles.

"That's it. Hold on. Let me show you how *good* it can be to let someone else be in control." With his knee, he spread her legs wider, then he twisted and lowered onto his back, placing himself beneath her thighs. Holding her steady with his palms at her hips, he made one long pass with his tongue, tasting her from end to end. Emily cried out and struggled against his grip.

"Oh. My. God."

Another pass and a flick of his tongue drew a whimper from her.

So damn good.

"You taste delicious. I could do this all night." He circled her clit and sucked the swollen flesh above it. He nipped and soothed his way along her folds until he found the source of her juices and dove in. Her hips bucked, but he held her in place, pressing her down tighter against his lips, stroking her more deeply with his tongue.

"Please." She rocked the headboard. "Please, I need more."

"Shhh… Let me pleasure you." A quivering sigh left her as he slid two fingers deep. He worked them, stretching her before adding a third.

"Oh…God," she groaned. "I can't take much more." Her hips thrust against his palm, straining to have more of him. "I want you. Okay? Please, take me." The words, edged with desperation, tumbled from her.

Kenric stroked once more across her clit. Her sudden loss of air silenced any further complaints. He placed her swollen clitoris between his lips and pulled on the sensitive nub with gentle sucks. His spread fingers worked inside her core, filling her. Within seconds, Emily screamed his name. He held on and rocked with her until her tremors settled to gentle waves.

Gently he lifted her hips, slid from beneath her, and maneuvered back onto his knees. Reaching forward, he removed her hands from the spindles and pulled her to him until her back rested against his chest. Her breasts overflowed his hands as he whispered in her ear, "You are so damn sexy. Do you have any idea what you do to me?"

She shook her head. "No. Tell me."

"Let me show you." He took her hand, brought it around between them, and wrapped it around his rock-hard cock. The instant her warm palm surrounded him, she left him starved for air. "I want you so much, it hurts."

Emily squeezed him gently, and his head roared with need, with hunger. He wanted in her—now, in every way possible, hard, fast, and unyielding. "Never have I craved a woman as much as I do you."

She shivered and released his shaft. Her buttocks pressed against his erection, and she brushed her back against his chest.

He trailed kisses around her ear and down the length of her neck. The salty sweetness of her skin coated his tongue. He licked her fluttering pulse. His gut was on fire, burning for her. "Will you let me have you, Wildflower?"

"Yes." The soft word left her on a tremulous sob.

"Everything?" Gently he pressed the tips of his fangs against her throat. He had to make sure once more that she wanted this. Wanted all of him. He wouldn't be able to stop once he got inside her.

"God, yes!"

Kenric urged her hips up with his hands, leaning her slightly forward, and then inch by splendid inch, lowered her back down onto him.

Fuck! So wet. Her tight, hot sheath surrounded the head of his cock, barreling him to the edge of release. And the cusp of restraint.

He tried to go slow, knowing he was a large man, but she pushed down and impaled herself.

"Oh, God!" she cried out.

He started to withdraw, but her short-lived exclamation quickly turned to a moan. She reached over her head and buried her fingers in his hair. Holding on tight, she squirmed on his lap and ground him deeper.

Damn. She turned him inside out. With his arms around her waist, he held her in place, even though she protested the sudden restriction. "Slow down, love. I want this to last."

He rocked against her, slowly at first, then with a building tempo. "So tight. You're fucking killing me."

Her moans and cries of pleasure enhanced the exquisite milking strokes of her walls along his cock. No way in hell would he last.

He loosened and removed the hold she had on his hair and kissed her shoulder. "Turn around. I want to see you while I love you."

She lifted, turned, and lowered herself onto the bed, spreading her legs in invitation. Never had he seen a more magnificent sight.

He moved between her thighs. "You're absolutely beautiful."

A shy smile played on her lips. "You're quite handsome yourself, vampire."

With his shaft in hand, he stroked between her folds and, in one swift move, buried himself inside. The moment his sac bumped her bottom, they both released a moan. So damn complete.

She dug into his hips with her fingers and wrapped her legs around his buttocks. He clutched her hands, slid them down his legs, and across her thighs to her juncture. "Touch yourself for me. Show me what makes you come undone."

Her eyelids closed, then slowly she slipped two fingers into her curls. Emily mewled and made gentle circles across her clitoris.

"Yes. Beautiful." He continued to rock deep inside her.

"More, Kenric. God, I want you so much."

He plunged deeper. Faster. Over and over. He had to feel her, skin to skin. Reaching forward, he pulled her from the bed and into his arms.

Sweat ran down his temples. Her inner muscles clenched around him. He scraped his fangs over her pulse. Chills lifted against his lips, and she shuddered in his arms.

He was right there.

Kenric sank his fangs deep. Her blood, so sweet and heady, flooded his mouth, spinning the world away and suspending time. Emily screamed and arched against his hold. His cock erupted — there were no other words for it — jetting its release in a never-ending wave of pleasure. One he was sure his heart, and the wall he'd built around it, would never survive.

Chapter Sixteen

"That was…"

Emily pulled her face out of the pillow she'd collapsed into and blew the hair out of her mouth. "Yeah." She couldn't form anything more coherent. Maybe she'd fried some of her brain cells with that last orgasm.

Wow. Sex with Kenric St. James ought to come with a warning label.

She glanced at the naked man lying partially on top of her. They had been in each other's arms the entire day. She should have been starving by this point in the evening, since the only time she'd gotten out of bed was to relieve herself. But the last few hours with Kenric had flown by, and he'd filled her—satisfied her—in so many more ways than a meal ever could. Who needed food?

"Sorry. Hope I wasn't crushing you." He rolled onto his side, sliding the rest of the way out of her.

The sudden loss of contact made her want to pull him

right back. "No. You were fine. More than fine." She flashed him a smile.

A grin spread across his face, and his blue eyes lit with mischief. Her heart skipped a beat. God, he was beautiful when he did that.

"Come here." He tugged at her arm. "I want to feel you against me."

He pulled her on top of him. Her breasts pressed against his firm chest. His roughened hands stroked her hair, then trailed up and down her arms. *Mmm, so nice.*

Lowering her head against him, she closed her eyes and listened to the rapid beat of his heart. He sounded and felt so human, all hard male beneath her.

Normal.

So unlike what they'd just shared. Not your typical sex. It had been out of this world. Leaving her to wonder if she'd ever want ordinary again. Speaking of normal sex... *Oh, no.* Emily shot up in bed. "I can't believe I did that."

"What?"

Emily swung her head around to look at Kenric. He stared at her, confusion written on his face.

"I can't believe we did that without either one of us thinking about a condom." She dropped her head into her hands. "Oh, God," she groaned. "What kind of health care professional am I?"

"You don't have anything to worry about, Wildflower."

Emily lifted her head from her palms at his soothing words. She glanced back over her shoulder. "What do you mean by that?"

"I mean, I can't give you *anything.*"

"Oh...because you're a..."

"Right." He nodded. "Seems that when you're transformed, you're... *sterilized* in the process." She must have appeared shocked, because what looked like a weak attempt at a smile formed at the corners of his mouth. "Hey, but on the upside, immortality makes you clean."

Emily turned and leaned over, resting her head on his chest. "Well, I guess that's something of a perk." She tried to make light of the conversation as she wrapped her arms around his chest in a gentle hug. Thank goodness he didn't carry any diseases she needed to worry about, but the way he'd said the word "sterilized" made her heart ache for him.

"I hate to bring up more uncomfortable memories." She lifted her head and brought her hands together, propping her chin on top of them. This was probably the best opening she was going to get to find out why this woman wanted her dead. "But can you tell me a little more about this—your creator, I think you called her—and why she feels like she has to kill me?"

He shifted beneath her. "How about you go first and tell me who hurt you so much that you would run from the person who wants to keep you safe?"

"Oh, no." She shook her head. "I asked you first. Besides, I think I should know something about the person who wants me dead."

A resolute sigh left him as he slid his hand down her back and squeezed her against him.

"From what she has told me, Marguerite is somewhere around six hundred years old. An ancient. She has always been incredibly strong for a female vampire, but she is obsessed with power. The greater her source, the more capable she is in manipulating and controlling not only humans with her mind and blood, but other vampires as well.

His heart pounded beneath her palms. She lowered her head back down and wrapped her arms around him, hoping her calm presence would help him tell her his story.

"I was thirty-two when I met Marguerite three hundred years ago." He chuckled, but she had a feeling it wasn't because of fond memories. "Well, if you could call it a meeting. I was on the battlefield, fighting back home in England with my regiment. I'd taken a blade to my flank and gone down. Next thing I knew, I woke up in a cold, dark cell chained to a wall like an animal."

Emily jerked her head up, enraged on Kenric's behalf. "Dear God."

"For three years, she kept me as her personal meal and… And any other needs she had." His gaze diverted from hers.

Three years? She shuddered, and her gut twisted into a painful knot. That monster had kept him as her slave for sex and blood. How could he have mentally survived that kind of hell?

A part of her didn't want to hear anymore. She couldn't bear the mental images his words conjured. Didn't want them burned into her brain cells. This proud warrior, broken and tortured, as no man ever should be—dehumanized. Emily's stomach soured. She couldn't even imagine the level of humiliation he'd suffered.

Suddenly, he clutched her face, startling her. The blue of his eyes darkened like the sea battling a raging storm.

"I didn't want her." He shook his head. "I *never* did. She had ways of getting into my head and making my body do things. You have to believe me. I never wanted her."

The desperation in his voice broke her heart. Dear God,

the abuse he must have suffered. Her jaw clenched, and her temples throbbed. She wanted to scream—cry out until her throat burned from the overwhelming sense of helplessness. She didn't know how to take his pain away. *Dammit.* She was a nurse, trained to ease suffering. Yet she was at a loss to how to make this all better. What she wouldn't give to possess the magic to turn back the hands of time, dive into the pit of hell where he'd been chained, and kill the bitch that did this to him. She brushed her palm across the back of his hand, wishing like hell she could somehow act as a wick and absorb some of the hurt.

"Yes, I believe you. Of course I do. It was rape." Emily leaned forward and placed a soft kiss to his lips. "You don't have to explain anything to me. I understand that kind of abuse." Maybe not the molestation, but the mental and physical abuse she could certainly comprehend. He hadn't asked for it, and none of it was his fault. He'd been a victim.

And he'd survived.

Marguerite may have destroyed his human DNA, but unwittingly what she'd unleashed back into the night was an even stronger version of the man than before. Emily's admiration of him soared to a new level. She had respected him prior to the revelation about his past, but now…. He'd risen out of Marguerite's clutches and turned his tragedy into a crusade to protect the innocent. In her eyes, Kenric was nothing less than a hero. Yet Emily knew if she tried to tell him the two were connected, he'd deny it. He would see it only as his duty—the right thing to do.

His hands softened on her face before he claimed her with a kiss of his own. Tenderly, he traced her lips. She opened up and invited him inside. Their tongues slid back and forth, stroking each other in a sensual dance.

With a sigh, Emily broke their kiss and brushed his coarse shadow of a beard with her chin before delving for more answers. "She made you a vampire against your will?"

Kenric nodded in silence before explaining to her how Marguerite had sensed his untapped psychic abilities while he was human. He'd always possessed a very strong second sense, an ability to see things before they happened, which he'd never told anyone.

The stronger the mind, the more powerful the vampire. In fact, he could become a Master, and Marguerite had always wanted to mate a Master. She'd become obsessed with creating a perfect male for herself. One who could control the elements, who had the potential for superior psychic influence and an ability to shift into multiple forms.

Emily rolled off him and pulled up the sheet from the foot of the bed to cover herself before sitting up. He repositioned and turned onto his side to face her. She reached out and brushed a wave of dark curls away from his brow. His jaw was rigid, but his gaze warmed her when he turned his cheek into her hand.

He lifted his head from her palm. "A vampire has the ability to mate for life at a soul level. What she wanted out of the deal was a share of my power. Marguerite is an anomaly among female vampires. She's very strong. Most females are pretty weak. Even with age, they are unable to become Masters themselves. If they mate, a female can tap into her partner's power through a psychic link."

"Ah. I see where you're going with this. If Marguerite got her claws into you, she would become even more powerful. More powerful than any master vampire alone."

"Exactly." He narrowed his eyes. "And I can't allow that."

"This woman—and I use the term loosely—has threatened everyone you care about all these years because you spurned her?"

"Yes." He lightly traced the side of her face.

"How bad has it gotten, Kenric?" She didn't want to know, but she had to. The depth of sorrow in his gaze choked her.

"I was engaged once," he mumbled.

"Oh." The bottom of her heart gave way. She took a deep breath, trying to push past the weight in her chest. "You've been in love before? I guess that's a stupid question. With as long as you've lived, I'm sure you've loved many women in your time." She was rambling, but if she kept talking, it didn't hurt as much.

Nothing to it.

She could do this.

"No. I haven't." He lowered his gaze. "Not since Annice have I allowed myself to get close to any woman. That was three centuries ago."

"What?" She placed a palm on his chest, and he lifted his lashes. "You haven't had a relationship in three centuries? You've been alone all this time?" she whispered. How in the world did anyone survive that kind of loneliness? "That must have been an incredible love you two shared."

He rolled onto his back and stared at the ceiling. Her hand fell away.

Oh God, how could she compete with the memory of a woman that had endured hundreds of years?

"Annice was…" His face wore a distant, lost expression.

"…a sweet, docile woman, who would've done anything for me."

A hard lump formed in Emily's throat. She didn't want to hear any more and opened her mouth to change the subject.

"But she didn't have half the fire you possess." He rolled his head to the side and burned her with the passion in his eyes.

The moisture in her mouth disappeared under the heat. She licked her lips with her too-dry tongue and asked, "What happened to her? Did Marguerite have something to do with it?"

"You could say that." He stared again at the popcorn ceiling of her bedroom and started to laugh but stopped, looking more pissed than amused. The tips of his fangs captured the light that shone through the open bedroom door and glinted under his lip. "It finally occurred to me one night that the best way to handle Marguerite was to play her game. Stop resisting. I convinced her that I was starting to fall for her, my distaste for her waning." Emily ran her fingertips over the back of his hand, tracing the raised scars that marred the skin.

"Marguerite started giving me small amounts of freedom and more frequent feedings as her trust in me began to build. I used those few weeks to gain strength, to learn how to use my new powers. And then one night, after she was finished with me, and I'd had my fill of her blood, I manipulated that surge of power and phased back home." His gaze darted to Emily. "She never saw it coming. Marguerite was so caught up in the fantasy that I would be hers, she never thought I would leave."

He looked away once more. Obviously, there was more

to the story. "I had to see Annice one more time. I wanted to ask forgiveness for having disappeared from her life for three years. We had been engaged before I had left for the battle." His Adam's apple dipped before he continued. "Marguerite had warned me that if I did not give myself to her, I would have no one. She would not share." His hand fisted in the sheet. "Foolishly, I thought if I could only glimpse Annice one last time, talk to her for a few seconds just to make sure she was okay, I would be able to move on. Let her be in peace."

"Marguerite followed you." She sensed what must have happened next. Marguerite had murdered Annice. He was remembering another woman, yet his pain tore her up inside. She should be jealous, but all she wanted to do was hold him.

"I saw Annice in the gardens of her home that night. She was alone. I thought it the perfect moment, so I stepped from behind the trees, and she ran. Right into my arms. She'd thought I'd died."

"Before I could explain, Marguerite phased in, ripped her from my hold, and slashed her throat."

Emily flinched and grabbed her rebelling midsection.

"It happened so fast. I was still a young vampire and hadn't sensed her presence. Annice died because of my ignorance."

The frustration and pain in his voice was almost unbearable. She wanted to say…something. Anything to ease the hurt. Yet she sat there, barely keeping down the contents of her stomach.

"My vision went red, and I attacked Marguerite, ripping and clawing at her with everything I had. I remember standing over her bloodied body, feeling not a shred of remorse, but before I could make my final blow, she disappeared from beneath me." He shook his head. "I would have thought it impossible, considering the damage I'd done.

"Marguerite went deep into hiding. She knew if I found her, I would do everything in my power to see her dead." For a moment, an eerie red glow appeared in his eyes, then faded.

"My God, what you've been through. How you must hate her." *For what that bitch did to him, she deserved to die.*

"I searched relentlessly in Europe, for a century, until I got a lead that she may have gone to America. I caught the next ship heading west. Not easy for a vampire, but I survived." He rolled back onto his side and faced her. Lifting his arm, he allowed his fingertips to follow the curves of her arms as he spoke. His hardened expression softened, as if the feel of her skin soothed him. "That's how I came to be in South Carolina. I didn't find any evidence of her here, but I decided to stay and try to start a new life for myself. That's when I formed the Enclave." He threaded his fingers into her hair, his gaze one of confident determination—and affection. "I knew there was a possibility that one day she would come for me again. But this time, I would be ready."

They stared at each other in silence, both digesting the weight of the reality between them.

"So, now she's here and she still wants you."

"And now, thanks to her new source of power and skill, she knows there's a woman I care about, because you're in my head."

Heat rose to Emily's cheeks. "Any idea how she's gained this new power?"

He told her of the info they'd learned about a vessel

containing the essence of an ancient Croatian vampire, Madunic, and its implications before adding, "When you came in before, she was in my head. She confirmed it. She's dosing herself with it to achieve whatever little feat she desires at the moment. Like what you witnessed—she wanted to prove that she had the strength to hold me and recreate the hunger I'd endured centuries ago when she had turned me."

Kenric's eyelids drifted closed, then he moved his arm down and encircled her waist, pulling her to him. He rolled her onto her back and in one move braced himself above her and opened his eyes.

"Emily, you know the truth. I can't let another woman I care about die because of me. Two women have already given their lives: my mother and Annice."

"Your mother?" Emily choked out the words through the emotion riding high in her chest.

"She died trying to protect me from my father's abuse, and Annice died because I didn't have the strength to stay away." He dipped his head and placed a kiss to her forehead, then each cheek. "Come home with me tonight. Let me protect you. I can't lose you, too."

Tears streamed down her cheeks. He brushed them away one by one. She laced her fingers through his raven hair and pulled him to her lips.

She wanted to kiss the hurt away. Kiss away the years of loneliness he'd carried in his heart.

"Marguerite may have taken away the sun from my life," he said. "But I won't allow her to have my light, too." Kenric cupped her cheeks. "I won't let her hurt you, Wildflower. You have my word."

A knot swelled at the back of her throat, blocking her ability to speak.

"I-I want you to know, you're the only person on this planet I've ever told the details of what happened back then." He closed his eyes and his Adam's apple bobbed. "Not even Guerin knows the extent of her crimes. Some I can't even bring myself to remember during my waking hours. The images plague me enough in my dreams that I don't really need to."

Emily brushed her fingertips along his jawline, the coarse feel of his whiskers tickling the sensitive pads. "You can tell me anything. I could never judge you for what you feel after the things she put you through. Nor would I ever betray your confidence."

"I want to make her pay," he growled. "With everything in me, I want to bring her down—destroy her for all that she's taken from me and all the others she's hurt in her path of destruction."

Air sawed in and out of Kenric's lungs, as if the admission had nearly exhausted him.

"I'm not proud of the fact I've allowed my need for vengeance against her to consume so much of my life. In fact, it pisses me off that even during her physical absence she's still been inside me, a never-ending source of fuel for my anger."

"Dear God, Kenric, if anyone ever had a reason to carry a grudge, it's you." Emily tugged his chin back up, bringing his shadowed gaze back to hers. "You have nothing to be ashamed of. That's all on Marguerite."

He cupped her breasts and rolled her nipples between his fingers, pulling a moan from her throat, then his mouth was on hers. The kiss hard and deep, as if she tasted of his salvation. And in her heart, Emily would give anything to be that for him—be whatever he needed.

A knock sounded at her front door.

"Ignore it," he grumbled against her lips.

Another rap against the wood reverberated through the condo, this one harder.

"Damn," he muttered and tumbled away from her onto his back.

Chapter Seventeen

Grabbing a robe from her closet, Emily hurried down the hall. "Who is it?" she called a few feet from the door.

"It's Jeff." A deep, grumpy voice sounded from the other side.

She skidded to a halt. Her heart flipped in her chest and landed in her stomach. *Dear God, what was he doing here?*

"What do you want?" God, she needed him here like she needed a toothache.

"Open the damn door, unless you want a scene on your front porch. I told you I would be here, woman."

A snarl behind her had her wincing. Kenric framed the entrance to the living room, his jeans hanging loose at his hips. The blacks of his pupils filled his eyes, and one hand hung curled into a fist at his side.

"It's my ex-fiancé." She tried to give a half smile.

"Your ex?" Two small words, but when he said them, they held such power.

"I haven't had a chance to tell you about him yet," she whispered. "I'll handle this." She motioned to the door with her index finger.

"Emily. You've got two seconds to let me in, or the whole neighborhood will know I'm here.

No mistaking the rumble that emitted from the other side of the room.

"Stop that." She shot Kenric an irritated look. "And get rid of the scary vampire look." She waved a finger in the direction of his dilated eyes. "I've got this under control. It's nothing I haven't dealt with in the past."

With a flip of the dead bolt, she opened the door. Jeff barged in, almost knocking her over, and then pulled up short. Kenric had made it across the room before the jerk had taken three steps.

"Well, I see you've been busy." Jeff scowled. "It didn't take you long to find someone to warm your bed." His gaze flicked from her to Kenric.

"I think I've heard enough of your bullshit and your insults." Kenric moved in, his face inches from Jeff's. "Apologize. Now. If you want to leave here on your own two legs." Each word eased from his lips, his voice dead calm.

Jeff stumbled back and bumped the wall. She thought for a second maybe he'd gained some common sense, but hell no. He curled his lips and straightened his shoulders. "Just who the hell do you...?"

Good Lord. Emily broke in on the testosterone display. "God, you're such an ass, Jeff." She grabbed his arm and pulled him to the side. "Let's settle this once and for all, and then you can get the hell out of my house." She glanced back and mouthed, *I'm sorry. One minute, please.*

Kenric wrestled with his raging need to kill the asshole following Emily into her bedroom. Thank God, she'd left the door open. He might have torn the damn thing off with his bare hands if she'd closed it.

She hadn't mentioned the asshole before, but he knew someone in her past had hurt her. Not hard to guess who the responsible party was after meeting good old Jeff. What an absolute prick.

Their voices rose and carried to the front of the house. Even without his superb hearing, their words were clear.

He braced himself against the wall.

Ten minutes.

That was it.

He would give Ms. Independence a few moments to handle this, and then *he* would take care of him.

"I don't have anything to give you," Emily yelled. "I've already maxed out the equity line on my home to cover the previous debts I created because of you."

Fuck. Fuck. Fuck.

His fingers dug into the plaster behind his legs.

Stay. Stay. She wants you to stay the fuck out of this.

"Bitch, you owe me. I know you've got something left you're holding on to. Your mama left you everything when she died."

"She barely had anything, and you know that. Dad's drinking took everything except this place. And I'll be damned if I lose it because of you."

Emily's voice broke, and Kenric's heart turned inside

out. He had no idea she'd held on to her life by an unraveling thread. She'd stolen his ability to think straight. This wasn't him, standing on the outside and allowing his woman to be treated like shit by some asshole jerk-off.

"Get out of my things!" Her voice rang out, followed by a crash of something onto the floor.

The bastard was dead.

Kenric bolted. Her jewelry case lay shattered on the floor, her few trinkets scattered around her feet. Jeff groped on his knees after some of the items.

"I said get your hands off my stuff!" Emily beat at his back with her fists.

Jeff glanced up, his brown hair covering one side of his face, but it didn't hide the sneer he aimed in Emily's direction.

That cinched his fate.

Kenric took two steps and swung. Jeff howled as his nose exploded under the impact of Kenric's fist, spraying blood across his face and down his shirt.

"Oh, my God!" The distressed sound of Emily's voice only heightened his need to get the bastard away from her. Permanently.

He wouldn't kill him. No matter how much joy it would bring to watch the asshole take his last breath. But…there were other ways.

Satisfied with at least some display of blood and pain on Jeff's behalf, Kenric gripped him by his nape and dragged him down the hall. "I guess you didn't have enough brains to heed my warning."

Jeff yelped and clawed at the hand holding him.

"Kenric!" Emily cried out, following close behind.

"Stop! What are you doing?'

Her frantic swats at his arms didn't matter. Old Jeff needed to learn a lesson. He hauled the vermin up and slammed him into the wall. The air left Jeff's lungs on a wheeze. Kenric dug his fingers into the asshole's chin and forced their gazes to meet. He reached in, wrapped his mind around Jeff's slimy excuse for a brain, and forced the other man's neurons into submission and readiness for his verbal command.

"You will never again set foot on Emily's property. Never will you call her or let her name fall from your lips again. For the rest of your life, Emily Ross does not exist to you. Do you understand me?"

Jeff blinked with a glassy brown stare and nodded.

"Good." Kenric released him and stepped back. "Now get the hell out of here."

Jeff immediately headed toward the front door and left without looking back.

The door closed with a soft *click*, and Kenric wheeled around, satisfied he'd taken care of that piece of shit. The look on Emily's face stopped him cold. She stood with her hands on her hips, sporting an expression that said she wanted a piece of his ass, but not in a pleasant way.

"What's wrong?"

"What's wrong?" She covered her face with her palms and groaned. "I can't believe what I just witnessed."

"I took care of the bastard." Another wave of satisfaction rushed through him. "He won't be coming back to bother you."

"I told you I could handle it," she spat. "I don't need some overgrown vampire fighting my battles for me and zapping people with all kinds of mind mojo."

"Emily…" He couldn't believe what she was saying. All he did was protect her. What the hell was wrong with that? "I think I did a pretty damn good job of controlling myself. He's lucky I didn't kill him for how he spoke to you."

She shrieked. "That's it," she said, sweeping her palm out before her. "That's what I'm talking about. This is exactly why this will never work between us. I can't live like that."

"Like what?" He crossed the distance between them and brushed his palms down her arms, then withdrew. "I care about you. You can't live with someone who wants to take care of you and protect you?"

She narrowed her eyes on him. "I know you thought you were saving me from him, but I didn't ask you to. I can't live with someone who wants to control and dominate everyone around him." She slowly shook her head. "I would never survive." Her eyes shimmered with tears.

A knife to his gut couldn't hurt as much as the words that fell from her lips.

"Emily…" He reached for her face. "I would never…"

She flinched from his touch and pulled free, heading in the direction of her room. "Go, Kenric. Please, just go. I need some time to think. Without you here."

"I'm not leaving like this. Not with you believing…"

"Go home!" She glanced over her shoulder. "Go home," she whispered this time. "You have a job to do, and so do I. I need to get ready for work." She turned, walked into her bedroom, and closed the door.

On them.

• • •

With the press of a button, her umbrella sprang open with a *snap*. Emily pulled her jacket tighter around her neck. The cold wind clawed to get in. Lifting her umbrella against the rain before her, she made a slippery dash to her car. No garages here.

The rain pelted the car's roof as she tossed her purse inside and dropped into the driver's seat. She slid the key into the ignition and groaned. *Remind me why I have to go to work again? Oh yeah, because if I don't, I'll lose what little I do have. And I need the work to take my mind off the vampire who wants to take me home and keep me as a pet.*

Pulling away from the corner, she spotted a dark figure in leather standing near a streetlight. She couldn't see his face, but it had to be Kenric. The man was huge. She'd thought he'd long since gone home. Guess he decided to play guard dog and didn't mind getting soaked.

Five minutes later, her cell phone buzzed. She reached inside her purse, slipped it free, and glanced at the display. *Private number.* Kenric.

Hell, no. She didn't have the energy right now. Dragging her purse over, Emily dropped the cell back in and noticed the slender dark vial lying on top of her wallet. Green flipped to red at the next traffic light, and she came to a stop. She lifted the blood sample and rolled it in her palm, studying the garnet fluid sitting within the glass. Strange how the vial felt heavier in her hand than its actual weight.

Where had her head been when she had taken this?

A car horn blew, and she jumped. The light had turned

green while she sat in a daze. She pressed the accelerator and made a right turn in the direction of Bean City. God, she desperately needed some caffeine.

She glanced at the tube of blood once more before returning it to her purse. Memories of their night together tugged at her mind. She didn't want to let them in. They made her heart ache. She shook her head, warding them off, but they breached her defenses.

He'd treated her with such tenderness, as if she'd meant the world to him. Every touch and caress had both eased and exhilarated her, as though he knew exactly what she needed. And then he had given it to her.

Afterward, he had revealed some of the most private parts of his life. He'd trusted her with his very existence.

She knew what she had to do.

Destroy the vial.

No matter how pissed off he'd made her, she would not betray him. She would not be responsible for inflicting more pain than he'd already suffered.

She hit the turn signal and pulled off the road into the vacant parking lot that sat between the closed Hallmark store and her favorite all-night coffee shop. A large vanilla latte and a glazed doughnut sounded like heaven to her growling stomach.

Ten minutes later, she finally had some caffeine to go, despite the fact that the barista behind the counter had refused to remove the ear buds from his ears the entire time he took her order. Thank God, since it was already eleven thirty. Maybe she'd be lucky and only be about twenty minutes late for her shift tonight.

With a steaming coffee in one hand and a warm doughnut

in a bag in the other, Emily shoved at the exit door. She could barely wait to get behind the wheel, break off a piece of that sticky decadence, and chase it with a gulp of sweetened caffeine depravity. *Oh, yeah, this is gonna be good.*

The door swung wide and a cold blast of wind hit her, sending a curl of steam up through the vented lid of her cup. Holding it steady, she made a sprint toward the end of the sidewalk, heading for her car. She'd left her umbrella on the floorboard, knowing she would have both hands full on the short jaunt back.

With one eye on her cup and the other on the car, she didn't notice the large man coming around the corner. Her shoulder bumped into his chest, knocking her bag onto the wet sidewalk.

"Oh, no! I'm so sorry. I didn't see you there." Luckily, she'd only lost a few drops of her coffee, and none of it on her or the guy she'd run into.

"Here you go, ma'am." The dark-haired man picked up her wet sack and handed it to her. He smiled, but none of it reached his gray eyes, which bore into hers with a cold stare.

"Thank you." She clutched the dripping paper bag and took a simultaneous step back. She shivered, but not from the cold rain.

Edging around him, she took off in the direction of her car. Lord, that man gave her the creeps.

Finally, she reached her car. With her foot only halfway inside the sedan, a large hand came out of nowhere and grabbed her shoulder, spinning her back around. She stumbled back, wedged between the car and the door. Her arm banged against the window, knocking her cup out of her hand and throwing scalding espresso onto her leg.

She cried out at the same time a hand came down hard against her temple and jaw. Stars twinkled behind her lids. The lights danced before her eyes. *How pretty.* She would have liked to stay there, but the throbbing pain in her face brought her back to frightening reality.

A massive palm against her mouth threatened to smother her, stifling any attempt at a scream. She thrashed against him as her vision cleared. *Oh, God. He's going to kill me.* She expected to see the creepy guy from the corner, but the thing pressed up against her was a hell of a lot scarier.

Solid black eyes, fangs that dripped with drool, and the smell… This had to be what Kenric and his Enclave hunted: a DEAD.

Her gaze darted over his shoulder. The dark, rain-slicked streets were empty, too late for most people to be out on a night like this.

Except for—oh, hell, he wasn't alone.

Another one of his blood-lusting friends stood behind him. He grinned and ran his tongue over his thick and shiny lips.

The DEAD holding her leaned in, squeezing her farther into the crevice formed by the door and car. His breath heated her cheek and singed her nostrils.

Her stomach roiled. She jammed her eyelids closed.

This could not be happening.

He sniffed her neck and along her jaw. Her legs trembled and threatened to fail.

"Enclave whore," he grumbled in her ear. Cold fingers crawled under her jacket and groped her breast. "Do you know what we do with whores like you?" With the weight of his hand across her mouth, all she could do was stare into those freakish black eyes. "Do you?" he shouted.

Emily shook her head.

"We eat them for dinner." He twisted her breast.

She screamed into his palm. The pain jolted her stunned brain, and she slammed her knee into his groin. The vampire cursed and doubled over, clutching his wounded genitals. She dived into her car. Dumping the contents of her purse out onto the passenger seat, Emily scrambled, looking for her keys. She couldn't think. "Where the hell are my keys?"

Sharp nails clawed at her through the open door. He'd recovered faster than she'd expected. *Shit!*

She clambered toward the other side of the car. The vampire snagged her foot, and her wet fingers made a sloppy attempt at the door handle. Emily kicked at the arm and head that was yanking her out of the car. Her arm hooked the umbrella sticking up from the floor. She palmed it and placed it against her body, holding it, waiting for the bloodsucker to pull her out.

Her lower body hung from the car. She twisted and lunged forward onto her feet with the sharp point of the umbrella extended straight for the vampire's chest. Boxed in by the car door and the protruding rod in her hand, the DEAD had nowhere to go but hell.

The crunch of cartilage vibrated through the handle as it made its way past his ribs to his heart. She cringed. A loud, rasping puff of air released from the vampire's mouth before he crumbled like a rag doll.

A hysterical giggle bubbled up and out of her throat. Her focus riveted on the curved handle sticking out of the dead male's chest. Good thing she always favored the large umbrellas that looked more like lightning rods than the miniature purse models.

A new set of hard hands dug into her upper arms and jerked her off her feet. She shrieked.

The other DEAD.

In shock, she'd blanked about the second vampire. Why hadn't she run instead of standing there, freaked out over a dead one?

The DEAD slammed her onto the wet pavement. Air punched from her lungs in a painful rush. The blow to the back of her head brought the pretty white lights back to dancing behind her eyelids.

Before she had time to recover her sight, the weight of his body covered hers. He tore at the turtleneck underneath her uniform. The loud popping of the stitches counted down the seconds left on her life.

Fangs stabbed into her throat. The pain forced the air into reverse, leaving a vacuum inside her chest. She tried to scream, but panic sealed her airway.

She beat at his back, pounded at his shoulders. Gradually, her attempts to battle him turned into clumsy, weak slaps.

The twinkling lights were back again. But this time, her eyes were wide open.

The bright lights didn't stay long. Their sparkle grew dim, like batteries losing strength.

Hypovolemia. Rapid blood loss.

She was dying.

Kenric, I'm so sorry. Please, don't blame yourself. It's not your fault.

Across the street, the glow from the backlight of a cell phone illuminated the night. The man punched the numbers on his keypad and waited for an answer. A *click* on the other end of the line connected him, and a voice answered with one word.

"Report."

"Tell our mistress, it's done." Markus didn't wait for a reply. The DEADs were still at work on her body, but at this point, she didn't have a chance in hell of surviving. He closed the phone and slipped it back into his leather jacket.

Turning his back on the macabre scene across the street, he sauntered to where he'd parked his motorcycle a block away. Straddled on his red ride, he reached for his helmet. Marguerite would be…

A stabbing pain sliced through his right eye. He ground the heel of his hand against the source of his agony, as if to hold the contents of his head inside.

What the fuck was going on? The headaches had to be associated with his fall at the warehouse. They'd plagued him ever since, and they were a bitch.

Markus scanned the area around him. What the hell was he doing out here? *Fuck!* He remembered leaving the Enclave for a ride, needing to relax a bit. But then… Nothing. His mind was blank. Markus grabbed his phone from his pocket and glanced at the time display. Three hours? What the fuck had he been doing for the last three hours?

The pain inside his head receded to a tolerable dull throb, replaced by a gnawing hunger in his gut. And something else. A stomach-churning emotion he wasn't overly familiar with but recognized its unsettling symptom: fear. The idea that he wasn't completely in control did not sit well.

But he wasn't about to reveal any of this to Kenric or Arran until he knew exactly what he was dealing with. If Kenric thought he wasn't fit for duty, he'd pull him off the streets. Markus couldn't risk that. He needed the hunt. Needed a reason to get up every night, and the battles that followed to keep him feeling…something at all.

His gut clenched once more, reminding him it had been too long since he'd last fed. Markus punched in his partner's number on his cell. He could use the distraction.

"Hey, man." Markus raised his voice over the sound of eighties rock in the background. Sounded like Def Leppard. Something about "love me like a bomb" began before Arran turned the volume down. "You free for some drinks, and maybe a sip on the side?"

"Yeah, I could use some chill time. Where do you want to meet?"

"How about Tail Spin? Nothing like some sweet ass to go with the bite."

"I see you're suffering no lasting aftereffects from that fall on your other head."

Markus laughed. "Bastard. No, that brain's working just fine. Meet me in twenty."

With his phone back in his pocket, Markus slid his helmet in place and cranked his ride. His back tire skidded on the wet street as he burned out.

He rolled to a stop at the traffic light and glanced at the street sign. Twenty-first and Ocean. What had brought him out to this section of town? He shrugged and flipped his turn signal. These headaches had him doing some fucked-up shit.

Chapter Eighteen

Kenric battled for control. The storm brewing inside him demanded to be unleashed. Every cell in his body clamored to go back, grab her, and haul her ass home with him. She wouldn't even answer her damn cell. He'd never met a more frustrating woman in his life.

Shower jets sprayed steaming-hot water onto his back while he lathered his chest with mechanical swipes of his palm. The bar of soap, fisted in his hand, surrendered under the pressure of his grip. Deep grooves caved the soap in on one side, creating four perfect replicas of his fingers.

This fucking sucked.

He had to stay put. The defiant, independent streak in Emily would rip his balls off if he showed up right now. He sighed. One step at a time. At least she would be working tonight. Marguerite wouldn't touch her with so many people around. Tomorrow night would be a different story. One that ended with her in his home and in his arms.

He swiped what was left of the soap off the floor and jammed it back onto the dish before shutting off the water. Reaching for the shower door, he staggered back under an unseen force that slammed into his chest and knocked him into the tiled wall.

The weight against his ribs held his air hostage. He grasped for the rail mounted on the wall beside him. He held on, sliding his hand down the slick, cool metal until his knees bumped the wet stone floor.

Dark edges crept over the corners of his vision before the pressure on his chest relented enough for a ragged breath. In its place, a wave of misery flooded his heart. He hoisted himself up and stumbled out into the fogged bathroom.

He grabbed the marble sink for balance, his knuckles blanching under the death grip. *Emily.*

Something was horribly wrong.

Yanking his blue jeans from the counter, he jerked them on along with a black sweater over his head. They stuck to his wet skin, but he didn't give a fuck. Each moment wasted sent a stabbing pain through his soul. Only one thing could make him want to claw his heart out. His brain couldn't go there.

It wouldn't go there.

He put his boots on, strapped his silver-plated dagger in place, holstered a nine millimeter pistol at his side, and phased, reaching for Emily's essence. With the distance that separated them, he could only target her general direction.

A dark street.

Vacant.

After the second attempt, her presence itched inside his veins. The next phase would bring him to her.

The image of a narrow parking lot came into focus. His world shifted under his feet. Emily lay on a glistening carpet of blood on the wet street with a DEAD at her throat.

The chain he had so carefully coiled and maintained around the monster inside him snapped.

His head flew back as an agonized war cry rent the night.

With claws and fangs extended, he leaped into the air. He landed with a solid *thump* near the vampire's crouched form. The DEAD's head drew back, and it hissed. Kenric's hands were at the sides of the vampire's face before the animal could flinch. With a single jerk, the DEAD's neck cracked.

He dug into the flesh of the vampire with his claws. A guttural cry, more animal than human, tore from Kenric's throat, and he launched the filth into the brick wall. The body dropped onto a Dumpster lid with a dull *plop* and rolled onto the pavement in a heap.

Kenric pulled his dagger and made his way over to the twisted corpse. A swift kick into the shoulder of the bastard flipped him onto his back. He palmed the hilt of his blade. The wet, silver-plating glinted in the streetlight a split second before he drove it into the DEAD's chest. A split-second later, he yanked the blade back out and spun on his heels, the rotting carcass forgotten.

Swirling, red-stained puddles of rain circled his boots as he sheathed his blade and crouched beside Emily's body. Uncertain of where to touch, where to begin, he hovered over her with shaking hands. So pale. His chest heaved, sucking for air. From exertion—agony—or both? His head and heart were so fucked, he didn't know. Kenric fell to his knees and reached for her cheek. The chilled surface of her skin had his stomach heaving. He swallowed back the bile.

"Dammit. Fuck." The words groaned from his soul. It wasn't enough. Nothing he said helped him take the pain away. He collapsed onto his rear, cradling her head within his lap. Grasping the tail of his shirt, he ripped a long section and pressed it to the gaping tear at her neck.

"Oh, God! Please, no." The pain in his chest surpassed any wound he'd ever received in battle. His eyes burned. Moisture clouded his vision.

"Emily!" he called to her, wiping at the water pooled within the corners of her eyes. "Can you hear me? Open your eyes." What the hell was he going to do? Dear God, she'd lost so much blood. Her heartbeat was but a weak thump to his ears. No hospital could save her now.

Goddamn you, Marguerite! He bellowed inside his head, when what he wanted was to scream until his lungs burned for air. But he couldn't risk drawing the attention. He groaned and curled over her body, both fists thumping his forehead.

He should have never let her go. *Fool!*

"Emily." Kenric tried again with a light tap to her cheek. No response.

He reached into her mind. "*Emily. Hear me. It's Kenric.*" A chaos of voices and flashes of her memories surrounded him. "*Focus on my voice. I'm here for you.*"

A whisper of a reply called to him. "*Kenric?*"

"*Come back to me, Wildflower. Please, open your eyes.*"

The flutter of her eyelids kick-started his heart. A weak groan escaped her throat.

"Shhh… Don't speak, love. I've got you."

Her lashes, sprinkled with drops of water, drifted back

down.

"Emily! Emily, stay with me!" he commanded with another soft tap to her wet cheeks.

Her eyelids slowly opened.

"You have to focus and listen to me. You've lost too much blood." His voice failed him, choking on the damning words, *you're dying*. "There's nothing I can do." He paused, swallowing the hard knot of pain back down into his gut. "There's nothing I can do as a man," he amended. "But there is another way."

He shifted on the wet pavement, needing to see her eyes, to know for sure she understood exactly what he offered.

"I can turn you. Make you like me—a vampire. Do you want that?" He couldn't believe the words spilling from his mouth. Never in his existence would he ever have thought to turn someone into the very thing he'd despised for centuries. But the idea of Emily no longer in his life trumped all his previous convictions. Having her here, with him, mattered more than all the other bullshit in his head.

She blinked. Beads of cold rain mixed with her tears and tumbled down her cheeks.

Bitten three times, she had enough of the antigen present in her system for the conversion, but he had to let it be her choice. Even if the thought of losing her felt like barbed wire shredding through his insides, he would never force her into this kind of life.

She hadn't answered.

He brushed the blood-streaked auburn curls away from her face before repeating the question. "Do you want me to turn you? You have to answer me now, baby."

He ran his hand over his rain-drenched face. "You're

dying," he whispered, unsure how he got those last words out past the constriction in his throat.

A slight dip of Emily's chin indicated her answer. More tears fell from beneath her lashes. Her lips parted on a weak cough. He leaned in.

"I...trust you." She swallowed. The massacred flesh of her neck barely withstood the movement. Waiting for her next words to leave her lips nearly destroyed him. "Do...it."

Kenric's gut discovered a new definition for agony. She trusted him. He'd never sired another, but he'd be damned if inexperience would stop him from trying to save her.

Already drained of most of her life's blood, he needed to only take her a step further, then feed her his own blood.

And pray.

Pray that she would survive the change. The next forty-eight hours would be hell on earth for both of them.

The last thing he wanted was to move Emily in her current condition, but if he was going to do this, he had to pull her farther into the shadows so that he could cloak them. Not that there should be much pedestrian traffic at this time of night and with the rain, but another vehicle pulling into the parking lot wasn't out of the question.

He cradled her body tightly and, using every ounce of speed he possessed, moved them to the opposite side of her car, away from the street and into the shadowed edge of the building. Gently he repositioned Emily in his lap, then lifted his arms, gathering the shadows into the palms of his hands, and pulled them around their bodies. No one would notice them now.

He lowered his lips over the wound at her neck. "Hold on," he whispered against her ear. "I'm not letting you slip away so easily." He found her weak pulse and drained the remaining essence of her life.

Jerking his head free from her with an anguished groan, he jammed his fangs into his wrist.

Her head lay limp in his palm as he pressed his vein to her mouth. The crimson stream trickled down her chin. His arm shook next to her lips. He willed his heart rate to a steady rhythm. He had to stay calm. For Emily to survive, he had to get a grip.

Reaching back into her mind, he called for her in the darkness. Wrapping a compulsion within the words, he willed her to swallow.

"Come on. Drink for me." He pressed his wrist tighter to her lips. "Hold on." Her cheeks filled, and her throat bobbed. A cough racked her body as the warm flow gargled in the back of her throat.

"Swallow," he commanded. "Come on, you can do this." Another cough. Another swallow. "That's it." Her lips sealed around the wound on his wrist and pulled. "Take from me, Wildflower. Take from me and live."

A burning ache spread up his arm from where she fed. He hissed as his cock hardened. An erotic high flashed through his veins. With every pull at his wrist, he soared. He shifted her in his lap. Damn, she didn't deserve this. Not his begrudged arousal, nor the change to her destiny.

After what seemed like forever in the empty parking lot, he slipped his finger between her lips and removed the source of her nourishment. She groaned. He eased back into her mind, familiar with the pathway now, and soothed her. "*There will be more to come, love.*"

He hadn't properly fed in days, and the amount he'd

taken from Emily earlier wouldn't sustain them both. With her life in his hands, he had to stay strong enough to get them both back to the compound—alive.

Lifting her carefully in his arms, he stood and phased.

The walls of the manor came into view, and Kenric's legs buckled. He went down hard on his knees, cradling Emily to his chest. The world around him shifted like those crazy funhouse mirrors he'd once seen at a fair.

Bloody hell. He'd given more than he realized.

Exterior lights from the house flooded the grounds. The sensors had detected his presence. Blinded, he threw his hands up to cover his eyes right before the anxiety-laced voices of Michael and Elle surrounded him.

"Sir, let me help. Let me take her into the house." Michael attempted to peel Emily from his clutches.

His gums tingled, and his fangs lowered. An ominous rumble surged from Kenric's throat. "Mine."

Michael flinched and jerked his hand away.

"I have her. Just get us inside and to my floor."

Buffeted by the two, Kenric weaved his way to his quarters. He barked orders to Elle for bandages and a hot bath for Emily before turning to Michael and ordering him to get Guerin on the phone.

Elle stood at his side and helped lower Emily into the large soaker tub. The room continued to tilt with his every exertion. He glanced in Elle's direction.

"DEAD attack?" Elle didn't look up as she asked the unnecessary question. She knew the unmistakable evidence in front of her.

"Yes."

"Good thing you got to her when you did." She looked

over at him this time.

"I didn't."

Her hands stilled for an almost indiscernible second, before she dropped her gaze and continued working with Emily's clothes. Kenric went ahead and answered the question he knew burned in her head. "I had to turn her."

Elle nodded and then muttered an "oh." The Enclave's only human female resident had been down a similar path, and Kenric hated having to ask her to care for another female in the aftermath of a DEAD attack. Luckily for Elle, the damage had not been so great that she had to be transformed to survive. But the trauma had left behind scars only the people who knew her best could see.

A few silent seconds passed between them before Elle spoke. "Make your call, Kenric. I've got her. I'll finish getting her clothes off, and the water will warm her." She pushed at his shoulder. Her concerned expression told his head she understood and would take good care of her, but his feet didn't want to obey. They had somehow attached themselves to his heart.

He didn't want to leave her in the hands of another, but things had to be dealt with at the scene.

"Yell for me if she starts to wake, or if you need anything." He backed away in what felt like slow motion.

"You know I will."

She peeled the bloodied and ragged piece of cloth from Emily's neck. He clenched his fist, but Elle didn't flinch. He had to give her credit: Elle was as tough as they came. He thanked God for Elle's help and her compassion. She moved to the shredded remains of Emily's blouse, and Kenric spun on his heels. Passing through the doorway, his fist connected with the sheetrock, leaving a lasting impression of his rage.

Michael met him in the sitting room with a cell phone in his hand.

"I've got Guerin on the line," he said, handing over the smart phone, then turned to show himself out.

Kenric gripped the slim case, pacing the confines of the room while he filled Guerin in on the details.

"Motherfucking bitch," Guerin growled back into his ear at the news.

Kenric's voice dipped into a grave tone. "I had to turn her."

"She's okay with that? That's what *she* wanted?"

"Of course, it's what she wanted," Kenric blasted into the receiver. His free hand ran through his damp hair while his feet continued to tread the room. "You think I would have done that to her without consent?"

"No, man. Don't get me wrong. I just know Emily is... She's special to you. And I don't know what I would have done in the same situation."

Kenric stopped and leaned back against the wall, pressing the heel of his hand to the incessant throb at his temple. The back of his head bumped the wall with a hollow thud.

"Let's just say this is a night I wouldn't want to live through again." Kenric swallowed hard, forcing the knot in his throat back down his esophagus. "About the scene. I need you or Logan to get over to Ocean Ave. Emily's car is in a parking lot there, a blue Corolla. Looked like it's next to a coffee shop. I need that scene scrubbed clean. Bring the car back to the compound when you're done and make sure you have Emily's personal items."

"Consider it done."

Elle's voice called out for him from the bathroom.

"I need to take care of something. Ring me when you have everything completed." Kenric hung up, already in motion back to Emily.

He stepped into the doorway, and Elle looked up from the side of the tub. "I could use some help getting her dressed and into bed."

Kenric stood spellbound, his gaze fixed on the beautiful, pale woman lying naked in his tub. His heart kicked in his chest. Thank God this was what she'd wanted. His meager existence would have shattered in that parking lot tonight if he'd had to watch her die in his arms.

"Hey, Kenric," Elle repeated, louder this time, grabbing his attention.

"Yeah, I'm here."

Chapter Nineteen

The hot richness of the female's blood flowed over his tongue and warmed his veins. Markus pumped twice more into the fishnet-and-leather-clad prostitute bent over the seat of his Ducati. Releasing his fangs from her neck, he reared his head back and groaned.

Sated for now, Markus slid from her and stuffed a Ben Franklin into her cleavage. He tucked himself back inside his pants before easing her around to face him. Dirty blonde curls hid her eyes. He brushed the tresses from her face, tucking them behind each ear. Her unfocused, glassy blue gaze searched his face. His hold on her mind distorted her ability to focus. A tipsy little grin curled the corners of her mouth. He chuckled. Her brain was on the vampire joyride of its life.

Markus leaned in and tended to the wound with his tongue, making sure the bleeding stopped prior to setting her on her way. With the small amount he'd taken, she would feel no ill effects. The bite would heal within twenty-four hours, leaving no sign of him. Until then, he planted a memory of a middle-aged customer with a kinky obsession, encouraging her to cover the mark.

His cell phone buzzed.

The hooker slid past him, shimmying her skirt into place. Her full rear jiggled with each rock of her hips as she swayed in her black stilettos.

Markus couldn't resist. He slapped her behind as he pulled out his cell. She squeaked and whirled back around.

"Watch it. That'll cost ya extra." She winked, giving her gum a smack.

Markus growled but pulled back on any further exchanges. He'd already set memories in place.

"Yeah?" he belted into the phone, half listening to whoever the hell was on the other end. The sway of the ass moving away commandeered his gaze.

"I need you both back at the compound." It was Guerin.

Arran stepped out of Tail Spin's back door, passing hot stuff on her way back in.

Markus dragged his attention back to the conversation. "What's going on?"

"There's been a DEAD attack on Kenric's friend Emily. He sent me to clean up the scene. I need you both back on premises. Kenric has Emily at the compound, and we need you there for security."

"She's alive?"

"Yeah." Guerin hesitated before adding, "He turned her."

Markus snapped his phone shut at the same moment a sharp pain pierced his brain, staggering him.

"What the hell's wrong?" Arran's voice penetrated the thick mental soup of anguish inside his skull but sounded a mile away. Markus pressed the heel of his hands into his temples and braced himself against the seat of his bike. His head was seriously jacked up.

The intensity eased to a pulsing ache.

He lifted his eyelids and forced a smirk. "I'm good, just a damn headache that's been giving me hell off and on ever since I took that fall."

"Well, you look like shit."

"Yeah? Well, kiss my ass." Markus threw up his middle finger for good measure.

"Sorry, think that's been taken care of already. Besides, you're not my type." Arran swung his leg wide to capture his ride between his thighs. "Was that Kenric on the phone? I heard you ask if she's alive. Who's been hurt? Is it Gabrielle?"

Arran tried to pull some kind of worried-comrade bullshit, but Markus had known him too long. Elle was a hell of a lot more than a fellow comrade to him.

"No. Kenric's female, Emily. DEAD attack. We need to head back."

· · ·

Not since he was newly turned had Kenric fed on this level, this fast. His head rushed from the overload. Striding into his room, he pulled his leather jacket off and rolled his shoulders, feeling hot and overstretched in his skin.

He found Elle at Emily's bedside, bathing her forehead with a washcloth. Beads of sweat covered Emily's face. She moaned and gripped the blanket covering her.

Easing down onto the other side of the bed, he lifted Emily's hand, wrapping his own around it. She shivered with fever, her hand a heated torch in his palm. The vampire antigens were in full attack mode, re-creating her. She thrashed and cried out, her spine arching from the bed. Her body needed more of what he provided.

"Gabrielle, thank you for taking care of her." Kenric glanced in her direction. She lifted her gaze from Emily, concern and worry wrinkling her forehead and lingering in her eyes. "I need you to leave us alone now."

"Are you sure?" Her voice was shaky, hesitant.

He nodded.

"By the way, I bandaged what looked like a burn on her thigh. I'm sure once she completes the transformation, it'll heal completely. Do you want me to come back in a little while and check on you both?"

She wanted to help, but there wasn't anything she could do now. He had what Emily needed, and he would be here to ride it through with her.

"No. I'll call down if we need anything." He removed the washcloth from Emily's forehead, wiping the droplets of perspiration that rolled from her temple. "Inform the others not to disturb us. It may be a day or two before you hear from me. In the meantime, I will need you to contact Emily's employer at Elizabeth Bay Memorial. Tell them she's been injured and may be out indefinitely, and that she'll contact them personally as soon as she's able."

"I'll take care of it. But before I go, Guerin asked me to make sure you got this."

He lifted his head.

She held out a handbag in his direction. "It's Emily's."

She glanced down at the item in her hand. "Guerin had to collect the things from her purse off the seat of the car and the floorboard." Elle skirted the bed and handed it to him. "There's something in there he felt you would want to see."

He stood, took the purse, and pulled it open. Lying on top of her wallet was a dark vial of what looked like blood. He lifted it from her purse and peered at the label. *John Doe ER 11/10/11.*

His gaze fell to the shivering woman in his bed. The center of his chest twisted into a painful constriction. The undeniable implications behind her having the vial bombarded him. *Not Emily.* Kenric couldn't go there—didn't want to go there.

No, no, no…

Betrayal.

Yet the word with its ugly connotation slithered through the recesses of his brain. A spasm seized his gut as if the world had just sucker-punched him in the midsection. Kenric didn't want to believe it. Their history—the way she'd touched him, cared for him, and him for her—demanded he give her the benefit of the doubt. But since when in his life had anything ever ended with a happily ever after?

Damn, he sounded like a cynical son of a bitch.

But why else would she have kept his blood? The last time they'd been together things had not ended well. Yet he'd never thought of Emily as a vengeful person. Besides, she would have had to have retrieved the sample before that night.

"Kenric…?" Elle's voice collided with his reeling head.

Without a glance in her direction, he ordered Elle from the room. "Leave us."

He dropped onto the side of the bed and stared at the evidence in his hand. What had she planned to do with this? How could she…?

He wanted answers.

Only Emily held them locked inside, and they would not be forthcoming for many hours. Until then he had no choice but to believe there had to be another reason beside the obvious one hammering around inside his head. The turning was in motion, and there would be no stopping it. He'd started it, and he would see her through.

Kenric shed the remainder of his clothes and slid into bed beside her. Emily moaned, tossed a slender arm over him, and sighed. His warm body had to feel wonderful next to hers. He wrapped his arms around her and pulled her close. Maybe he was a damn fool, but no matter what her intentions were, he couldn't decelerate the changes occurring inside her. He cared for her, a hell of lot more than he wanted to wrap his head around, and until he could hear her side of the story, he'd give her the benefit of doubt.

"I've got you, Wildflower. I'm not going to leave you."

"No. Daddy, please. Don't leave me," she mumbled. "It's dark in here. I promise I'll be good. Daddy! *Daddy*!"

Her head rolled back and forth against him. Tears streamed down her face while she pounded on his chest.

"Shhh—It's okay. Emily, it's okay." *What kind of hell tortured her dreams?* He realized, at that moment, how little he knew about her past. He stroked her hair, attempting to soothe her. "I'm not leaving you."

Her tears slowed, and she snuggled against his chest. Somehow, his comfort must have gotten through. He shifted, pulling them both higher up on the bed and into a partial sitting position. She needed another feeding.

This time, Emily took to his wrist with little coaxing. Her lips sealed around the wound and nursed hungrily at the flow. A spark of desire leaped through his vein and burst into a raging flame, threatening to consume his control. Air staggered from his lungs. He gripped the blanket with one hand and stuffed it between his body and Emily's.

This was going to be the longest forty-eight hours of his life.

Feeding and sex.

Each one intensified the need for the other. A large part of the reason he'd kept his sexual desires caged for so long. He never wanted to succumb to what he'd witnessed in Marguerite's dungeons. He never wanted to become someone who was maddened by sexual bloodlust. As a master, losing control would make him a danger to everyone around him.

After a few more pulls that distorted the line between pleasure and pain, he removed her from his vein. She appeared at peace for the moment and settled down at his side. Her body glowed, satisfied with its feeding.

Moments later, her breathing returned to a more natural rhythm, and her temperature dropped from its fiery state. It wouldn't last long, though. A temporary reprieve for what was yet to come.

With her sleeping peacefully, he had time for a quick shower. His body reeked of sweat and blood, and he couldn't shake the throbbing reminder between his legs. He needed some relief. The second he slid from the bed, she moaned and rolled into his warm spot.

He brushed a damp lock from her cheek. "What made you take that vial and hide it from me?" There had to be a damn good reason. Please, let there have been a damn good reason. Otherwise… He didn't want to consider the alternative. The thought of her betrayal threatened to shatter him.

Leaning over, he placed a kiss to her tousled mass of curls. His shaft flexed toward her with a mind of its own. Yeah, he needed that shower.

Ten minutes under some cool water did help. He smelled a lot better and had gained some semblance of relief. Well, at least his erection had gone down. For now.

Rubbing his hand across the rough stubble of his chin, he thought about a shave, but the moment he reached for his razor, Emily's scream pierced the room. He barreled into the bedroom.

"I'm on fire!" Her gaze found his, and her look of panic ripped him apart. "Kenric, what's happening to me? Dear God, I'm burning up inside." She clutched her stomach and doubled over. "Oh no, I think I'm going to be sick."

He dashed for the nearest trash can.

Chapter Twenty

Kicked back with his boots propped up on the conference table, Markus tossed his dagger into the air. The silver blade flipped end over end as Guerin and Logan strode through the sliding steel door of central command.

The chill on Guerin's arrival said he'd shelved his easygoing nature for the night. In its place, he wore the lethal aura of a pissed-off three-hundred-year-old vampire. Dressed in dark leather, Guerin matched his killer attitude; even his eyes glowed red. An unnatural sight beneath the sheen of brown hair turned black from the rain.

He took his seat at the head of the table in Kenric's absence.

The focus of Guerin's sinister eyes tracked Arran as he pushed away from his computer and joined them. "I'm sure Markus has filled you in on what happened tonight to Emily Ross."

"Yeah, I heard. That's fucked up." Arran switched his

gaze from Guerin to Logan, who'd decided to prop himself against the smooth cement wall. Neither warrior twitched under the heat of each other's glare. Markus stayed out of range, glad he hadn't been the one to put the stink in Arran and Logan's shit.

"What I didn't get into over the phone was that Kenric believes it was a deliberate hit since there was a recent threat made on her life."

"Son of a bitch!" Logan bit out.

Markus dropped his boots to the floor with a thud. *Damn.* Only yesterday had Kenric mentioned her to them.

"Kenric suspected she might be in danger from Marguerite." Arran pulled up a task chair. He spun it around before straddling the seat and leaning over the back. "He filled me and Markus in when he asked for backup at the hospital."

Guerin worked his gloves from his hands. "What I can't understand is how in the hell they located her so fast in order to pull off an ambush on her way to work?"

"Where was she when she got hit?" Markus palmed the hilt of his dagger. Uneasiness slid through his limbs. Why was his gut crawling because of a woman he didn't know?

"That's another reason we believe it was a deliberate hit. The DEADs were completely off their usual hunting grounds. They ambushed her about three hours ago near Magnolia Island. Right outside a coffee shop on Ocean Ave."

The dagger hit the concrete floor with a clatter. The street sign of 21st and Ocean glared in Markus's head.

"Hey, watch it with that blade," Arran snarled beside him. "You take out my foot, and I'm going to show you how a Highlander deals out payback."

"Fuck you." Markus scooped up his dagger from the floor. Three hours ago. That's when he'd been there. Blood pounded at his eardrums. Why hadn't he sensed that DEAD hit? Images of an auburn-haired woman clutching a bag and running in the rain toward her car flashed across his mind's eye.

The pain that tortured his skull seized his chest, going slice and dice on his heart and lungs. He had to get out of here.

Now.

Or suffocate.

He jumped to his feet. His chair whirled and slid back, slamming into the pool table. All heads swiveled his way.

"I gotta go." Markus forced the three words out of his throat and made for the door.

As he rounded the table, Guerin lunged to his feet. "Where the hell are you going? We need you here tonight. Logan and I still have patrol."

Air. He needed air. Needed away from here. He rubbed his temples and kept moving. His damn head hurt. Pain. The fucking pain wouldn't leave him alone.

"Markus!" Guerin's bellow echoed across the expanse of the room.

Markus willed himself to stop.

"Where you're going is more important than your duty here?" His commander's question trickled into his brain and battled with the mixed-up shit swirling in his mind. Markus pivoted slowly on his heels. Guerin's dark eyes narrowed on him, waiting for his answer.

And he gave him one.

"Yes. It is."

Markus lowered his torso over the fuel tank and throttled down hard on the grip of his bike. The wind fought to tear him from his ride. The speedometer read one hundred ten miles per hour. Rain sprayed his visor, blurring the road at his wheel. Oncoming headlights formed starbursts of colored lights on his wet face shield.

He didn't give a flying fuck.

Better off dead.

They'd all be better off if he'd eat some serious-ass pavement and fry with the sunrise.

He was a traitor.

During the last hour since his realization that the auburn-haired girl was Emily, the seal on his duality of memories had cracked open. The images spilled into his conscious mind like some cancerous sludge regurgitated from hell. He remembered. Remembered it all.

Such a sick SOB.

He'd followed Kenric to Emily's at sundown, completely covered in leather and a black-out helmet to combat the lingering rays of the sun. He'd waited all evening for them to part.

Trailing Emily hadn't been hard in her aged sedan. She'd been an easy target, alone late at night in an empty parking lot. One phone call was all it had taken to have the pair of DEADs lying in wait for her.

He'd done some vile things. Images from his time spent at Marguerite's lair flickered across his mind's eye.

Sick, depraved things.

Flashes of him in various stages of sex and bloodlust gripped him. Multiple bodies, male and female, writhed against him on a floor littered with white furs.

They had stroked, licked, sucked, and fucked. Him and everyone around him.

Markus shook his head, trying to knock the degrading images from his mind. His rear tire slipped on the wet road, but he countered the effect with little effort, bringing it back under control.

Wind and rain beat at the sleeves of his coat and ran down his back, finding their way under his shirt. Spider veins of ice formed at the edges of his field of vision, but he didn't feel the cold. Strange.

He really should be cold.

Maybe it was because the last shred of what held him to his humanity had severed. Broken by the vampire his leader knew all too well: Marguerite.

What she'd left behind he didn't recognize. Markus worked his throat, trying hard to swallow the acidic taste of self-disgust threatening to choke him.

A horn blared, jerking his attention back to the road. Throwing his body to the right, he willed his bike around and away from the blinding, fragmented prisms of color.

Somehow, he avoided the head-on collision. The pissed-off sound of the horn blasted into his ear as it passed him. Breathing hard, he geared down and popped his visor.

Too late.

He leaned hard into the sharp turn of the road, but his rear tire lost its traction. The bike spun out from beneath him.

The force of the crash sent him flying. Time slowed to a crawl, and the world went mute.

Suddenly, the ground sped forward and slammed into him with a lung-exploding force.

Sound returned at a full-volume blast.

He tumbled down the embankment. Tree limbs and loose gravel chewed at the leather covering his arms and legs, ripping it apart and peeling back his exposed skin. A blow to his back brought his momentum to a halt. He lay on his side, sucking hard to feed the rush of adrenaline. The stench of burned rubber and gasoline filled the air and stung his nostrils.

Markus lifted his eyelids and groaned at the unnatural arrangement of his right leg. *Dammit!* He was still alive and conscious. This had to be somebody's idea of a sick fucking joke. Not one damn branch had pierced his heart or removed his head, taking him out of his messed-up life. Throwing his head back, he raged into the blackness.

Inch by inch he dug his fingers into the soil and pulled himself along on his stomach. Every breath felt like muscle gliding over shards of glass. *Damn!* He must have blown every rib on his left side.

Getting into a sitting position was a maneuver born in Hades. The metallic taste of blood flowed into his mouth as he brought his leg forward. The bottom half of his calf dangled at a grotesque angle. A jagged piece of bone protruded through what remained of the leg of his jeans.

With the last vestige of strength left in his body, he reached for his wolf form. Fuck his clothes. No way in hell did he have the strength or desire to undress in his messed-up state.

The crack of bones shifting into place, along with the sound of tearing fabric and popping threads, echoed through the trees. Markus howled from the morphing of wounded flesh and bone. A necessary marathon of endurance. With the shift came a swifter tide of healing.

Black fur sprouted from his pores and spread across his extremities. He rocked up and onto four solid legs, whirled about, and leaped deeper into the unfamiliar woods, leaving the shredded remains of his life behind.

In his head, he ran into the night with no general direction or purpose.

Deep inside his gut, a different story unfurled. It knew exactly where his paws took him.

Mud caked all four limbs when he exited the dense cover of trees onto the shoulder of a dark paved road. God only knew how long he'd run. His sides sawed in and out. He snorted and twitched his ears as clouds of vapor curled from both nostrils.

Fur receded from his muzzle, and his limbs elongated. Uncurling his spine, he braced his stature on two legs. He rolled his newly re-formed shoulders and sucked in a deep, pain-free breath.

The road sign to his left read HWY 505 SOUTH, below it, mile marker twenty-five. A single mile from Marguerite's lair. *What the fuck? Who are you kidding, asshole? You knew where you were heading the moment you walked out on the Enclave.* He whipped around, one foot back into the underbrush, and phased.

His feet settled on the hard-packed dirt of an empty driveway as a dingy white Victorian porch came into view. Taking the steps two at a time, he headed straight for the front door.

He didn't knock.

Enrique could kiss his ass.

With his mind clear for the first time in days, he had to face her. Face the reality of what he'd become.

Markus sauntered naked into the candlelit foyer and straight for her receiving room. She might kill him for his arrogance—hell, he wished she would—but he seriously doubted she'd dare.

He held the key to what she wanted most. .

He heard several sharp intakes of breath the moment he threw open the double doors. Before he could blink, Enrique appeared before him and wrapped his hand around his throat.

"I don't believe you've been announced, minion." Enrique sneered with a shiny white display of fangs. "An ill-conceived move like this could have the unfortunate effect of death."

Markus pulled back his lip to unveil his own set of sharp teeth. "Something tells me, *minion*, that you won't risk pissing off the mistress by killing her new play toy."

Enrique's face twisted, and his eyes lit with seething anger. Enough rage, Markus knew, to be a formidable threat. Instead, Enrique shoved him into the room.

"Well, if it isn't my handsome Enclave warrior come to pay me a visit." On her chaise, Marguerite rose from the lap of one of her half-naked male slaves. "I've been expecting you."

Markus planted his feet at the base of her platform.

Enrique's fingers dug into his neck. "Kneel before your mistress."

"I'd rather stand." Markus cocked him a sideways glance.

Pressure landed on his shoulders, driving him to his

knees. He swallowed back a grunt as his hands saved his face from eating the floor.

"I'd rather you kneel." The threat contained in Marguerite's words was unmistakable.

Guess he'd fucking kneel. He eased his head up and rolled back onto his knees. In his periphery, Marguerite's commander stood to his left, his arms crossed over his chest, weapons galore strapped to his body.

"Much better, slave."

He'd pick his battles.

"Did you come for your reward, minion? My commander tells me your mission was a successful one with Kenric's newest, or shall I say *former*, bedmate."

Marguerite glided down the steps before him. Her silver gown parted at her thighs with each step, offering him glimpses of her bare pussy. Hot blood engorged his cock. Oh, she knew how to play the fucking game well. Pun definitely intended.

A rumble vibrated in his chest.

By sheer will alone, he pulled his gaze away from the show. Her lips curled into a slow smile. She could see his arousal, and he smelled hers.

Her feet touched the wood floor, and she lifted her hand to her neck. Without hesitation, she dragged one hooked claw across her flesh. A swell of blood rose along the open trail.

A ribbon of red flowed down her pale white skin and disappeared into her cleavage.

The rich and heady scent of her blood short-circuited his brain. He groaned, his gut a wretched coil of hunger, of need.

"Come, Markus. Come to me, and let me show you how

delicious it can be when you make me happy."

Her words crawled inside his head and seeped into his veins. His cock jerked as the pressure within his balls shot to an aching overload and the whore took him to the brink of release. He coiled his fists at his side.

It wasn't enough.

Dear God, he was so lost.

He lunged and grabbed the blade sheathed at Enrique's thigh. With both hands wrapped around the hilt, he drove the serrated end straight for his own heart.

"No!" Her single word filled the cavernous space.

Every muscle locked. *Fuck!* The blade ceased in its path, the biting edge of the tip burned in his flesh. Yet he lived. The bitch wouldn't let him die.

Deep inside, the remaining piece of his soul that belonged to the Enclave cried out. *Forgive me, my fellow warriors.*

She'd won. He'd failed to take his life. There would be no going back.

He couldn't resist her. Drinking from her black well had fed the stain on his soul—renewed its vigor.

She owned him.

And God help him, but he *wanted* her.

And in a way, it was a release. He didn't have to fight any more. The choice had been made, and he wasn't the one who had made it. He'd been spawned from the seed of evil, born and bred to become a killer. Even though he'd tried with the Enclave, for the last few decades, to become something more, as a bit of redemption for the crimes he'd committed while human, a part of him knew this was inevitable. Sort of a self-fulfilling prophecy.

Marguerite wrenched the knife from his chest. The jagged metal ripped at his flesh as she twisted the blade free. Cold sweat erupted from his pores.

"What the hell do you think you are doing?"

He tumbled forward from the sudden loss of her mental hold. "It was better to take my life than reveal my failure to you, mistress. There is nothing to be rewarded for."

Enrique grabbed his hair, jolting the back of his head. Markus hissed from the stab of pain at his scalp.

A chill swept his body, telling him Marguerite had come closer even before her face loomed over his. With another jerk, Enrique released him. His head dropped forward, wet strands of his hair clinging to his cheeks. He glued his stare to the floor. Waiting. Wanting.

Icy fingers gripped his chin, bringing him to his feet. "What do you mean, minion, that there is nothing to be rewarded for?" Marguerite's fangs lengthened, the tips glistening below her upper lip.

"Kenric's whore lives."

Chapter Twenty-One

Every muscle in Emily's body screamed for mercy. She curled into a fetal position. The horrific pains were back, growing more intense in her abdomen and spreading like burning tendrils down her arms and legs.

The only thing that stayed her stomach and calmed the flames was Kenric's blood. Dear God, she hated to admit it, but she craved the taste of him.

The bed dipped behind her.

"It's time." Kenric's deep voice rolled over her as his hand smoothed her hair. She moaned. Even the movement of her hair felt like needles piercing her skull.

After helping her to sit up, he presented his wrist. She winced at the condition of his flesh, mangled from the numerous bites he'd inflicted on himself. The frequency of her need for him left him little time to heal.

"How long can you keep this up? This has to be hell for you." She stared at the crimson stream dripping onto the towel beneath his arm. Hunger twisted in her stomach.

"As long as I need to," he whispered near her ear.

Bringing his wrist to her mouth, she eased her tongue out and licked the trail of blood back to its source. He hissed and drew her closer to his warmth, her back to his side.

She froze. "Am I hurting you?"

"Not in the way you're thinking."

"But I *am* hurting you." She pushed his arm away. "There has to be another way. I can't stand the thought of you in pain for me."

"No, there is no other way. And you're misunderstanding me." He encircled her with his arm, bringing his wrist back to her lips. She couldn't resist. Gently, she placed her lips to his addictive offering. "It's not the type of pain like you're experiencing. To feed another, the act is very…sensual."

"Oh." She released the seal around his vein, suddenly aware of the hard ridge pressed into her back. "This happens every time?"

His stubble brushed her ear with his nod.

"Oh, Kenric, I'm so sorry. In so many ways, this has been torture for you." She owed him a debt she couldn't begin to repay. Their last time together… She'd been a royal bitch. And what had he turned around and done? He had saved her life.

"Feed, love." He rocked his open wrist at her lips, stopping her protest. "Let's get you through this night. Dawn is approaching, and I need you further along in the process before we sleep."

The taste of his blood filled her mouth. Thick, rich, and oh so *good*. She whimpered from the flavor and the feel of its magic working on her insides. Each swallow rained cool water on a raging inferno.

A muffled grunt came from behind her, and Kenric stiffened.

She lifted her chin. "Kenric, please. It wouldn't bother me if you need to… You know."

"That's not necessary. Focus on you."

"Come on, you're not fooling me. You could shatter a brick with your…uh…the tension in your body. I might not be up to joining you, but it would make me happy to know you were enjoying this." She lowered her head and gave his vein a long, deep pull.

His breathing quickened, and seconds later, his arm left her waist. The sound of a zipper and shifting clothes sent her pulse escalating. *Yes*. That's what she wanted.

Within moments, he jerked in time with each sip to his vein. The fact that her feeding brought him to such a fevered state gave her a thrill. She swept her tongue out, enjoying the addition of the salty taste of his flesh mixed with the savory spice of his blood. His breath heated her neck, and the pace of his movements intensified.

His body suddenly grew rigid, and a deep groan shuddered from him. She smiled against his wrist. Both of them satisfied.

That was her last thought before her world faded to black.

A cool cloth brushed her face, waking her to his brilliant blue eyes, hooded by the longest raven lashes she'd ever seen. Beautiful, but the lines around them worried her.

"You need to rest," she whispered. "How long have I been out?"

"It's a little over an hour after sundown, and I did rest. You slept much longer this time, but you've started to perspire again." He wiped her brow. "I'm sorry I woke you."

"Don't be. You've been so good to me." She reached out and followed the hard line of his jaw with her fingertips. "Lie with me. Please."

"Sure." He smiled. "But let me take care of this first." He dropped the cloth into the bowl on the bedside table, then reached for something from the floor. "I went by your place and collected a few things I thought you might want." Kenric sat the duffle bag beside her on the mattress, gathered the bowl, and headed toward the bathroom.

Emily studied the large brown canvas satchel, her mind wondering what sort of items he would have thought to pack for a woman. She grinned. For a badass vampire, he could be such a considerate man. Emily pushed up against the headboard, then reached for the zipper and opened the bag. And her world shrank, narrowed down until the only thing remaining in focus was the framed photo sitting on top of her clothes.

How had he known she needed this?

Emily stared down at the frozen black and white moment in time of her mother, father, and an eight-year-old Emily Ross. The pictured captured one of her favorite memories: a sunny day she'd spent on the beach with her parents—before the alcohol had claimed her father and her family. She missed them, especially her mother. God, how she would love to talk to her one more time. But what would she say? "Hey, Mom. Guess what? I met a man who stopped my heart in more ways than one." She couldn't help but quirk a smile. For the first time, Emily was grateful they were already gone. This way she wouldn't have to try and create excuses as to why she'd stopped aging, or worse, had to disappear from their life all together.

The clank of glass against tile drew her attention to the man in the other room. Kenric stood over the sink, rinsing the bowl. She couldn't believe he'd thought to fill a satchel of memories from her human years and bring them to her. How could she have ever believed being with Kenric would have been a prison sentence? When she was with him, he filled in all the hollow places inside without crowding her spirit.

Emily turned her gaze back to the photo in her clutches, and it suddenly dawned on her—she hadn't truly lost anything by becoming a vampire. Instead, she'd gained so much more. She'd been holding on to the past with such a fierce grip that she couldn't reach out and grab hold of her future.

Kenric slid into bed beside her, propping his elbow onto the pillow and his head on his hand. "Did I do okay? You approve of my choices?"

And that future now lay beside her. She would always have the beautiful memories. Moving forward and letting go didn't mean she would be empty. She would be free. And with room for centuries more of living with the man who had captured her heart and changed her life in so many ways.

"Yes." She nodded and smiled. "It's perfect." Emily stuffed the frame back inside and moved the satchel gently back to the floor. "I haven't had a chance to thank you for saving my life." She turned and brushed the back of his hand laying between them. Gratitude, anxiety mixed with excitement, and, yes, a little fear coursed through her veins. The rawness of her emotions kept her eyes downcast. "We haven't really had much time to talk since my turning began."

It was time to face the next step and find out what she could expect in her new life. Emily swallowed hard, summoning her courage to hear the answers to her next question. "What kind of changes will happen to me other than the obvious: inability to tolerate sunlight, a thirst for blood? Will I be able to change into a wolf like you?"

That would be kind of cool.

Kenric smoothed his free hand down her arm. "Soon you'll be stronger than you were before, faster."

She liked the sound of that, being able to kick ass if the need arose.

"But as an unbonded female vampire, you'll be weaker than most male vampires. As far as shifting into a wolf, yes, but that takes time. Most vampires can't shift until they're at least half a century into their turn. You should be able to phase a short distance pretty soon after your change is complete. But a vampire needs to be at full strength to do so."

"Okay." Emily released a long exhale and gave her head a slight shake. "So much to digest. It's all kind of surreal right now." She placed her palm next to his heart. He'd given so much of himself for her. After the brutal way Kenric had been forced into his life as a vampire, what he'd done for her, even if it had saved her life, could not have been easy.

"When I found you so near death, it almost destroyed me. Waiting for you to choose…"

She glanced up under her lashes. Storm clouds hovered in his gaze.

"I barely refrained from making the choice for you."

"Are you happy I said yes?" She had to ask. Even if she didn't like his answer, Emily had to know if he regretted having been forced into that situation.

A flash of lightning lit the blue in his eyes, and his palm cupped her cheek. "I've never offered another person what I gave to you. Through all the centuries, I never wanted to release the choke hold on my resentment long enough. Not for a second. Until you." He leaned forward and placed the gentlest kiss to her forehead, yet it held the power to command her heart. Kenric made her want to forget. Forget all the reasons why she'd feared his strength. His passion.

The moment he'd offered her his world, she'd grabbed hold. The thought of not living to feel his embrace again, and causing him more pain by her death, had outweighed any of her reservations.

Her mind strayed to the night in the hospital when she'd discovered the stray vial of blood. How could she have ever thought to betray him? She needed to tell him. No secrets. He deserved that much.

"Kenric…" She cleared the tightness in her throat.

He leaned back to look at her but continued to hold her cheek.

"There's something I need to tell you." Her gaze darted from his eyes to the wall behind him and the framed art of waves breaking the shore on some imagined, sunny beach. If only her heart held the peace depicted there.

What if he hated her for what she was about to confess?

Don't tell him. He doesn't have to ever know. The little demon whispered away in her ear, and she oh-so-wanted to follow his lead. But she knew better. Secrets like that had a way of rearing their ugly heads and devastating lives when least expected.

Dragging her gaze back to his, she started again. "You

deserve to know about what happened the night you left the hospital after I helped you in the lab."

His eyes narrowed on hers, and his palm dropped from her cheek. He pushed into a sitting position. "What do you mean?"

She tipped her head back to catch a glimpse of his face. His body grew tense, as if he sensed the news wouldn't be pleasant. The queasiness that was the perpetual state of her stomach ramped up another notch.

"You know, when you left, I was pretty ticked off about the way you informed me I would be moving in with you. I'm sure you can tell by now, I don't do well with commands."

He grunted. "I kind of got that idea."

After a deep breath, she told him everything. About finding the vial of blood in the trauma room, and what she'd done with it.

"I kept it."

His bare feet dropped to the floor, then suddenly, he was up and across the room. His open palms slapped the wall, causing her to flinch.

He stood with his back to her, his rigid body braced against the hard surface. "Why did you keep it, Emily?" His words sounded tortured, uttered like torn bits of his insides.

She grabbed the headboard, pulled herself up, and opened her mouth, but nothing came out. How did she explain it without losing him forever?

He whirled around. A second later, he was beside her, dropping her purse on the side of the bed. Slowly, she tilted her head and met his glare. Her throat tightened, until she was sure she'd choke from the cold look in his eyes. He'd already known.

"I'll ask again. Why did you keep it, Emily?"

"Fear? Bad judgment? Anger? Probably all. None of them a good reason, and all of it a sorry excuse for hurting you." She searched his face for some sign. One that said he might not hate her. What she found cut with a sharper edge than hate. Disappointment.

"I've been chewing on the revelation I found in your purse over the last twenty-four hours." He whipped around and grabbed the corner post at the footboard, holding on to it like a lifeline. "I couldn't wrap my mind around a good reason why you had my blood and never told me." He pivoted. The grimace on his face stabbed straight into her soul.

"When I made the choice that night, for a split second, your blood seemed like the answer that would keep me from drowning with the sinking ship called my life."

"You didn't need the damn blood for that!" He punched the wall. "All you had to do was come to me. I would have never let you go under."

"I couldn't ask you for money," she cried out. Sweat dripped into her eyes, forcing her to rub at the stinging corners. "Right then, I was pissed at you for wanting to control my life… Do you really think I would have wanted to be indebted to you for money?" She lowered her head in shame. "It made me sick even thinking of using you to save my own ass, but at that moment, I was out of options. Jeff wouldn't leave me alone, and I love my home." Risking a glance in his direction, she lifted her chin. Maybe it was her imagination, but his expression seemed a little softer. "I didn't want to risk losing it."

His palms went to his face. He gave it a quick scrub

and moved back to the bed. The headboard creaked as he dropped onto the mattress's edge and eased her purse to the floor. He didn't say anything. Just sat there with both arms resting on his thighs.

"If it makes any difference, the night of the attack, I…" She swallowed hard. God, she was so nauseated. "I had already made the decision to destroy the blood when I got to work. Even though you had made me mad as hell that night with Jeff, I couldn't do it. I couldn't bring myself to hurt you like that."

He lifted his arms from his legs and smoothed his palms over his pants.

"You mean too much to me, Kenric. I don't want to be the person who brings you more pain." She clenched her teeth against the growing knot of her own pain and nausea. Gulping for air, she added, "And if there was a way possible, I would sell my soul to go back in time and erase this mistake." A slicing lance of pain curled her over, but she clamped her mouth over a sob. Chills raced over her body. "Kenric! When will this end?" She shook from the wave of cold marching across her skin.

Edging over into the bed, he rubbed her back. "Soon. I know it hurts, but you're almost there. After this feeding, I'm going to need to leave for a little while. I have to feed again."

A growl rumbled from her throat. Her eyes flew open, startled from the sound. Her heart raced, but the speed of the beats didn't come from pain alone. The very idea of him at another woman's throat sent a violent streak of jealousy coursing through her.

A tingling sensation zinged her upper gums, then quickly turned into an ache. Her skin itched, creating a frantic need to move.

Lunging into a sitting position, she flung the covers from her.

"Something's happening." Panic shot like lightning down her spine. "What's going on?" She clawed at her skin.

"Tell me. What are you feeling?"

"I itch all over, and my gums ache."

A tearing sensation exploded in her gums. She screamed and dropped her head into her hands.

That's when she felt them.

Placing her tongue to the front of her mouth, she found two sharp points sitting beneath her upper lip. She reached with trembling fingers to explore. The tip of a right fang poked her finger. "Shit!" A bright red drop bubbled to the surface.

She lifted her head. Her focus zoomed to the vein at Kenric's neck. Each beat lifted the skin there. *Fascinating*. Every rush of the beautiful, dark fluid moving through his body played like an erotic melody to her ears.

She *wanted* him.

Wanted to sink her fangs and drink until his hot blood filled every inch of her. And then she wanted to do it again. And again.

"Oh. Dear. God." Every inch of her pulsed with need.

He reached for her. "You're okay. Breathe. Just breathe. Your transformation is complete. That's all."

She scrambled from his touch. "You don't understand. I want you. More than anything I've ever wanted in my life," she growled. "I want...to sink my teeth in you."

"I know, sweetheart. And you can have me."

"Oh, no... No." Emily shook her head. "I can't. I don't

know if I can control this…this need." She hugged her chest and rocked, wanting to curl as far away and as close to the man who wanted to give himself to her.

"Yes, you can." His tone oozed confidence. And complete trust in her.

"You sound so sure." She scoffed. "How do you know, when I don't know myself?"

In the sexiest move she'd ever beheld, his gaze boring into hers, he reached behind his neck, grabbed a fistful of his sweater, and jerked it over his head. His muscles shifted and flexed across the expanse of his chest. She licked her lips and tried to find enough saliva to swallow. The impulsive need to climb up his rippled abs had her gripping the sheets.

"What are you doing? You're insane. Get away from me!" He'd lost his mind. She might kill him.

His hands gripped her upper arms and dragged her against him.

"Please, Kenric," she groaned against the fine hairs of his chest brushing her cheeks. "It's too much." She shook her head and whimpered. "Don't you understand? I don't know if I can stop." The unique scent of cinnamon mixed with pine drove her mad. "It can't be you. I don't want to hurt you again." Her abdominal muscles cramped. She wouldn't be able to hold out much longer. "You have to get out!" She wrenched at his hold.

"Don't you understand?" His voice was hoarse against her hair. "It will always be me."

Large hands clasped the sides of her face. She lifted her lashes as he tilted her head. A warm trail of tears rolled down her face.

"I won't let you go too far," he said. "But I don't believe

I'll have to do anything. You're much stronger than you realize."

She couldn't find her voice. Even after her confession… He still trusted her. Wanted her.

He rotated and leaned against the headboard, bringing her down on top of him. "Come here," he said, sliding her closer to the pulse at his throat. With one hand at her nape and the other placed possessively at her right hip, he breathed into her ear, "I'm dying to feel your bite. Take from me."

The beating of his heart called her. Irresistible. She licked once at his skin and choked on a moan. He shivered beneath her. *Please, God, don't let me hurt him.*

She opened her mouth and struck.

His blood filled her mouth, but the man who held her filled her heart to overflowing. She snaked her arms around his neck and her palms into his hair. The thick, silky locks slid through her fingers while her lips and tongue pulled his delicious essence into her. Nothing in her life had ever felt so right.

Chapter Twenty-Two

Kenric slipped back into the house through his private entrance. Leaving Emily, though he'd craved more, had been difficult. He'd ached to have her beneath him, his cock buried deep inside. But she'd fallen into a deep sleep after her feeding, and he'd neglected his own nourishment for too long. He'd also had to check in with his Enclave. Two nights had come and gone, but as he'd expected, Guerin had everything under control, and he was glad to hear Emily had survived her transformation and all was well.

Nearing the bed, his heart swelled. A pink tinge colored her cheeks. Her reddish brown locks lay spread across her pillow in a sea of curls that he hungered to sink his fingers into. Taking care of her, feeding her—nothing had ever felt so right.

Before their earlier talk, he'd questioned his sanity. As leader of the Enclave, he couldn't fathom how the woman whom every cell in his body said was his soul mate could so easily stab him in the back. Though she'd confessed, her fleeting thought to betray him had hurt like hell. But the hopelessness that had driven her actions had shattered his defenses. How could he not forgive her? She owned too much of his heart, and the thought of not having her in his life… His fist clenched. He'd rather walk into the dawn.

At least between them everything was resolved, and they could move forward, because he still had a psychotic vampire bitch on the loose who wanted the beautiful woman in his bed dead. Unfortunately, that was only one part of her agenda. He was sure she wanted more.

When he found that sadistic whore, he would rip her apart bit by bit. Anticipation juiced his veins. Oh, there were many, many ways he wanted to dole out his vengeance. Ripping her apart was just the beginning.

With his clothes shed, he eased under the covers. Emily's body matched his perfectly. He wrapped his arms around her. She'd brought an almost forgotten emotion back into his life: happiness. A feeling that had been absent for what had seemed like an eternity. And he never wanted to let her go.

She stirred. He loosened his hold, allowing her to roll over. The sleepy smile she gave him had his pulse racing and his mind and body wanting to grab her and never look back. Never reflect again on the mistakes he'd made in the past and his failure to save the lives of the two women who had loved him.

He could not let Emily down again. There would be no more second chances. He had to keep her safe, until he'd personally handled the extermination of Marguerite.

"Hello, there." Her voice had that husky, just-woke-up

sound. It fueled an already kindled fire.

The curls that graced her pillow tumbled in chaotic ringlets around her face. Too enticing. Kenric worked his fingers into a handful of her soft locks and smiled.

"I see you're most definitely up." With a mischievous grin on her face, she brushed her thigh against his erection.

"Why don't you come a little closer and see for yourself."

Her lips glided over his in a seductive, playful dance of desire. She parted for a breath, and he dived in to capture a taste.

A moan escaped her throat. He didn't need any more encouragement. Almost seventy-two hours without her touch had proved to be too many. He dropped to her shoulder, then lower, to the gorgeous, dark nipples poking through the material of her nightshirt. He pulled at the neckline until he exposed one sweet nub. Perfection. Under the attention of his tongue, the tip pebbled, and she gasped, arching under his palm.

He wanted to imprint her taste and texture into every molecule of his senses. *She was alive*. Here, breathing and responding with every touch he showered over her.

What an excellent idea.

With one last kiss to the glistening bud, he rolled away.

The frustrated cry of a disappointed woman came from behind him.

He rotated and offered her his hand. "Come with me," he said with a grin.

Her eyes narrowed with a speculative look, but she took hold of his palm anyway. "What are you up to?"

Drawing her against his chest, he spun and backed her into the bathroom. At the shower door, he jerked on the handle and opened it.

Understanding lit her face. If she only knew all the wicked things he'd love to do with her. With one deft move, he grasped the hem of her nightshirt and lifted it up and away from her delectable body. No more secrets between them. No more clothes. The passion in her eyes mesmerized him. He swooped her into his arms. Where she belonged.

A startled rush of air tickled his ear before she wrapped her arms around his neck and tucked her head under his chin.

Gently, he lowered her feet onto the tiled shower floor and closed the door shut behind them.

"Wait right here," he said.

"No." She grabbed his arm. "Please."

"What's wrong? Are you feeling weak?"

"No. I feel fine. I…" She lifted her chin. "After what I did, I need to know if we're still okay."

Fear.

It swirled in her beautiful hazel eyes. A sight he never wanted to see there again. One he planned to erase tonight, and if he had his way, for eternity.

He slipped his arms around her and pulled her close. Her nipples brushed against his skin, and for a second, he forgot how to breathe. "You want to know how I feel about last night. About your confession?"

Her nod brushed her hair against his chest.

He arched his pelvis and traced the curve of her spine with his fingertips. The head of his erection bumped her abdomen, and a soft gasp escaped her lips. "I understand what drove you to do what you did." He smoothed his palm across her hair and curled his lips in a half smile. "I don't want you to ever feel afraid or helpless again. I'll always be there for you. And that's not ever going to change."

The tension in her body eased under his hands. "So we're okay?"

"Yes." He nodded. Kenric pulled her in, enjoying the warmth of her body and the feel of her heart beating next to his flesh. "We're more than okay."

"You have no idea how much it means to me to hear you say those words. I can't imagine, after everything we've been through together, having to live the rest of my days without you."

Kenric flinched. The idea of something coming between them or someone taking her away seared through him like the hot edge of a blade, leaving him raw and exposed. He drew her closer, tighter. "Never going to happen," he growled.

A few moments later, Kenric stepped away and quirked an eyebrow. "Now, let's get back to my plan." With a quick adjustment to the dials, he found the right temperature and set the showerheads at the proper angle. He grinned as he picked up a large sponge before turning back to Emily.

Twirling the irregular-shaped ball of yellow around on his fingers, he cleared his throat, choosing his words carefully.

"As a nurse, aren't you supposed to be licensed in the use of one of these?" He glanced her way and back to the item rotating in his hand. "There seem to be a few spots I just can't quite reach. Think you can help a guy out?"

Her throat worked, and he could sense her attempt to hold back a laugh.

"Yes, I'm *fully* licensed." She plucked the sponge from his hand with a playful smile. "In fact, I believe I excelled in that area. But you, my darling, appear to be completely healthy." Her devilish gaze dropped between his legs to where his cock stood at full mast.

"You've got one thing right." His voice deepened. With an arm, he pulled her in close, making sure she felt every rock-hard inch of him. "Very healthy."

She nuzzled against him. God, he loved the way she felt against his skin. Soft. Warm. And so…right.

"Like you said, though," she said, glancing up with a grin before slinking her body down his chest and dropping to her knees. His heart rate leaped into a gallop, and his cock bobbed, the tip brushing her upturned cheek. Her twinkling eyes never left his. "I'm the nurse here, so let me be the judge of that."

Her warm fingers gripped the base of his shaft as her mouth closed over the head. Blood left his brain in a dizzying rush. At the first pull of her sweet lips, his fangs exploded into his mouth. He gripped the shower walls at his sides with a hiss.

Slowly, she engulfed the near length of him. Then she pushed his control to the breaking point when she dropped her head back and took even more. The head of his cock bumped the smooth, slick surface at the back of her throat. *Bloody hell!* Never before…

His hands dropped to her head, and he buried his fingers in the damp curls of her auburn hair.

"Emily…," he rasped. He would never get enough of her.

She cupped one hand to his sac and the other around the base of his shaft. His head fell back with a moan. Her hot tongue bathed the underside of his cock while working its way up the rigid length. His head fell forward on the special attention she paid to the sensitive rim. The hands he'd entwined in her hair trembled with restraint. Her lips, hands, and tongue drove him insane. The way she watched him as if in ecstasy—the hottest fucking thing he'd ever witnessed.

The tip of her tongue lapped at the leaking bead of precum before drawing it in for a long suck.

"Shit! God, sweetheart, you're killing me."

She paused long enough to give him a lazy, sexy smile.

"You like?" She applied a gentle squeeze to his shaft and balls. He cursed and fisted the back of her head.

"What do you think?" he growled.

"I think I'm not finished with my assessment yet." And damn if she didn't thoroughly assess every curved inch of him.

Back and forth she worked, battering at his self-control. His hips rocked of their own accord, driving his cock into her mouth. So damn good.

The sight of her surrounding him, swallowing him... He had to stop before it was too late. When he came, he wanted to be pumping deep inside her. He wanted to hear her scream his name.

"Stop, sweetheart." His voice came out hoarse. "I need you to stop." It took every ounce of strength he had to extract himself from the haven of her mouth.

"I wasn't done yet." She scowled, then curled her lip into a smile.

"But I have to get inside you. *Now*." He drew her back up his body and into a desperate kiss, silencing the start of a proud giggle over a job well done. He nipped and sucked at her full lower lip, reveling in her little mewls with each tweak of his fang. "You're destroying me with that wicked mouth of yours," he muttered against her lips.

Emily loved the way he kissed and gasped for air as he broke away. She needed him. Needed him on a level she hadn't known existed before he came into her life. It terrified her to crave another so much that every fiber of her being cried out for him. Yet she couldn't run anymore. To never touch him again, or feel his touch, would be an agony she knew she would never survive.

His large and callused palms guided her to the bench on the other side of the shower. "Kneel here."

She did as he requested and climbed onto the heated tiles. "Do you know how beautiful you are to me, Wildflower?" he whispered and caressed her bottom. The rough texture of his hands sent shivers over her skin. Her nipples puckered, yearning for his touch. She reached behind her head and dug her fingers into his hair. He encircled her waist, then slid his palms up her belly to cup her achy breasts. "You bring me to my knees. No woman has ever stirred me the way you do."

The way he touched her, his words, made her feel… cherished.

He rolled her nipples between his thumbs and forefingers, then gave them a slight tug. Her back arched, and her head dropped onto his chest with a moan. The hot ridge of his erection pressed between her cheeks and worked back and forth on the slickened path of her arousal. The erotic sensations at her breasts, coupled with the torture of his hard shaft at her rear, had her begging for more.

"Now. God, Kenric, I want you inside me *now*."

His hand left her breast and followed the curve of her raised derriere. Large fingers slid between her cheeks and folds before dipping a shallow inch into her pussy. She cried out.

He hissed against her neck. "So wet for me. Do you know what a fucking turn-on that is, sweetheart?"

She loved that he seemed to lose his hold on his control, and how his voice and language turned primal. "Only for you."

Soft kisses, laced with a growl, trailed down her throat and shoulder. His hand slid up her arm and drew her fingers from his hair. Before her, he gently pressed them against the wall with a command. "Don't move."

The thrill of his control, and only *his* control, accelerated her desire, heightening her awareness of every touch.

Of him.

Tears welled in her eyes from her escalating need and unfettered emotions, blurring her vision of the tile before her. The muscles in her thighs trembled.

God, how had she ever denied her attraction—her visceral need for this man?

At last, the broad head of his erection pressed against her opening—where her body throbbed with emptiness. She gasped, riding on the wave of pleasure.

"I've got what you need." He bathed the tip of his cock in her wetness. "Remember that."

How did he think she could ever forget? Her body would forever crave his. From the first moment he'd touched her, she had belonged to him.

"I'll always have what you need." His deep voice stroked her, making her center ache from its void. "Right here." He surged forward, burying every inch of his hard cock deep inside her.

She cried out, and a spasm worked over her body as he slammed into her pussy, stretched her, and filled her to the brink of rapture. Rapid intakes of air burned a path through her chest. "Kenric... Oh, God. *Yes.*"

"You were made for me," he groaned.

She wanted to move, but his arms held her tight to his chest.

He rocked into her, slowly at first, then with glorious, hard pumps of his cock. The large, smooth head of his erection bumped her womb with each thrust and stoked fevered nerve endings higher, giving her exactly what she needed. Her nails dug at the tile wall as her orgasm broke.

She screamed, riding the waves that shook her with ecstasy. He gripped her hips, thrusting inside her with delicious friction, extending her mind-altering bliss.

The sharp sting of fangs at her neck had her crying out his name as another orgasm shattered on the heels of the last. A deep groan vibrated against her throat, and the warmth of his ejaculation saturated her deep inside.

For a brief moment, the weight of his body covered hers before he slid from her and onto the bench. He pulled her over with him and onto his lap. His lips claimed hers before she could utter a sound, but she didn't care. She could kiss him for the rest of her days and never tire of his taste. Her fingers mindlessly wandered up into his dark and wet waves. She loved his hair, loved the way the silky texture caressed her skin.

She moved to his jaw, lightly spreading her kisses along his shadow of a beard. "There's something I want to tell you," she breathlessly uttered. The words were busting to get out. She couldn't go another night without letting him know how she felt.

He stared down at her expectantly. "What is it?"

"When I thought I was dying the other night, when that animal was at my throat..." His arms tensed. She brushed his cheek with the backs of her fingers. "There were many things I thought would have flashed in my mind at the moment of my death." She threaded her fingers through his damp hair. "But the only thing I saw was you." She turned to touch her lips to his. "I only saw you," she repeated and lost herself in his kiss.

Chapter Twenty-Three

The smell of blood, sex, and death clung to the air. Kenric's eyes were closed, but he didn't have to see to know precisely where she'd placed him. He tugged his lids apart. The dark gray walls of his former slave cell met his retinas.

"Marguerite, this is getting old," he said in his most bored tone.

The shackles holding Kenric imprisoned on the cot dropped from his wrists and ankles and clattered against the stone wall. He rolled to his feet and strode across the dirt floor. His fingers gripped the rusted iron of the bars that once had held him. A pair of cold palms slithered up his back. Fangs dropped into his mouth, and he unleashed a sharp hiss of warning.

"Unlike with Annice, you got lucky—this time, Kenric."

"There won't be a next time." He roared and spun, driving Marguerite's body into the opposite wall with his mind.

Her back crashed into the rock. A shower of loose dirt

littered the floor and air around her.

"Tsk-tsk-tsk. My, aren't we touchy about the female." She emerged from the cloud of dust. "You must be fucking her." Her green eyes darkened to a pitch black, and her hips swayed as she sauntered closer. "Bet she doesn't make you come as hard as I do. Does she, darling?"

He curled his lips into a purposeful, lazy smile. "You have no idea," he said, closing the distance between them, his chest a whisper from hers. Her eyes widened. "When I come for her, she leaves my lungs burning, starved for air, and I shout her name from my soul." The tips of her fangs dropped into sight. "My cock may have come for you, but your name never left my lips."

Her head reared back, red lips stretched in a hideous contortion of rage as a shriek tore from her throat.

She lunged.

Kenric pivoted, and Marguerite whirled, her long hair fanning around her like a black cape.

"What exactly do you want, Marguerite? You have Goran's blood. What do you plan to do with it?"

"There are things you don't know." She shook her head. "You turn down my offering of a place at my side so quickly, like swatting a fly." She batted her hand and stepped forward. "It's more than power that I've come for." Her green eyes shone in the darkness. "But you won't give me the opportunity to show you what's in store for our future. Trust me. I guarantee you won't be disappointed with the outcome. Together, our union would make everything right." Marguerite's lashes lowered as if she savored the vision in her mind.

Trust her? Goran's essence had infected her, taking her deep inside a version of reality that she alone understood. She *was insane.*

"And if you won't come to me willingly…" Her expression morphed into a sneer. "I will make it happen." She sprang into the air, aiming straight for him.

"I'm done, Marguerite." He spread his arms wide. "Game over."

His eyelids sprang open. The warmth and darkness of his bedroom enveloped him as an echo of an outraged scream rang in his mind. *Damn, that felt good.* Rolling onto his side, he pulled Emily's soft body close, spooning her backside. He needed to make sure if Marguerite ever came close, Emily stood a fighting chance. That meant one thing: Emily needed to be his in every way. She had to become his mate. A slow smile tugged at the corners of his mouth, and his cocked twitched. Damn, he liked that idea.

She mumbled in her sleep and squirmed in his arms. Holding her tighter, he smoothed her hair. Her murmurs grew in intensity, the beat of her heart a rapid pounding drum in her chest.

"Get off of me! No!" She broke into a sob and thrashed against his hold. "I said no! Stop, please."

"Emily! Wake up, love. It's me." She rolled, facing him. He grabbed her forearms, blocking the fists going for his face and chest.

"Stop! I won't let you do this," she snarled through her fangs.

"Emily!" He gave her a shake, hard enough to get her attention but not enough to hurt. Her lashes lifted. For a few moments, wide hazel eyes gazed unseeingly into his before recognition took hold.

"Kenric," she whispered. She threw herself into his

arms, rocking him back. His heart ached with each shudder running through her. In silence, he held her. He had a feeling what she needed most were his arms, not his words.

After a while, her tremors stilled. "Sorry about that. I don't know what happened." She shrugged. "Bad dream, I guess."

He lifted her chin, the lingering shadow of pain impossible to miss.

"It's more than a bad dream, and we both know it. When are you going to let me in so that I can take that pain from you?"

A rush of moisture filled her eyes, but she blinked it away. She shifted from his hold and leaned against the headboard, her face a stoic shield.

"I haven't asked you any more questions. I wanted to give you time to come to me, when you were ready. During your turning, you cried out about your father, and now this." He slid next to her and caressed her cheek with his palm. "I know you're hurting. Talk to me, love."

She dragged her face from his touch and tucked her chin. "It's embarrassing," she mumbled. "I'm a grown woman, letting the scars from my childhood and the actions of another still affect me."

"Emily…" With the palm of his hand, he cupped her chin. "Look at me." She clutched his hand with her own and allowed him to bring her face to his. "I'm the epitome of that statement. I have allowed the past to define me for three centuries."

She reached out, turned, and sank into his arms. Fine with him. No place in the world he'd rather be than wrapped around her.

A deep sigh released from her chest. "After my ninth birthday, not a day went by that my father wasn't drunk, and when he was…anything would set him off." He held her a little tighter. "Something as simple as not moving fast enough when he called or not cleaning my plate at dinner. I never knew what I would get. His fist, his belt…or his favorite punishment, the closet." Chills lifted under his palms, and she shivered. Lightly, he brushed her arms, warming her and hoping to encourage her to let go of the horrible memories.

"I used to pray for the belt. At least it would have been over faster." She grew quiet and still in his embrace. Then a soft voice whispered, "I hate the dark. My dad would lock me away when he said I was bad. Our coat closet didn't have a light. I would lie there with my face as close as I could get to the narrow slit of light under the door."

Both his hands curled into tight fists. Son of a bitch. His gut rebelled at the image of her, a sweet little girl, abused in such a way. A damn good thing her father was already dead. Daddy wouldn't have wanted to experience the punishment *he* had in mind for him.

He placed a kiss to the top of her head. She cleared her throat and rubbed the back of his fist. "I never knew when he'd get around to coming back. Sometimes he would pass out, forgetting I was in there. Mom was too scared of what he'd do to her if she let me out before he gave permission. She let him control her every move and virtually her every breath." Her voice grew bolder. "I promised myself I'd *never* allow any man to treat me or my chil…" She stilled, the rest of her words left hanging in midair. "I'm never going to have children, am I?" The sad plea in her voice wrapped around his heart and squeezed.

Kenric closed his eyes and breathed deep. Would she hate him now? "No, Wildflower," he whispered. "Just like we talked about, as far as I know, male or female, the result is the same: sterility."

Her curls brushed his chest as she nodded. "Well, I won't lie and say it's not disappointing. But sometimes you may not see why you're led down a certain path in life. You just have to hold on in the dark and have a little faith that you'll end up exactly where you're supposed to be."

"You're amazing." He gave her a light squeeze. "You know that? Amazing."

She laughed. "Well, you may think so now, but you haven't heard the rest of the brilliant decisions I've made in my past."

"Like what?"

"Like the time I went and got myself engaged to someone even worse than dear old dad. I'd promised myself not to let myself be treated like my father had done to me and my mother. But not only would my fiancé lock me in our room when he wanted to punish me, but afterward, in the bedroom, he'd remind me exactly who was in charge. Those are the dreams I can't seem to shake."

"This is the bastard you didn't want me to kill?" The words rumbled from his chest. "My God, if I had known the extent…"

She uncurled herself from his arms, and her soft hands wrapped around his neck. "I hurt you before—when you were only trying to protect me, and I'm so sorry."

"You've been through hell in your life, and I'm sure my actions, from the moment we met, didn't make things any easier on you."

Emily arched one delicate brow with an unsaid, *you think?* "When you showed up, I was desperate to reinvent myself. To regain control of my life. When Jeff knocked on the door that night, I needed to feel like I could hold my own against him. To prove to myself that he didn't intimidate me anymore."

"I never want you to feel like a prisoner with me."

"You make me feel cherished and, at the same time, amazingly free to be myself. I realize I would never be in prison with you." She rose to her knees, punching the air from his chest and grabbing the reins to his heart with the smoldering heat in her gaze. "Just the opposite. With you... Because of you, I'm empowered. And I'm not running anymore. I love you, Kenric St. James."

Emily knew she'd laid it all on the line. Like a giant bull's-eye, she'd stuck her heart out there, and it was open season. But the way he touched her, held her, and wanted to know everything about her, said he cared.

"You have no idea what a miracle you are to me, do you?" Both of his hands burrowed into her hair. "You've brought happiness into my life again. I'd built a wall around my heart so high, I didn't believe it would be possible for anyone to scale it." His lips brushed her forehead, and the slight touch flipped her heart over. He drew back and gave her a smile that brought a hitch to her throat. "But you did." His thumb stroked her bottom lip, sending a tingle of desire down her spine and a rush of arousal between her legs. "You not only scaled it, but you brought the son of a bitch crashing down."

He laughed, and it played like beautiful music to her ears. The tune carried notes of pure, unabashed joy, and it filled her heart to near-bursting.

"Stay there. I have something I want to give you." He left the bed before she could reply.

He sauntered naked across the room, each step powerful and sure, the rippling flex and extension of his muscles declaring him a warrior. The man made her blood overheat.

Moments later, he stood at the bedside holding a black leather pouch. He held it out. She opened her hand, and he dropped it into her waiting palm. "What is this?" She held the lightweight package up and studied it.

"Open it and see."

She pulled at the ties and spread the material open. Inside laid a coiled bundle of leather straps lined with a silver band on one side. "Uh… Thanks?" She glanced up, and one corner of her mouth rose in a smile.

He grinned but didn't elaborate. Instead, he climbed into bed and stretched out like a big cat waiting for a scratch to its tummy. And damn if she wasn't itching to oblige, but first, she had to figure out what the items in her hand were intended for.

"Kenric, what is this all about?"

"Come here," he said in a deep and sexy-as-hell voice. A voice that he had to know damn well would have her doing anything he asked.

As if she were feather-light, he grasped her, placing her astride his hips. His thick shaft nestled in the groove of her bare bottom, chasing her breath away. The storm returned to his eyes, the one named desire. And it consumed her. She rode the waves cresting there, and he took her out to sea. No lighthouse to find her way home, but she wasn't afraid. She wanted to stay there—with him—forever.

"Since the first moment I met you, I knew you were something very special. But because of the danger and the darkness that surrounds me, I didn't want to acknowledge the reality of what I'd found." He brushed her cheek. "You're my soul mate, Wildflower. And I know that with every fiber of my being. You were meant for me."

It was as if he were reading the script etched on her heart. She believed it as well. He was meant to be in her life. "You're my rock, my anchor, Kenric St. James," Emily said, her voice cracking. She placed her palm over his breastbone, and he gripped her fingers.

"For a master vampire, the discovery of a mate that's a perfect match, body and soul, is a powerful and rare experience. But I didn't want to believe it had happened. Because caring for any woman has proven in the past to be a death sentence to the one who chose to be a part of my life. I couldn't bear the thought of losing you, too." The tender look on his face tied her up in knots. She sat the gift bag on the washboard of muscles before her, then slid her palms down the sides of his arms and into his hands.

Suddenly, a smile curved lips so delectable, she had to resist the urge to lean forward and steal a taste. "But look at you, sitting there, having defied death." His hands left hers and followed the curve of her arms down to the tops of her thighs. "My Wildflower, you're so strong—beautiful—and the other half of my soul. I love you."

She chewed her lip to keep from sobbing once more in front of him. *Shit*. The man made her snivel like an idiot.

"Kenric…" He stole her words, her mind. Placing her hands to his abs, she leaned forward and tasted his lips before claiming his mouth.

He kissed her like a man starved. Famished for the love he'd denied himself for years. She returned his hunger, wanting to be the woman who gave him everything his heart had been missing.

Without warning, he took his lips from hers. "There's something I want to offer you," he whispered breathlessly.

"I don't need anything else. I have all that I need right here." She placed a finger to his lips.

"Please, I want to do this, but I want you to think before you answer, because it cannot be undone."

"What are you saying?"

"Remember when I spoke of vampires having the ability to mate? Blend with another at the level of their very soul?"

"Yes."

"That is what I want with you. To share the rest of my days as a part of you, Wildflower."

She rocked back. Her hands shot straight to her face and covered her mouth. Speechless. With a shake of her head, she rattled a few coherent syllables together. "There are no words …"

"Think about this clearly. I have. And I have no doubts that we were meant to be together." His gaze dropped to the leather pouch still sitting between them. "Those straps that I gave you, if you decide you want this, are for you to bind me with. I must submit to you."

"Kenric, you're joking." She shook her head. "I have to tie you down?"

He took her hand in his. "Yes, we would become a part

of one another, and at the end of the blending, you would share in my strength. That is why the male submits. I know this probably feels like we're moving fast."

A chuckle bubbled up from Emily's gut. "Everything about us has moved at lightning speed. But that doesn't mean it's wrong."

"With Marguerite's power escalating, we don't have the luxury of a long courtship. As the other half of my soul, and for as long as we live, neither I nor any male will ever control or dominate you again. Not that any would dare touch you, if they wished to continue living."

She smiled, having seen the proof of that statement with Jeff. The man before her was incredible. He understood her fears and offered her the power to conquer them. To free herself. Never to be at the mercy of another man again. Bound to a fortress of power, yet at the same time, she would maintain the strength of her independence. Her head spun. "Kenric, what you're offering me is staggering. That you're willing to give yourself to me in this way touches me so deeply." She squeezed his hands. "You said a blending. How is this done?"

"It would require you to drain me. My soul would leave my body at that moment and enter yours, blending with your essence. Afterward, you would need to compel me to feed from your vein, and, as I revive, my soul would return to me as a blended version of us both. You will sense me as never before and gain the ability to communicate with me telepathically."

"But I have to kill you. Is that what you're saying?" She jerked her head back and forth and snatched her hands free from his. A horrific panic gripped her, and she wrapped her arms under her breasts. "What if something goes wrong and I can't bring you back?" Submission of his body, that in itself moved her, but he wanted to give all of himself—his power, his soul, his life—to her, and he trusted her to return it to him.

"It won't. To actually kill me, you would have to remove my head or put a dagger through my heart. In this situation, I would neither be dead or alive. But that's not going to happen."

She scoffed. Mr. Always So Confident. For some crazy reason his explanation did not make her feel any better.

"Nothing will go wrong," he repeated. "Because I know this was meant to be." His hands encircled her arms. "The most important thing here is…" Roughened palms loosened her hold and stroked her forearms. "Is this what *you* want? Marguerite is still a threat, and she will be enraged when she learns of this. I promise you, I will protect you with my life and all that is in my power. It sickens me to know that my world puts you in danger, but I can't exist any longer without you. In here." His fist struck his sternum.

Ever since she'd found him lying injured and unconscious, her body and soul had yearned for him. Her life had changed forever that night. His words rang true in her heart and mind. Destiny had brought her to this moment in time.

"Yes," she breathed.

"Are you absolutely sure?" His fingertips glided across her cheek. "There's no way to reverse this once it's done. No divorce like in the human world. We will be married on a plane so deep, death will not even part us."

She took his hand in hers and laced their fingers. "Look at me." She leaned in a little closer, her voice hoarse. "I would choose to die tomorrow, having shared my life with you—having been loved by you, rather than be gifted an eternity without you." She sealed her pledge with a greedy kiss, yearning for the future he offered.

The leather pouch tumbled to the bed, reminding her of what they must do first. She removed her lips from his and scooped it up from the mattress. "I take it I need to secure you with these." She lifted the small bag, indicating the bindings inside. He nodded before reaching behind his head, stretching his arms wide to grasp the headboard.

"Be sure you wear the gloves that are inside," he said, lifting his chin to indicate the bag in her hand. "Dump the contents out first and find them. The silver on the underside of the straps will burn you, if you're not careful. They were made specifically to contain a vampire."

Her hands trembled, making it difficult to slide her fingers into the black leather gloves. With the gloves in place, she shifted off his body. The hardwood floor chilled her bare feet as she made her way to the headboard and the large wrists waiting for her there.

"When you bind me, be sure you place the silver to my wrist." His darkened gaze flicked to hers.

"You want me to put this so it will burn you?" She took a step back from the bed. *Oh my God.* She couldn't stand the thought of intentionally hurting him.

"This is about complete submission. I want this, Wildflower. I want to give myself only to you." The tone in his voice clenched her core. He was hers.

Emily cinched the strap tight around his flesh. Within seconds, a tendril of white smoke curled from where the silver met his skin. The stench of burning flesh stung her nostrils, shooting the taste of bile to the back of her throat. Her gaze darted to his face. He hadn't flinched. How could he stand the pain?

"Kenric, please… This has got to be excruciating." She gripped the top of the headboard to keep herself from ripping the silver off him.

He tilted his head in her direction. "It's not too bad. Don't worry." A slight shrug lifted his shoulders. "It's going to be worth every minutc, because when this is over, I'll have you forever."

"God… If I didn't love you so much, I'd have you committed." Even through the agony she knew coursed down his arms, he graced her with a smile that beckoned her to take him. She ran her fingers through her hair and sucked in a calming breath.

With his wrists secured, she tugged the leather gloves from her hands one finger at a time, enjoying the way he watched each movement, raking her body with his smoldering stare.

Her fingertips grazed the top of the silk sheet as she circled the four-poster bed. The air left her chest in shallow bursts. He was magnificent. Nude and fiercely aroused, the warrior lying bound to the massive bed met her perusal with equal intensity. She loved how he made her feel. Desired before all others. Powerful. In control, yet out of her mind at the same time. It had all happened so fast, and she could barely remember the trip. But she'd take it again in a heartbeat if it would bring her here. To this very moment.

Like a predator with her prey, she climbed onto the mattress beside him. She traced the rapid rise and fall of his chest lightly with her fingertips, following his ripples down the center of his abdomen. She mapped the hard lines, ending with the length of his straining erection. As she reached the tip, his back lifted from the bed, and a bead of moisture appeared in the slit. She smoothed the liquid over the flushed head and circled the ridge, wringing a hiss of approval from the back of his throat. She adored the way he responded to her touch.

"I love you." His velvet voice caressed her, drawing her gaze to his. "I'm yours, now and forever. Take me for your pleasure, my love. My flesh, my soul, and my blood, they're yours. Draw me into your body. Blend your essence with mine, and spend the remainder of eternity with me."

Never in her wildest dreams had she dreamed that she would find someone who loved her so completely. She believed that someone found their one true love, a hero, only in fairy tales or romance novels. Somehow, by some divine intervention or destined fate, she'd found one, and he'd just offered her his life.

Emily straddled his hips, relishing the feel of his hard cock parting her swollen folds. This was it. Once they fell together over the precipice there would be no turning back. Two would become one. She wrapped her fingers around the hot shaft, smooth silk over hard steel, holding herself completely still. Her breath trapped in her lungs. Kenric moaned with anticipation, the head of his cock waiting at her entrance.

And she'd never wanted anything more in her entire life.

With one firm press of her hips, she claimed him. Her head fell back, and the room winked out for a split second. A deep groan, her own and his, returned her to her senses. No one had ever filled her the way he did. It wasn't penetration with Kenric. Rather, it was a joining of two bodies.

Her fangs burst from her gums, coaxed by the lust for her mate. In slow, precise glides, she slid over his cock, every nerve on fire, and eased forward, seeking the pulse she craved. His head fell to the side. Her tongue flicked at his throbbing vein, her own heartbeat pounding away at her skull.

"Kenric," she whispered. "Please tell me if you have any doubts before I can't turn back."

"I want you," he growled. "Do it. Take me."

Thank God. She struck. Hot blood spilled into her mouth, and she drank with greedy swallows. His back arched, followed by the driving thrusts of his hips. She matched each upward lunge with her own downward stroke. Each swift meeting buried his cock deeper, stroking the sensitized nerve endings until the dam on her orgasm broke.

A muffled scream wrenched from her throat.

Spasms of sheer ecstasy centered where his hard cock speared her core. Her muscles clenched, trying to capture and hold on to the rapture.

Beneath her, Kenric moaned her name, and the headboard protested. It creaked under the abuse of the warrior tied to it. With a loud bang of wood against plaster, he stiffened, and a guttural shout of pleasure filled the room. She swung her head from his neck. The straps remained intact, but the headboard lay broken and sagging against the wall.

Her gaze fell to his open vein. A trickle, instead of a stream, flowed from the wound. This was it. God, what if she lost him?

"Don't stop." His command came, as if he sensed her conflicted emotions. She gripped the pillow beneath his head. "Finish it," he said on a ragged breath. "Drink, Emily."

She returned, pulling at the wound, encouraging it to continue to give. His body grew cool and still beneath her. A wave of panic and dizziness inundated her. *Don't leave me, Kenric. Please don't leave me.*

A tidal wave of intoxicating blood raced through her system. The potent essence of her mate had created her, but she wasn't accustomed to so much at once. Her heart sputtered, and her limbs trembled. Chills ran down her spine, and a shiver skated across her skin.

Suddenly, the cold subsided on the heels of a firestorm, building inside her. "*Emily.*" Her gaze swung to Kenric's lips. "*Emily.*" His voice, except his mouth never moved. She'd heard him in her head.

"*It's you.*" She closed her eyes and spoke inside her mind. "*I can feel you. Your warmth consumes me.*" Her palms roamed her body, pursuing the trail of his soul. It danced under her skin in a kaleidoscope of heat, then flame. Behind her eyelids, colors whirled in dazzling reds, yellows, and blues.

"*Bring me back. It's time. I must return, before it's too late.*" The urgency in his words yanked her back to the present and into action. Bringing her wrist to her fangs, she bit.

With the flow of blood at his mouth, she prayed and worked the stream into the small part between his lips. A trickle of red seeped from the corner of his mouth. He wouldn't swallow.

"Kenric! Damn you. Drink, you hardheaded vampire!" She choked back a sob. Wrapping what he'd taught her about compulsion into her voice, she threw her words at him. "I swear, I'm going to kick your ass if you don't swallow and come back to me."

His eyelids flew open. Wild, dilated pupils searched her face with a glassy stare. He gulped, then released a strangled cough from the overflow in his mouth. His chest rose on a long, deep breath. The warm feel of it at her wrist melted her. If she'd been standing, she knew her legs would have failed her.

Fangs pierced the flesh at her wrist. She cried out from the sharp dig of his teeth. Ravenous hunger drove him to sink deeper. With her free hand, she wiped at the fine layer of sweat popping at her brow.

The hairs on her arms and her nape stood on end. A hot, tingling sensation leaked through her pores as a portion of her, merged with Kenric's returning soul, left her body. She would have thought to feel empty, but the remaining essence of her mate left her complete.

Her heart skipped in her chest as his eyelashes lifted. The summer blue of his eyes cleared. Her warrior had returned.

His fevered pace at her vein slowed, replaced by the warmth of his tongue. He applied pressure at the wound they had both formed before pulling away. The growing light in his expression told her that he felt a new acute awareness of her.

She dropped onto the bed beside him and grabbed her gloves to release the restraints she'd almost forgotten were in place.

As soon as his arms slid free, he pushed into a sitting position. With trembling fingers, she climbed the planes of his abdomen and chest. She'd never fully realized the extraordinary power that lay restrained within the vampire she now called her mate. Her mind hummed with it.

His hand met hers, his fingers brushing her skin, before he brought it to his lips. The link they shared flooded her senses.

"You feel incredible in here." He tapped the place above his heart with their joined hands. "I honestly don't know how I've walked this world without you for so long."

She squeezed his hand, her mind spinning, overwhelmed with the depth of his emotions. "My love, you'll never again journey alone."

Chapter Twenty-Four

Arran shifted in his seat for the third time, trying his best to appear disinterested in the chestnut-haired beauty helping Michael clean the kitchen. He should find something else to focus on before someone noticed, but the sway of her hips and the curve of her back captivated his imagination. All the things he envisioned doing against those rounded curves tortured him. The endless places he wanted to bend her sweet ass over, or spread her naked on, or…

Shit. He needed to get a grip.

None of those fantasies would ever make it out of his head. Gabrielle was too precious. Too innocent. If she knew him, really knew him, the look in her eyes would turn to hate, instead of the adoration she touched him with now that made his heart turn inside out.

Arran pushed to his feet, sliding the chair back with a scrape along the hardwood floor. Across the table, Logan shot him an irritated glare. The heat of Gabrielle's gaze tracked him out of the room. No one dared to ask about his abrupt departure. Excellent. The aura he wore did its trick.

Halfway up the stairs, his cell vibrated. He slid it from his jeans pocket and glanced at the blue-lit display. Markus. About damn time. "Nice of you to check in, bastard," Arran said with a blast of sarcasm.

"Kiss my ass."

"Where the hell have you been?" Arran flung his bedroom door closed and plopped down on the edge of his bed.

"I had to go. It was…personal. Something I couldn't put off any longer."

"So damn urgent, it had you walking out on the Enclave during a crisis? Kenric's going to have your head."

"Yeah, he probably will." Markus grew silent on the line for a few seconds before asking, "Who's all around tonight?"

"Guerin and Logan just came in from patrol. We're all here."

"So Guerin still has you on security detail for Kenric and his woman? I take it she survived."

"Kenric gave Guerin an update earlier tonight. Looks like Emily's going to make it. What's up with you and the twenty questions, man? Why don't you come in and see for yourself?" Markus didn't sound right. Arran didn't know what the hell was going on, but his partner hadn't been the same since his freak accident.

"Yeah, I'll be there soon. I have some loose ends to tie up first."

"Markus…" The line went dead.

• • •

The sliding door to the Enclave central command hissed open before Arran could enter the password. Guerin exited, still dressed in patrol gear. A couple of hours remained before sunup, but he and Logan had called it for the night because of Markus's stunt. With Kenric occupied with Emily's transition, Guerin wanted a team on base at all times.

"Hey, man. I was looking for you," Arran said as the steel door slid shut behind Guerin. "Markus contacted me, said he'd be in soon."

Guerin brushed past him with an aggravated huff. "I want some food. So, if you see him before we do…" He pulled up short, long enough to glance over his shoulder, his dark eyes edged with frustration. "Tell him to find me the moment his ass crosses this threshold."

"I'll let him know."

With a grunt, Guerin resumed his trek for the kitchen, and Arran trailed him up the staircase. As their boots struck the first floor, a perimeter-breach alarm blared throughout the compound. Gabrielle and Logan bolted from the kitchen door a few feet down the hall, heading for the security office. Shock resonated throughout the compound, a palpable wave off each warrior. For years, the Enclave's residence had remained a secured location, miles away from any DEAD activity. Though they were prepared for any assault, a direct attack on their headquarters blindsided them.

The locker for weapons on the main floor stood outside security. Arran slammed to a halt beside it, while Guerin headed straight to security to join Gabrielle and Logan. Arran entered the password and yanked the door open as a distinct shadow fell across his arm. Without looking back, he tossed several blades to Kenric and loaded himself down with as many as he could carry. When the last weapon passed to his leader, Arran banged the door shut and spun. Kenric appeared to have dressed in a hurry, since the only thing covering him were faded blue jeans and a row of bite marks on his neck. Damn. He jerked his gaze way. No time for jealousy over those telling marks. Arran bit down, clenching his jaw hard onto his resolve, and fell in behind Kenric.

"Report." Kenric targeted Guerin inside security.

Guerin glanced over his shoulder. "We've got six intruders at various locations around the perimeter about two hundred fifty yards out."

"They're low-level heat signatures. Vampires," Gabrielle said, her focus riveted to the computer monitor.

"I agree," Guerin replied from his position opposite Kenric's at Gabrielle's shoulder. "Dammit and motherfucker!" Guerin's fist collided with the oak desk. "More just appeared less than twenty-five feet from the compound walls. I count five. They're moving in phase leaps across the grounds, never in the same location for more than a few seconds."

Gabrielle jumped to her feet, grabbing earpieces for each warrior. For a brief moment, her gaze held Arran's as she placed one of the wireless devices into his hand. "I'll keep you updated as their locations change." Her voice carried to everyone, but when her hand slid from his, the look in her eyes sent a clear message for him alone. *Be careful.* He coiled his fist around the piece and tightened the hold on his heart. She needed to stop wasting her prayers and wishes on him.

He'd been dead long before she had even been born.

Arran wrapped the receiver around his ear and headed

down the hall with his team. "Where's Emily?" The question came in loud and clear over the device.

"Armed and secured in my quarters." Kenric's voice. "Where I told her to stay put."

"You really expect her to follow your orders?" The underlying humor in Guerin's tone was hard to miss. No verbal response came, but up ahead, Arran caught the kiss-my-ass glare Kenric threw Guerin.

They reached the end of the corridor as the sound of breaking glass echoed through the house. Michael rounded the corner and pointed to the blade Arran carried. "You got an extra one of those?"

Arran pulled the spare from the small of his back and handed it over, hilt first. "Keep close."

"You can count on it." Michael gripped the hilt and rotated it until the blade lay flush against his wrist.

"We've got six in the house now," Gabrielle's soft voice whispered in Arran's ear. "One heading upstairs. Two at the entrance to operations. The others are heading straight for you."

Kenric pivoted. His gaze tapped Arran, then Logan. "You two take the bastards down here. Guerin and I have the others." No sooner had he given the orders when the commander and his second phased.

The house went dark, and a cry filled the dark void. One down. The emergency lights clicked, flooding the house in a soft yellow glow layered with shadows. Vampires attacking vampires, and the intruders took the time to kill the lights. A waste of fucking time. Except for two humans, everyone in the battle possessed superior night vision. Apparently the DEADs had a flair for drama. The Enclave had a flair for killing the stupid fucks, and no loss of light would lessen their advantage.

Adrenaline flooded Arran's system, contracting his heart into a rapid battering of the walls inside his chest. For some, the hormone made them less effective, nervous, and edgy. For Arran, he soaked it up like a junkie, becoming more alive, alert, and ready for anything.

Logan panned right, and Arran took the left, spreading out across the main level. A slight breeze followed by the stench of decay invaded Arran's nostrils seconds before a DEAD materialized in his path. The bloodsucker lunged with his blade drawn.

Arran tucked and rolled, dodging the initial attack. He regained his feet, whirled, and slashed the rear of the DEAD's neck. Blood flashed from the wound, and the vampire's head lolled forward, severed from his spine.

A curse rung out from Logan's mouth, and Arran glanced across the open expanse of the living area. A DEAD intruder battled the warrior. A long slice to Logan's arm smoked like a pan of damn fried bacon. How the hell did these DEADs get their hands on silver-plated daggers?

Marguerite.

She must have armed them with the Enclave's own weapon of choice.

The bigger fucking question of the night was, what traitorous asshole ratted out their location? His feet rooted to the floor. The earlier phone conversation with Markus replayed in his mind. *No.* He shook his head at the nagging suspicion making him ill. Markus wouldn't…?

"Three more. I detect three more intruders on the first floor." Gabrielle's alarmed voice filled his ear.

• • •

Markus watched from his vantage point five hundred yards outside the compounds' sensors. Like clockwork, the lights had gone out, sending the house onto emergency power. Why the hell not? Make them all scurry like rats. Kenric had to be out of his fucking mind right about now. Never would he believe one of his own had betrayed his perfect order. It had been so easy, just like Marguerite had predicted.

He chuckled, riding high on his mistress's blood. His body ached, not yet completely healed from the punishment of her whip, claws, and fangs.

When his mission was over, he would savor his reward. He stroked the hard length of his cock in anticipation. Marguerite would make all the pain and deception worth it. Relinquishing the Enclave's fucked-up hold on his mind had been difficult, at first. They'd been the only taste of honor he'd ever known. Then Marguerite had opened his eyes to what truly lay in the darkness, and it was more than he had ever imagined. She was powerful and beautifully exotic. And she was delicious.

The dimly lit sitting room came into focus as Markus phased to the third floor of headquarters. With the house under full attack, he knew Kenric would leave Emily in the one place he believed to be most secure: his private wing. Only Enclave warriors would have visual knowledge of Kenric's living quarters, thus the ability to phase into the location. Surely, his fuck-toy was safe, locked away inside the master's den. What foolish arrogance on his *former* commander's part.

No one was ever truly safe.

Dressed in a man's white T-shirt and oversize sweats, the woman paced the floor, working the hilt of a blade inside her fist. A muttering of various curses rolled from her lips. Left behind and fucking pissed, she didn't sense his presence behind her.

Markus glided forward, sticking to the shadows, his body a transparent veil of a human form. He palmed the dart gun loaded with Ketamine buried inside his pocket. Two feet from him, she came to an abrupt stop. Her head dropped into her hands with an exasperated sigh.

Perfect.

Aiming straight for her exposed neck, Markus fired.

Bull's-eye.

She whirled, yanking the dart out of her neck. Her wide eyes scanned the object and the surrounding room, but she would find nothing but dark corners. Within seconds, her knees buckled, and her unconscious body wilted.

Breaking free of the shadows, Markus kneeled and scooped Emily from the floor. The sensors would detect the extra presence in her quarters, but he'd be long gone. And Kenric, too late. He grinned and phased them both on a trip to his mistress's arms.

• • •

Something was wrong. A sudden emptiness—a void—welled inside Kenric's chest. He reached for his mate with his mind, but there was nothing on the other end, only stillness. Across their connection, he called to her, but she didn't answer.

"Emily!" he cried out and bounded up the stairs. Why

wouldn't she answer?

Like a madman, he burst through the security door to his residence. Empty. His soul couldn't find the essence that matched his. He didn't need to search, though he did, tearing through every room. Agony constricted his heart to the point that the blood in his veins felt like sludge, too thick and heavy to circulate.

Please, God, don't take her from me. Not when only a few hours ago, because of her, he'd learned to breathe again. And that air smelled like wildflowers.

From the floor near the baseboard, a glint of light bouncing off metal caught his eye. He dropped to one knee. He found her blade, and something else lying beside it.

Boots pounded the stairs outside his room. Kenric straightened as his warriors filled the room, his gaze transfixed on the black and silver dart between his fingertips. His fangs ached to rip into the throat of the one who had dared touch his mate.

The room shook from his rage. Lifting his gaze to his team, he pronounced, "Marguerite dies tonight."

Chapter Twenty-Five

"When do you think she'll come around?"

"I don't know. Mistress said to let her know when she shows any signs of waking," a thickly accented voice answered. "That new slave didn't go under like this. No matter if she's fucking a master, she's still female—still weak. The same dose that just dazed him kicked her little vampire ass."

Emily cracked an eyelid to get a look at the assholes discussing her. She didn't risk further movement. The blurry image of bars crashed into her brain and sent her pulse racing.

A cell.

They'd locked her in a cell. She bit her cheek to keep from screaming. The metallic taste of blood leaked across her tongue.

Every muscle knotted in rebellion as she fought the surge of her fight-or-flight reflex kicking into high gear. The ache in her bones and the grit in her mouth confirmed they'd left her lying on a dirt floor. The dank, earthen smell filled her nose with each rapid breath she failed to control.

"Well, look who's waking up and come to join in on our fun? Open those eyes, Red. I know you're hearing every word."

Shit, they must have noticed the changes in her heart rate and respiration. She dragged her eyelids open. No use pretending anymore. Two young men leaned against the bars. To her surprise, they were quite handsome and wore finely tailored white silk shirts and black slacks. Both grinned through the iron bars as if she were the prize catch of the day. Okay, so not a good analogy. She might very well be dinner.

After a few ungraceful attempts to stand on her legs, she finally made her way over to the bars.

"Inform Mistress Marguerite that her…guest is awake," the man with what sounded like a Spanish accent and long chocolate brown hair instructed the blond to his left. Without hesitation, the blond raced away.

"Sleep well?" The Spaniard swung his dark gaze back to her, jamming his hand through the bars and into her hair.

Emily hissed and jerked back, stumbling into the damp wall. "Keep your filthy hands to yourself," she spat.

"Admirable." His lips curled into a smile, displaying two long fangs. "But that feisty attitude will do you no good here. You belong to our mistress now. And I'm going to enjoy every minute of the show while she puts an end to another one of her precious Kenric's whores."

"Enrique, I suggest you watch your tongue if you wish to keep it. I'll decide if I want an audience." A serpent-like hiss of a feminine voice filled the dirt and stone space. "I would hate for you to lose a body part with which you are so talented."

Every hair on Emily's body stood on end. An exotic beauty, wearing sheer green silk held together by black netting down its center, glided into view. The gauzy fabric and strategically placed fishnet did little to cover her breasts or hide the top of a nether region Emily had no desire to see. Enrique tucked in his chin and inched away from the bars.

Guided by self-preservation, Emily backed into the corner of the small cell. The raven-haired woman with jade green eyes radiated pure evil. "Marguerite Devonshire, I presume?" At least she could be proud that she sounded steadier than she felt.

"That is correct, dear. And *you* are Emily Ross, Kenric's newest and most fleeting interest."

"Kenric will kill you for this." Emily pushed away from the wall, striding a few steps forward. She wouldn't go down without a fight. And she sure as hell would not let this bitch see her beg.

Marguerite's head tilted back with a laugh born in hell. "Oh, dear, I sure hope he'll try. Don't you realize that is *exactly* why you're here? Kenric needs a reminder of the place he is destined to take at my side. So you be a good girl and let your latest fuck find you. And when he does, I'm going to enjoy making him watch while I kill you."

Insane laughter followed the monster as she exited Emily's prison. Her Spanish guard turned to follow his mistress, pausing long enough to purse his lips in an exaggerated kiss between the bars. Her stomach heaved.

Emily stumbled backward until she found the wall, and her false sense of bravado gave out. From her spot on the floor, she reached for Kenric in her mind, praying that by some chance she might find him there. If only they'd had more time, she would have learned how to tap into her mate. Instead of becoming a pawn in Marguerite's sick game.

. . .

The stranglehold of the sun had never driven Kenric as close to the point of madness as it had today. It had taken every ounce of self-control not to lash out at his warriors earlier and possibly kill one of them for keeping him from his mate. But they'd been right. Emily had been taken less than an hour before sunrise. Not enough time remained to find her.

Sunlight continued to paint the sky outside. He felt it in the way his skin prickled and itched. But he wouldn't last another minute banging around like a damn pinball within the confines of his residence. Dressed in black leather and with every inch of his body armed, Kenric hit the stairs.

Time to bring his mate home and put an end to Marguerite once and for all.

Outside the entrance to central command, Kenric punched in his access code and placed his right hand on the identification screen. A blue beam of light scanned his palm, and the heavy steel door slid open. The door sealed with a brush of air behind him as he entered the expanse of the room. His boots ground to a halt. Swallowing hard, he worked his throat while his brain attempted to churn out some intellect befitting for what waited for him.

The entire Enclave—except for Markus, which he found odd—had assembled. Damn impressive. With the exception of Guerin, his warriors were young, under two hundred years old. An early rise would have proven quite a feat.

Guerin came forward and met him.

"Don't look so surprised. We pledged to protect her as our own, even before she became your mate. And your Enclave would gladly give their lives to bring her home to you." Kenric gripped Guerin's forearm with a firm shake that needed no words.

Gathered around the conference table, the team plotted their strategy. Kenric stood with both arms braced on the back of his chair. "I want all of you to know how much I respect and appreciate your commitment. Not just to the Enclave, but to Emily and me as well. You've demonstrated that tonight, with the strength it took for you to be here at this hour. I won't forget." Kenric studied his knuckles as they gripped the black leather of his chair. "Marguerite took Emily for one reason. It's her way of saying, *you want her? Come and get her.* She doesn't realize Emily is my mate, but she would have assumed I'd taken her blood, knowing how easy that would make it to track her." Heads rotated, and brows lifted around the table at the clear implication. "Yeah, it's a trap. Not only does she want Emily dead, she wants me there to witness it." A muttering of curses drifted from his team.

"Marguerite alone is an incredible adversary, but as you've seen, she has a colony of loyal minions and DEADs at her disposal. This may very well be a suicide mission." Kenric met each fierce gaze of his warriors. He would never force any of them into a battle they didn't wish to take on as their own. Emily was his life. His world. And if he had to go alone… Nothing could stop him from finding her and bringing her home. Alive.

"If you're waiting to see if any of us want out"—Logan grabbed his attention—"I can assure you, my oath to the Enclave had no strings attached. From what I've witnessed, taking Marguerite out will be a great service to the world." Logan kicked back in his chair and cracked his knuckles.

Around the table, the crew added their parallel sentiments and their desires to remove Marguerite's head and smoke some DEADs.

"Very well." Kenric nodded. "Let's bring my mate home and make sure Marguerite and her minions never see another sunset."

While the team readied their comm links and gear, Kenric met with his second-in-command. "Guerin, have the team ready. Once I'm as close as I can get to Emily without detection, I'll contact you with my coordinates. I'll take to the air for a recon of the surroundings and inform you of what resistance to expect once I shift back."

"Don't go in there alone, Kenric. You know that's what she's hoping you'll do."

He wouldn't promise a damn thing. Instead, he turned and headed to the door.

"Dammit, Kenric. You fucking wait for us before you go in," Guerin shouted to his back.

"Just be there." Kenric closed the door and phased.

• • •

At the end of his first phase, Kenric rematerialized from his atomic state onto the rooftop of an aluminum and steel warehouse building. He sat back on his haunches, searching once more for a sense of his mate's presence in order to head in her direction.

"*Kenric, can you hear me?*"

The soft echo of Emily's voice in his head rocked him. He hadn't been deluding himself. She was alive. Grabbing the edge of the roof, he braced himself before responding.

"*Kenric, please… Can you hear me?*"

"*Yes. Emily… I hear you.*" A relieved sigh filled his mind.

"*Thank God. Marguerite—*"

"*Yes, I know. And I'm on my way. I* will *get you out of there.*" If only it were as simple as a touch of their minds. He'd be by her side in an instant.

"*No!*" Her voice rose into a terrified pitch, slicing a new hole in his heart. "*That's exactly why I've been trying to contact you. Marguerite knows you will come for me. Oh, God, Kenric. She plans to… She wants you here when she kills me.*"

His nails lengthened into claws, puncturing the metal of the roof. They dug into the structure as he tightened the lid on the rage that threatened to rob him of his better judgment. *Keep it together.* Nothing short of thinking with his head, not his heart, would do if he hoped to save Emily. Marguerite wanted him enraged enough to lose his mind.

"*It's not going to happen. Marguerite remembers the young master vampire who escaped from her three hundred years ago. Through her dream visits, she's aware I've grown stronger, but she has yet to meet me in the flesh. You will not die. But she will,*" he assured Emily.

"*Please be careful. I love you so much.*"

"*Wildflower… I love you, too. We have to focus on getting you out. Can you tell me anything about who took you and where you are?*"

"*Not much. Someone shot me with a dart containing some sort of drug. It knocked me out, and I woke up here, in an underground cell.*"

Her omission of the details on how she was actually holding up told him all he needed to know. Locked away like some kind of animal. He of all people knew what that felt like. His skin crawled from the memory. But Emily… Putting her behind bars was hell-on-earth.

"*I'll chew my tongue in two, Kenric, before I give that bitch the satisfaction of seeing me squirm.*"

He couldn't help but smile. There was the fire of the woman he had fallen in love with. "*Do you know how much it turns me on when you talk like that?*"

"*Turns you on…? Nice try, buddy, but all the dirty talk in the world can't make me forget the evil on the other side of these bars. Hold on… They're back.*"

"*What do they want?*"

"*They've come for me. Marguerite wants me brought to her. She wants me ready for you. Whatever that means.*"

"*Stay strong, and know that I'm coming for you. You* will *be in my arms tonight.*"

Silence followed his last statement. He wouldn't allow himself to think about what they were doing to her, or he'd lose it.

After his fourth phase he arrived at the end of a dirt road. Taking cover in oaks laden with Spanish moss, he surveyed the outline of an old Victorian house. *Very Marguerite.* Of course she would love something so nostalgic.

A tap to the back of his earpiece activated his comm link, and Guerin responded in less than a second. Kenric provided the needed GPS location for them to take action.

ETA, thirty minutes.

In the form of a raven, Kenric took flight. Spreading his wings, he sought and found the air currents that took him high above the trees. He circled the house and noted several guards strategically placed around the main dwelling and the entrance to the property. It would be a fight for his warriors to gain entrance, but they were the best. Before landing, he risked a closer look in the windows of the house, hoping for a glimpse of Emily.

Through the large first-floor window at the back of the house, he spotted her. He seated his talons on the paint-chipped exterior ledge for a better look. Marguerite had made sure she wouldn't be missed. She'd stripped Emily naked, and Emily lay with her arms and legs cuffed on a parallel rack. From what he could tell from his angle at the window, her body appeared to be intact. No doubt, Marguerite was awaiting his arrival before damaging her flesh. Much more painful for both him and Emily that way.

He took to the sky again and, seconds later, landed without a sound near his clothes. In human form, he activated his link and informed his team of the geography of the property and the position and number of guards.

Re-dressed and rearmed, Kenric blended into the shadows and headed for the house. His mate lay strapped to a torture device. Not even Hell could keep him from her.

• • •

Marguerite leered over Emily's naked body. Her lip curled in disgust, showing off the tip of one fang. "What he sees in you, I'll never know. I can smell him all over you." The long fingers of one hand gripped Emily's cheeks, the tips of Marguerite's nails digging into her flesh, forcing her to stare into Marguerite's insane eyes. Emily didn't know what hurt worse: the searing pain of the silver cuffs that pinned her to the wood or the sharp fingernails making a new hole in her face. "I can understand why you wanted him. He can fuck like a beast, can he not?" Marguerite sneered. "And I bet you loved the taste of his cum filling your throat. So sweet, wasn't it?"

Emily pursed her lips and spat. She couldn't have asked for a better shot. The ball of saliva landed with a splat near Marguerite's right eye.

"How do you like that? You insane bitch!"

The hand that had held Emily's face reared back and scalded her left cheek with an ear-ringing slap. The warm taste of blood seeped into her mouth. Emily blinked, trying to clear her vision.

A cool finger traced her bleeding lip. "Don't make me kill you, whore, before our lover arrives." Marguerite licked the smear of blood from her fingertip. As if in slow motion, she paled, then tilted her head and met Emily's stare. This time, the jade green of Marguerite's eyes disappeared, replaced by the eerie glow of red.

Oh shit.

"You didn't…" Marguerite screamed. "I can taste him in your blood. You filthy fucking whore! How dare you mate him!" Emily flinched and jammed her eyelids tightly shut, waiting for the worst to come. The high-pitched squeal pierced her skull and went on and on until she knew her eardrums bled.

The sound finally faded, until the only sounds were her

rapid pants for air. She risked a peek from under her lids. Marguerite stood a few steps away. Two of her fingers were dipped inside a crimson vessel the size of a fist. It had to be Goran's blood, the ancient relic that Kenric had mentioned. Marguerite pulled her digits from the relic, her flesh coated in the thick dark matter, brought them to her mouth, and shoved them between her lips.

Oh God!

Marguerite's expression morphed, drunk on the ancient's essence. Before Emily could form a scream of her own, fangs sank into her throat with brutal precision. The DEAD attack had been nothing compared to the agony tearing into her neck. Marguerite chewed into her, making sure Emily felt every piece of her life rip into bits and drain away.

No! Think. She couldn't allow the pain and Marguerite to win.

A familiar warm vibration in her soul alerted her to Kenric's approach, helping to jolt her memory. As his mate, she should possess the ability to draw on his strength. Not knowing what to do, or how it worked, she was desperate enough to try anything. Anything to get this crazy bitch off her. Emily pictured a field of energy, buzzing with life, separating Marguerite from her. Marguerite flew from her vein with a furious wail.

Yes! It worked. A swirling pale blue haze covered Emily in a blanket of protective energy.

"He was to be *my* mate!" Marguerite whirled with her arms spread wide, crazed. "Both of you will pay. Kenric will hurt as he's never hurt before. Such betrayal," she wheezed. The once-exotic beauty had transformed into a wild, evil beast intent on pure destruction.

With fingertips more animal than human, Marguerite clawed at Emily's energy barrier. "You're not fit. I *made* him! He was to be the glue that would bring us together."

What the hell is she raving about?

"You don't deserve the gift of such a powerful vampire as he."

"Deserving or not," Emily said. "He's mine."

Kenric materialized in the center of the large room the moment Emily's declaration fell from her lips. At that instant, he loved her even more than he had thought possible.

"Truer words have never been spoken," he said. Marguerite's head swiveled in his direction. The image of his mate, beneath a power shield of her own making—as she tapped into his power *and* protected herself from the talons of an enraged Marguerite—would remain forever burned into his mind.

Marguerite knew. He'd taken a mate, and it would never be her. In her delusional world, the news had to be a bitch.

Immediately, her guards formed a circle with him at its center. The tips of their swords aimed at his back and chest. Their points pricked at his skin, but with his mind, he maintained control over the advance of their weapons. For the moment, he allowed them their show of force. Why waste energy on the wrong enemy? He needed his full strength for Marguerite.

They wouldn't kill him, anyway. Not without Marguerite's command. And the last thing she wanted was him dead. Well, at least not by another's hand. No, if he was to die, she would want that honor for herself.

Marguerite straightened to her full height and approached the top step of the elevated platform that held her and Emily. "You realize you've ruined everything," she said to Kenric, running her fingers through her wild hair. "Together we could have ruled the world. Now… Now you've mated with *this*." She gestured wildly at Emily, who still lay bound behind her.

Her red eyes blazed with fury as she glided down toward him. The guards parted. He'd waited for this moment for centuries. The blood in his veins surged in anticipation. Patience. His assault would need perfect timing.

She stopped less than a foot away. "Leave us." Her guards' heads turned to one another in confusion. "I said leave us!" she roared. "This is between me and the master of the Enclave."

The door clanked shut as the last vampire exited, sending an echo across the room.

"I loved you."

"Dear God. Your tongue defiles the very meaning of the words."

"I loved you, Kenric." Her head slowly shook from side to side. "I did. No other did I covet as much as you. The others beg incessantly for my attention. Freely, I offered it to you." Her face twisted. "Yet you have spat on me at every turn. I gave you the gift of becoming a master vampire and tossed it into your lap. And this is how you repay me?" Her voice rose into a hysterical frenzy. "All I asked was for you to share it with me."

"You don't love *me*. You love the power, Marguerite. You took what was not yours to take." His palms gripped the hilts of the daggers at his thighs. "You expect love and gratitude from one you chained and fed upon like an animal. And then you stole my life. You went too far, Marguerite. It ends tonight."

Like cannon fire, explosive discharges of energy from both of them resounded throughout the room. The sound waves bounced around inside his head like a mallet against his brain before his back slammed into a solid wall. Kenric shook off the haze from the impact. He steadied himself at the same time he spotted Marguerite across the room, picking herself up from the floor.

"*Kenric!* Emily's voice slipped into his mind. "*Get me off this thing so I can help you kick her ass.*"

"*She's my fight, Wildflower. Believe me, she won't be winning this battle.*" He launched into the air less than a second later, rolling into a somersault and landing behind his target. With his blade in his right hand, he struck. Marguerite ducked, but not before he grazed the back of her neck.

She whirled, throwing out another blast of energy that knocked him sideways. Kenric hit the floor but continued to roll until he was back on his feet. This time, he hit her with a blast and spun on his heels in her direction.

Caught off guard by his sudden recovery, Marguerite didn't have time to dodge his counterattack. Her feet left the floor under the brute force of the wave of energy. She flew backward, slamming into the lead glass window that covered half of one wall. The window shattered.

Marguerite's body lay unmoving on the shards of glass. Silence fell over the room.

"Kenric?" Emily's voice, like music from heaven, rang in his ears.

He took the steps by three, making it to her before he

could breathe a reply.

Silver cuffs held Emily's wrists and ankles. His chest throbbed at the sight. "One last step," Kenric said. "And then yes, it's over, and we're going home." He wanted the validation of seeing Marguerite personally turned to dust.

"Thank God," she said.

With his blade, Kenric popped the locks and eased his mate into a sitting position. Blisters circled her wrists from the prolonged contact with the metal. She winced with each movement, and her pain echoed through his soul like it was his own. Based on the sounds of battle coming from outside the chamber doors, his team had arrived.

He ushered Emily to the edge of the platform, but they both skidded to a halt before the top step. Marguerite stood in the center of the room, glaring like a demon waiting for her next kill. She reached up, and with the flick of her wrist, a broad sword left the wall and flew into her waiting palm.

In an equal move, Kenric lifted his hand, pulling the second sword from its mount on the wall and into his palm. A strangled cry of war rent from his lungs as he sailed into the air. Marguerite raised her sword and deflected his strike above her head.

His boot struck the floor behind her. She whirled and lunged straight for his gut. He pivoted, but the blade sliced into his side. The hot flash of pain shot through to his spine. But he didn't have time to assess the damage. Marguerite had drawn blood and was coming back for more.

They parried blow for blow, back and forth. The strike of steel on steel ricocheted off the plank floors. Years of buried anger, rage, and pain drove him.

Faster.

Harder.

He pushed Marguerite back. She dodged another swipe at her head, then leaped into the air, whirled, and came down behind him. Hyped up on Goran's blood, the move was too fast for him to counter.

Her sword appeared at his neck. "I could so easily take your head, darling." She pulled in, bringing the serrated tip to his throat. The sting of the blade said she'd nicked the flesh. "Why do you push me to such lengths? Was she worth it?"

"Marguerite!" The sound of Emily's voice had them both whipping their heads to the elevated platform. Emily stood on the top step, a dark red vessel in her hand. She thrust a finger into the opening on top, then jabbed whatever she'd gathered on the tip into her mouth.

Christ! Had she found Goran's blood?

Kenric's heart surged to the back of his throat.

"Emily…what are you doing?"

"You bitch!" Marguerite hissed behind his head. "You cannot have them both."

The hazel gaze that mesmerized him now glowed with a fire that he'd never seen. She lifted the fist-sized vessel up in her palm, holding it out before her. "I don't want them both." Emily shook her head. "Just one." As if the world had suddenly slowed to half-speed, Kenric watched as Emily flipped her hand over, dropping the relic to the floor below. The jar slammed into the wood with a shattering *crash* that bounced off the walls, dueling with the cry that rang out behind him.

Marguerite dropped her sword from his neck, but lunged for his mate. Emily took to the air, her auburn waves billowing. She slammed into Marguerite, ducking her head inches from Marguerite's broadsword. The sight trapped the air in his lungs. Marguerite lost her momentum and crashed to the ground along with Emily.

"Join me," Kenric instructed in Emily's head.

Kenric darted for her and grabbed his mate's hand, pulling her back onto her feet.

Picture the wind in your mind. Emily glanced his way and gave a quick nod.

Now wrap it around Marguerite.

Together with his sword arm outstretched, the wind kicked up, rushing through the broken window with gale force. Dirt and loose debris funneled around Marguerite, the force lifting her several inches off the floor.

She whirled, a roar thundering up from her lungs as her long hair whipped across her face. Kenric squeezed Emily's hand, and they dropped the now dazed vampire back to the floor. Somehow Marguerite managed to stagger, but regained her balance and she hoisted her sword once again. Seeing an opening, Kenric dropped his mate's hand, swung his sword in an upward arc, connecting with her weapon and knocking it from her hand. His blow tumbled Marguerite to the floor as her sword flipped blade over hilt into the air, landing with a hard *clank* several feet away.

Both hands gripped the hilt of his sword, and with a cathartic roar, he lifted it overhead, preparing to erase the blight that had infested his life and the planet. In midswing, Kenric locked his muscles. He'd barely missed cleaving one of his warriors in half. Markus had materialized before him, blocking the intended path of his blade.

"What the hell are you doing?" Kenric shouted. His

biceps trembled from his sudden restraint and the weight of the sword. "I almost killed you. Get the fuck out of the way!" Markus's stoic face looked as if he'd recently stepped out of one hell of a battle. Two black eyes, and one side of his face was chewed with deep claw marks, giving every indication of a torture all his own.

"I won't let you kill her, Kenric." Marguerite eased up and against Markus, snaking her arms around him.

"What the fuck are you saying?" Kenric's mind reeled. The image of the two before him…together… *No!*

"She's mine." Markus clutched the hands that stroked his chest.

Marguerite cocked her head to the side and lifted one curved black brow in Kenric's direction. "You've lost more here than you'll ever know, darling."

Markus and Marguerite vanished.

Chapter Twenty-Six

Homecomings weren't supposed to be bittersweet.

Emily was thrilled to be alive and have the love of her life at her side. Kenric had survived his encounter with Marguerite, but more importantly, he had severed the woman's hold on him, and the possibility of Goran's blood ever falling into another's hands had been eliminated. The war still raged, yes, but a monumental battle had been won.

But there had been a price to pay.

The Enclave had lost a warrior: Markus.

The same man, she'd remembered after seeing his face, who had bumped into her outside the coffee shop the night of her first attack.

The same man, evidence revealed to the devastation of all the warriors, who'd orchestrated her attack and kidnapping.

He'd been working for Marguerite.

The entire ride home, Kenric had held her in his arms

as she'd dealt with the aftermath of the ancient's blood in her system. He'd soothed her with his presence, told her how much what she'd done had meant to him. But what he hadn't spoken of, the pain of Markus' betrayal, she wished she could take away. She held the key to incredible powers, thanks to him, though none were the antidote for that kind of hurt.

To make matters worse, upon their arrival, Arran had announced that he, too, would be leaving. He felt responsible for not picking up on the change in Markus. The Enclave wasn't the right place for him, he'd said. He wanted out. Kenric had done his best to change the warrior's mind, insisting Markus had fooled everyone. Not just Arran.

None of his arguments had made a difference.

One woman saved. Two warriors lost.

In the privacy of their bedroom, Emily wrapped her arms tighter around her mate, finding comfort in the warmth of his body pressed against hers. The steady rhythm of his heart beat in her ear.

"We'll need to relocate." Kenric's rich voice brushed her skin. Emily lifted her head and rested her chin on the backs of her hands. "We can't risk everyone's safety since Markus has switched sides."

"Do you have somewhere in mind?"

"South Carolina has been my home for two centuries, so I would prefer for us to remain in the state," he said, then planted a kiss to her forehead. "Besides, after Marguerite's recruiting efforts, a large number of DEADs will need to be mopped up around this area. I'll have Michael contact a real estate broker and begin a search for available acreage." He slid the backs of his knuckles down her sides, then placed his arms around her, hugging her tight. "We're down two warriors, and finding vampires who are willing to make the kind of commitment it takes to become Enclave is difficult, to say the least. But I, Guerin, and Logan will get the job done. It's who we are."

"And it's who I am, too," she said. "You've got me. Always."

His hands dropped low on her back, caressing the skin there. "And we're going to be fine, Wildflower."

"I know we will." She gave him a reassuring smile. "In fact, I've got to call work and let them know when I'm coming back. I don't want to quit my job. Maybe I'll just cut back to part time. You never know when being on staff there could be beneficial to us. Looks like I'll be on permanent night shifts." Emily turned her smile into her best devilish grin."

"That's very true. Look how it worked out for you and me." His hands darted lower and gave her ass a squeeze, making her yelp.

"You are so bad."

"And don't you forget it." His voice dipped into that lazy growl that got her juices flowing, but first, she had to get something off her mind.

"Kenric?"

"Hmm?"

"Marguerite's last words—they keep buzzing in my head. What do you think she meant when she said, 'You've lost more here than you'll ever know?'"

"I'm sure she truly believes me not mating with her is one of the biggest mistakes of my existence. And that I will have lost an incredible opportunity or something to command a colony of minions." He kissed the top of her head. "Christ, who knows what her mind saw for us? But nothing could be further from the truth." His hands left her back, blazing a path along her curves until his fingers brushed the sides of her breast. "I'm exactly where I belong."

His gaze darkened, and without warning, he rolled her on her back. "You are *everything* to me. When we blended, you were so afraid that something would go wrong and I wouldn't come back. But the truth is, that night, you're the one who gave me life. For the first time in centuries, I truly wanted to live."

His lips singed hers. She opened her mind and allowed the provocative sensations of their bond to wash over her.

She didn't know how she had ever made love without this euphoric rush.

Kenric's thoughts filled her mind, guiding her to the sensitive areas of his body that drove him mad. Likewise, his movements followed every desire she relayed. Her mate knew exactly how she liked her nipples sucked. He engulfed the entire areola with his mouth, bringing the bud into an instant hard crest, and with the roughness of his tongue, he stroked the sensitized point.

Within minutes, he had her writhing. Aching.

"Fill me now, Kenric. I want you inside me, a part of me again."

He lifted her legs, placing her calves over his shoulders. The head of his cock brushed her pussy, wringing a pleasure-filled gasp from her throat. She gripped his biceps, digging in her nails as the exquisite burn of penetration stretched her.

"God, yes!" she cried out.

"You feel so damn good," he groaned. "I love you."

Slowly and thoroughly he made love to her. Bringing her to climax again and again, until she thought she'd die from the pleasure.

Emily collapsed onto her pillow, and Kenric plopped down beside her. She'd never walk again. Maybe never move again, period. Her mate's fingers played in the curls of her hair. She grinned, knowing she'd never been happier in her life.

"I have something for you." He rolled to his side of the bed and reached for the nightstand.

"Kenric, you've already given me more than I ever dreamed possible." The man was unbelievable. She had nothing to offer him but her love. Yet he kept giving.

An envelope sat in his hand when he turned. "Here, I want you to have this." He stretched his arm out and placed it on her chest.

Emily slid her fingers around the edges and picked it up. "What is this?"

"Open it."

She gave him a puzzled look. What in the world had he done?

"Can't a mate surprise his woman?"

"Your woman…" She giggled. "You are a total caveman."

"And you love it," he said in that beautiful, deep timbre of his that turned her liquid. Suddenly, he leaned forward and nipped her breast.

"Ouch!" She popped the top of his head with her hand.

He rolled back, melting her heart with the warmth of his smile. "Open the envelope, woman."

"Fine." She laughed and sat up before tearing open the seal. A single piece of folded paper lay inside. She pulled it free and unfolded the document. *Impossible.*

Tears welled and distorted the words before her, but she'd seen enough to know what she held in her hands. Her heart fluttered.

The deed to her condominium.

"Kenric St. James…" Emily lifted her head long enough to glimpse his face. He beamed. "How did you know? And when did you do this?"

"I overheard your…conversation with Jeff about what you'd had to do because of that bastard. I could tell how much that place meant to you." He brushed her wet cheeks with his fingertips. "You deserve to own it free and clear, and I wanted to make sure it happened. So I made a few phone calls. This came today." He leaned in and gently kissed her. His lashes tickled as he mapped her face with his soft lips. "I take it you're happy," he whispered at her jaw.

She nodded. Her emotions spilled free, unhampered by the fear of rejection or retribution from the master vampire who could so easily control her every move. Kenric sucked in a hard breath. His gaze sought hers, eyes darkened from the overload of both their deepest desires.

Through their bond, she shared everything. It was wonderful. Miraculous. She'd found freedom in allowing herself to become bound.

"Thank you for my gifts. Your forgiveness. There are no words needed, I can feel it in my heart." She gently placed a palm against the coarse shadow of his beard. "You continue to amaze and surprise me at every turn, and I couldn't love you more. This deed…" She glanced at the paper, then back at Kenric. "It really does mean a great deal to me. But you, my love…" She slipped her hand behind his neck, stroking her fingers through the short hairs at his nape. "Wherever you are, that is my home. No matter what city or town, you and the Enclave are my sanctuary."

About the Author

Almost every author's bio states they've been writing since they learned to read. It's what they've always wanted to do. Well, my journey wasn't so straight and narrow. I've been a nurse for more than twenty years and hold a bachelor's degree in Science with a major in Biology. So, as you can see, my career path had originally gone in the opposite direction. I didn't discover my passion for the craft until after I'd had my son and decided to work part-time.

I've always loved to read but had never read a paranormal romance. Then one night at work on break, I began reading Karen Marie Moning's *Spell of the Highlander*. I couldn't believe what I had been missing and I immediately fell in love with the genre.

I wanted to write like that. I wanted to create worlds that others could find the same excitement in, as I did, when I read my first sensual, paranormal romance.

And I hope that is what I've accomplished in my work.

Please dive in, hold on tight, and enjoy the adventure. Just be careful in the dark; you might find more than you expected waiting for you there. *wink*

. . .

Jessica Lee lives in the southeastern USA with her husband and son. She loves writing, and can't wait for that quiet time each day when her son is in school and she can get lost in another place and world with the fantastical, sexy creatures in her head.

She's a member of Romance Writers of America, FF&P, and Carolina Romance Writers.

Acknowledgments

This book would not have been possible without the support and friendship of some very special people in my life:

The ladies of We Are The Women Writers: Lanna, Julie, Mur, and Naima. You rock!

The Carolina Romance Writers: I'm so proud to be a part of such a wonderful group of authors. Your encouragement and advice have meant the world to me.

Lanna Lejeune: Your wonderful insight and never-ending patience, during many a late-night phone call, have truly been a blessing. You are an angel.

Annette Hill: Everyone should be so lucky to have a friend like you. Thank you so much for your support and encouragement. I know you've always got my back.

Printed in Great Britain
by Amazon